Dear Reader,

Years ago my husband Peter and I took a trip around the United States in a camper van, traveling from Oregon to New England. It was summertime, and we sweltered as we drove through the Midwest and on to the East Coast. However, when we reached Maine, we breathed a sigh of relief as the breeze from the Atlantic Ocean cooled us. I remember the wooded campground we stayed in, the craggy coastline, the quaint villages, and the stunning landscapes. It was a trip to treasure.

As I wrote *Beacon's Call*, I recalled those memories but also the years in between. Like the four characters in the novel, I've suffered challenges to my faith. But I've also witnessed God's continuing care in my life, mainly through the family and friends He's given me.

Currently, my husband is deployed to Afghanistan, and I'm trusting God with his safety as well as with the needs of our children and me as we soldier on at home. Writing this novel has been a sweet reminder of God's continuing goodness. Once again, He's providing what we need through His presence and the support of family and friends.

You'll see that theme carried through *Beacon's Call*. My hope is that, as you read, you'll be reminded of that theme in your own life too.

Leslie Gould

MIRACLES *of*
MARBLE COVE

BEACON'S CALL

LESLIE GOULD

New York

To my niece Sydnie and nephew Noah,
remembering our time on the beach

And to my friend Lucas, thank you for
your idea of the "familyship"

ACKNOWLEDGMENTS

Thank you to my husband Peter for his never-ending encouragement and support, even from halfway around the world. My gratitude also goes to Jenna Thompson, a member of my critique group, for sharing her experiences in Maine, and to the other women in our group as well: Kelly Chang, Melanie Dobson, Kimberly Felton, and Nicole Miller. Many thanks to the other writers in this series, the editors who make everything work, and the entire Guideposts staff. It's been a joy to be a part of these stories.

BEACON'S CALL

CHAPTER ONE

"That should do it!"

Beverly slipped her laptop into her briefcase and snapped it shut. She was alone in her office in the Maine State House of Representatives, ready to head back to Marble Cove for the rest of the week of telecommuting. She stood, pushing her chair back with her leg. As she did, her eyes landed on the photo of the Orlean Point lighthouse that was the desktop image on her computer monitor.

She'd come into Augusta on this Monday morning for a staff meeting at the request of the new director of her department. Each time she left the community on the coast, the urge to return grew stronger. She lifted her jacket from the back of her chair, folded it under her arm, and had started to reach for her case, when she heard a rustling at the door.

Phil Miller, the new director, stood with one foot still in the hallway and the other in her office. On paper, he seemed qualified for his position. But with his thick brown hair and boyishly round face, he didn't look like he could be a day over thirty-two. He moved a file folder from one hand to the other and cleared his throat. "Bev?"

"Yes?" She strategically placed her hand on her desk next to the placard that read BEVERLY WHEELAND-PARKER. No one called her *Bev*. She'd already pointed that out to him at the morning meeting.

His expression didn't change. He wasn't getting the hint.

"It's *Beverly*."

"Oh, right." His face reddened as he stepped all the way into her office, opening the file as he spoke. But the contents sprung out, tumbling to the floor in three directions.

"Oh dear," Beverly said, bending to help.

Phil swooped down, picking up the papers and cramming them back into the folder. Once they'd collected all the papers and he had them back in the file, he looked at her briefcase. "Were you leaving?"

She'd talked through her telecommuting schedule with him a couple of hours ago. "I'm headed back to Marble Cove," she said. "Remember?"

"That's right." He seemed even more flustered.

She nodded toward the file and stood. "What do you need?"

"A budget report. By tomorrow afternoon." He straightened and extended the folder toward her.

"No problem. I'll do it this afternoon and e-mail it back to you."

"Actually," he said, looking timid, "I may need you to present the report. I'll be out of the office."

She raised her eyebrows.

He wrinkled his forehead. "I'm scheduled to go on a tour of some of the state properties tomorrow. Do you mind sticking around another day?"

She took the file from him. "I'll do the report this afternoon and then be back tomorrow afternoon to present it." The thought of driving out to Marble Cove today and then back to Augusta tomorrow didn't thrill her, but neither did spending the night in her big empty house above the river. She wasn't going to tell Phil that, though.

"Thanks, Bev. I really—"

She grimaced.

"Beverly," he corrected. "I'll let you know if I come across any more information that needs to be added." He turned and left her office.

Beverly wanted to groan, but instead she thumbed through the file. It was a mishmash of information collected over the last year by the previous director. She would need to make some phone calls to verify that the statistics were still current.

A few years ago the challenge of a quick turnaround on a project and the chance to present a budget report would have thrilled her. She would have poured extra research and then hours and hours of time into her work, far more than what was needed. Now all she wanted was to get to the little town on the coast.

She slipped the file folder into her briefcase and turned off the light. A minute later, her high heels were clicking down the polished floor of the corridor, her usually long stride hindered just a little by her pencil skirt. She took the stairs quickly. She'd be in Marble Cove in no time.

As Beverly drove across the Kennebec River, leaving downtown Augusta, her thoughts turned to Marble Cove instead of to the budget report. She couldn't stop thinking of the photo of the little boy and the man that her friend Shelley had found in the Orlean Point Lighthouse. Surely the image held a clue to the history of the lighthouse.

Maybe Mrs. Peabody, who helped out with Beverly's father, would know something about it. The woman was in her eighties and had lived in Marble Cove her entire life. Maybe she even went to school with the little boy. Mrs. Peabody would be working this afternoon.

As Beverly left the city limits behind and accelerated on the open highway, she decided she'd go straight to Shelley's and ask if she could borrow the photo. As she drove, she had intended to think through the budget report, but instead, over and over, her mind went back to the photo and the image of the little boy.

★　★　★

"I don't have it." Shelley was wearing her blonde hair in two low-hanging pigtails. She stood in the open doorway with her baby daughter Emma, who wore a miniature version of her mother's hairstyle, clinging to her leg. "I gave it to Diane last night."

Shelley's son Aiden sat behind them playing with a Lego spaceship in the middle of the entryway of their split-level house. His dog Prize must have been playing most of the day, because she slept a few feet away.

Beverly glanced across the street. "Is Diane home?"

Shelley shaded her eyes and squinted into the sun. "Her light was on in the middle of the night when I was up with Emma. I figured she must have been writing. So maybe she's sleeping now." Shelley lifted Emma over the threshold and lowered her onto the porch. "Or maybe she took the photo into town to show August Jackson."

"All right. Thanks, Shelley."

"Sure. Good to see you."

Beverly started down the walk, stepping around the red beach bucket and yellow shovel in her path. August "Augie" Jackson was a retired reporter and the unofficial town historian. He was in his late eighties so he could have been a contemporary of the boy in the photo, and might know who he was.

Beverly glanced back over her shoulder and waved toward Shelley and the kids.

Aiden was circling his mother and sister now, making engine noises as he swooped the spaceship up and down. Emma was still attached to Shelley's leg, so when Shelley took a step back into the house, she lugged Emma with her. The girl let out a wail, but when Shelley tried to scoop her up, the little one sat down, still deadweight, on Shelley's foot.

Beverly shook her head at the sight of poor Shelley anchored to her house. She turned and hurried across the street, where she stepped onto Diane's porch and knocked gently on her door. If she was napping because of a late night of writing, Beverly didn't want to disturb her. But Diane's car was gone, so unless she'd parked it in the garage, she'd probably headed into town. After a minute Beverly knocked again. This time, Rocky, the dog Diane had rescued a few months before, let out a bark— confirmation enough that his mistress wasn't home, or else she'd be coming to the door.

Back at the sidewalk, Beverly turned toward the ocean instead of going back to her father's house. She walked along the sidewalk until it ended on a little knoll above the trail that led through the tall grass and down to the beach.

The wind tugged at the strands of hair that had escaped her bun and lashed them against her face. The tide was out, and tourists were walking the beach from town to the lighthouse. The salty air stung her eyes, causing them to water. She breathed in deeply and exhaled slowly. The frothy waves crashed against the rocks where the tide pools formed. A handful of children and two adults scurried around the area, jumping from pool to pool.

She longed to be on the beach too, not to play but to run with the warmth of the sun and the rush of the wind.

She focused on the lighthouse way down the beach. She couldn't deny that it intrigued her, just as it did her three new friends.

If she'd learned anything in the last few years, it was that some things in life were better left forgotten. And while Beverly loved her new friends, there were some things even friends didn't need to know.

She tucked behind her ear the strands of hair that were whipping against her face, and turned back toward the street. She would put in another couple hours of work and then run on the beach before dinner. That would be her reward. And then she would ask Diane about the photo.

Her heels clicked along the sidewalk as she made her way up the slight hill. Ahead, her father's two-story Victorian beckoned to her, just as it must have to all its other occupants through its 150-plus-year history. The soft cream exterior and green and butter gingerbread trim glowed warmly in the bright afternoon light.

Beverly went to her car in the driveway and retrieved her briefcase. She veered around to the side yard, staying on the flagstone walkway beside the overgrown laurel hedge, and walked to the back door. The bayberry, viburnum, and Virginia rose that lined the yard all needed to be trimmed, and a pile of branches knocked down from last month's storms still sat beside the garage. She bounded up the back steps and opened the door. She stepped through the mudroom and made her way through the kitchen.

"Hello," she called out, but no one answered. Mrs. Peabody often went home in the afternoon to rest, and her father was probably reading in the library.

Beverly pushed through the swinging door, stepped into the dining room, and put her briefcase on her desk in the alcove. A minute later she pushed open the door to the library. Her father sat in his chair, his feet propped up on the ottoman and a book in his lap. His head was tilted back a little, and a snore rumbled out of his mouth.

She wouldn't disturb him. Not now. She closed the door quietly. She sighed as she returned to the alcove. She wished she could be as enthused about the PowerPoint presentation she needed to whip together as she was about being home.

CHAPTER TWO

Two hours later, PowerPoint presentation started but not nearly as far along as she had hoped, Beverly stood in the kitchen wearing a pair of shorts, a Lycra T-shirt, and her running shoes, drinking a glass of water. She turned at the sound of the back door opening.

Mrs. Peabody limped into the house, a plate of brownies in one hand and a loaf of French bread in the other. Although she was no longer using crutches after spraining her ankle, she wasn't as spry as she had been before her fall.

"Hello," Beverly said, eyeing the snacks Mrs. Peabody had just brought in.

Mrs. Peabody started a little. "Oh, you're here." The woman's short gray hair was pulled back in two clips. She wore a cotton dress and a white sweater, even though the day was warm, especially for Maine.

"I arrived a couple hours ago." Beverly put her cup on the counter and reached for the brownies. "How about if I put these in the cupboard?" Mrs. Peabody occasionally seemed to forget that her father really had to curtail sweets to keep his diabetes under control. She'd probably try the

French bread, but she'd sneak the brownies into the garbage after Mrs. Peabody went home.

As she closed the cupboard door, she turned to Mrs. Peabody. "Please help yourself to the brownies. Just don't let Father know they're here." She winked, hoping to encourage the woman to cooperate.

Mrs. Peabody gave a quick nod and stashed her purse in the drawer Beverly had cleared out for that purpose. "I thought I'd make fish chowder for dinner to go with the bread." She held up the loaf. "Diane Spencer gave it to me."

Beverly put her glass in the sink. "Is she home?"

"Just talked to her. She'd been to town—asking questions again, no doubt. That one's a real snooper, especially for being new folk. Always asking about this and that. Oh my, I've never seen the likes of her."

Beverly smiled at the irony of Mrs. Peabody, the snoopiest neighbor of all, interpreting Diane's interest in the history of the lighthouse as being rude. "Mrs. Peabody, I'll be right back. I'm going to go talk to Diane for a minute. Hopefully I'll have something to show you when I get back."

Sure enough, Diane's car was in her driveway, and Rocky was bounding around the yard, dashing to and fro.

"Come on in, boy," Diane said from the front porch of her cottage.

When Rocky saw Beverly, he bounded out into the street.

"Rocky!" Diane shouted.

Beverly grabbed the dog's collar, keeping hold of him so he wouldn't jump up on her. "I've got him."

Diane was on the sidewalk now, shielding her eyes. In the sunshine, it was warm and bright, but as Beverly stepped into the shade of Diane's yard, the temperature dropped. "Thank you," Diane said, reaching for the dog. Diane was tall and thin with brown shoulder-length hair, and she wore jeans, a short-sleeved shirt, and a fleece vest, her usual attire.

"He saw me," Beverly said. "That's why he ran."

Diane laughed. "He sees everything: squirrels, birds, cars, bikes." She nodded across the street to where Aiden was playing on Shelley's porch, the front door open. The sound of Prize's barking came from their backyard. "Children, puppies, neighbors—you name it."

"Speaking of," Beverly said. "Shelley said she gave you the photo from the lighthouse."

Diane patted the pocket of her vest. "I have it... somewhere." She patted her other pocket and then reached inside. "Here it is. Augie didn't have a clue who they could be. He said he'd located a few logbooks for the lighthouse at the Coast Guard station in Portland, but most are missing. There's one from the late 1880s through 1910, but then after that there's not another one until the 1950s, just before the lighthouse was decommissioned. No one seems to know what happened to the other books."

Beverly snorted. "That doesn't surprise me. It's just like our search in the newspaper morgue—the records we really need are mysteriously missing."

Diane patted Rocky's flank. "I had the same thought."

Beverly held her hand out. "I thought I'd show the picture to Mrs. Peabody."

"Good idea."

Beverly took it, holding it around the jagged edge between her thumb and forefinger. "I'll return it in just a few."

"No hurry. Oh, and give it to Shelley when you're done."

"Thanks."

Diane yawned, quickly covering her mouth.

"Shelley said you were working late into the night."

Diane smiled. "I'll probably pull another late one tonight. I'm on a roll."

"Nearly done?" Beverly asked.

"We'll see," Diane said, a twinkle in her eye.

"What is a 'cozy mystery,' anyway?" Beverly had wanted to ask Diane more about her writing and was thankful for the opportunity.

"It's a mystery that doesn't get too dangerous," Diane said with a chuckle. "They're usually about a female amateur sleuth solving crimes in a small town or village."

"Like Marble Cove?"

Diane nodded with a gleam in her eye.

"Sounds intriguing." Beverly turned to go. As she walked away from Diane's, Beverly held up the torn black-and-white photo. Surely the boy and man in the photo, most likely the boy's father, were clues to the mystery of the lighthouse. Neither looked happy. The boy had a somber expression and big, sad eyes, and he wore an old-fashioned cap and knickers. Beverly knew she'd seen family photos of a little boy dressed that way before. Probably her father. He'd been a child of the Depression. Most likely, the boy in the photo was now in his late seventies or early eighties, close to her father's age.

*   *   *

"I could ask my sister," Mrs. Peabody said, turning the photo over to the back for the third time. The faded inscription read "Robert and Edward, 1933."

"Ask who what?" Beverly's dad stood in the doorway to the kitchen, looking a little bleary-eyed from his long nap.

"Shelley found a photo at the lighthouse," Beverly said. "I was hoping Mrs. Peabody would have an idea of who it might be in the picture."

"But I've never seen these people in my life," Mrs. Peabody said. "Thought I'd ask my sister. She's a couple years older than me. She might remember the boy."

Beverly's father reached out his hand.

"We're thinking the boy lived in Marble Cove," Beverly told him. "Long before you moved here."

Mrs. Peabody held the photo so he could see it.

Beverly's dad studied it for a long moment. The expression on his face softened, and Beverly felt sure he was remembering his own knickers and little cap. After a minute he shook his head. "You're right. He must have lived here before we did."

Mrs. Peabody handed the photo back to Beverly. "You keep it. I'll get it later. It might be weeks—or even months—before I see my sister. She lives about an hour away, and I just don't get out there much anymore."

Beverly's heart sank. "That long?"

Mrs. Peabody turned toward the stove to stir the soup.

Disappointed, Beverly retreated to her alcove, slipped the photo into a manila envelope for safekeeping, and headed out for her run.

★ ★ ★

The evening light waned outside the window of Diane's office as she stared at the words on the computer screen. She reread the sentence she'd just finished and then took off her reading glasses and rubbed her tired eyes. She'd intended to take Rocky for a walk, but it had grown late.

Time kept getting away from her. With news writing, she might spend hours on an article, even days, but she never stayed up all night. The process never consumed her the way writing fiction did. Now a five-hour block could feel like fifteen minutes.

When her children were home and her husband was still living, she would sometimes play with an idea for a novel, maybe sketch out a scene or a character. But she never spent much time writing on it. She couldn't have dedicated the time to a novel back then. Other things, more important things, would take precedence. Now was the time for her to dedicate herself to writing.

Rocky barked from the middle of the room, and Diane stood, leaving her glasses on her desk. Poor dog. She'd been neglecting him. She reached down and petted his soft yellow fur and then shuffled into the hall and on to the kitchen, opening the back door for the dog to go out. He stopped at her feet and looked up, his big brown eyes sad and moist.

"What's the matter, boy?" She patted his head again, and he responded with a yelp. It wouldn't hurt to take him for a walk. The fresh air would do her good—maybe even rejuvenate her to work for a few more hours. "Okay, okay. I'll get your leash."

She grabbed it off the peg by the door and put on her jacket, pulling her safety vest over the top of it. She wouldn't go down to the beach. She'd just stay on the sidewalk and walk toward town.

The cool air greeted her. After the sweltering summers in Boston, she'd always found the mildness of Maine's August seaside refreshing. She started down the front walkway, breathing deeply.

Across the street at Shelley's house, Dan's pickup came to life with a shudder and a rev of the motor. It was unusual for him to go to work in the evening. And last night, when she'd been up writing, she'd heard his pickup come home around two thirty. She knew the young family could use the extra money, but she also knew they didn't need the extra stress. She turned toward town. When Dan's truck passed, Diane waved, but the young man didn't see her.

She glanced down at her reflective vest, thinking she was hard to miss. Dan must have had other things on his mind.

Rocky trotted along beside her, his head held high and his tail waving behind him. She accelerated her pace up

Newport Avenue, wanting to make it a quick walk so she could get back to her story. She'd read the manuscript straight through, copyediting as she did. She needed to expand the ending a little and rework the first chapter, but she was pleased with how the story had come together.

Smiling, she turned the corner by the Wheelands' house. The light in the library shone dimly through the curtains, but the rest of the house was pitch dark. She thought of Mr. Wheeland. Her own father had passed on when her children were babies, followed by her mother a few years later. Beverly was fortunate to have her father still alive.

Diane thought of her husband. How she wished Eric were alive now to read her novel. Her little cozy mystery paled in comparison to the classics he taught, she knew, but still she would have appreciated his opinion on the plot points and character development, setting, theme, and voice.

She waited for a car to pass, then crossed Main Street and headed north. What if she never sold the story to a publisher? What if the agent she'd met at the writing conference didn't like it? What if it was never published?

She sighed as she reached Marble Cove's little downtown area. If that happened, she could chalk the first novel up to experience and start another one. But what if a second one didn't sell? How long could she justify writing if she didn't see any return on her investment of time?

Diane stopped in front of the Shearwater Gallery and gazed in the window. Margaret had changed the display. The dim lights showed three paintings of birds: a giant black cormorant; a small golden crowned kinglet; and a common loon. They appeared to be by a new artist.

At the end of the street, she turned toward the wharf. As she grew closer, her heart swelled. Lights illuminated the docks. A lone figure was walking down toward the last boat. She peered into the darkness, sure it was Dan Bauer. Another man stepped forward, greeting him. Maybe Dan wasn't going into work. Maybe he was simply meeting a friend.

She turned to the right and stepped onto the boardwalk, strolling away from the docks and breathing in the salty air as she headed toward home. Whatever Dan was doing, it wasn't any of her business.

Rocky seemed reluctant to be headed back so soon, and he slowed his pace. Diane urged him forward. Then she smiled to herself as the thought struck her: she had all the time in the world to write as many novels as it took. She'd send this first one off to the agent and then get started on the next one as soon as possible. All the experts said that the more one wrote, the sooner one learned the craft. There had to be a reason she loved so dearly what she was doing.

She had to be honest with herself, though. When she was writing and lost in the imaginative world of her characters, she didn't miss Eric as much. It helped her forget, and she didn't grieve for him the way she did nearly every other minute of the day.

She didn't miss her two children, Justin and Jessica, as much either when she was absorbed in her work. They were thirty and twenty-seven, both launched and independent.

She was thrilled they didn't need her. It was exactly as life should be.

She was definitely happy to have her writing. She needed projects to keep her busy. Marble Cove had turned out to be the perfect place for her to make new friends—Margaret, Shelley, and Beverly—and to embrace her writing. Maybe God just wanted her to write for herself as a sort of escape from her grief. Or maybe He had a bigger audience in mind. She'd never know until she tried.

She looked down at Rocky. "I'm going to send the manuscript off before you know it." An invigorating rush of energy bolted through her, and she increased her pace again. The dog yipped but kept up.

Diane couldn't wait to get home and rework the first chapter. Again.

CHAPTER THREE

The next morning, Beverly rose early, showered quickly, and was at her desk in the alcove by 6:15 to finish the PowerPoint presentation. She would rather have gone for a run, but if she didn't buckle down and gather the rest of the information she needed, she'd make a fool of herself at the meeting in the afternoon.

Ten years ago, her goal had been to be the director of the department by now. Today, her goal was simply to not make a fool of herself. What was happening to her old driven self?

At eight, she took a break to fix her father breakfast, and she grabbed a granola bar for herself, taking it back to her desk. At eleven, she decided the presentation would have to do, even though it wasn't her best work. She'd stay at the office for the rest of the day after the presentation, working into the evening, and then to spend the night at her home in Augusta. She'd drive back to Marble Cove tomorrow morning.

As she grabbed a few overnight items from her bedroom, her eyes fell on the dressing table that had been her maternal grandmother's, and then to the top of the matching bureau, to the photo of her and her parents on the day she'd graduated from college. The room, even though it contained her things, was essentially a guest room. For some reason, that made her sad.

Beverly shook her head. Did she really want to live here? The thought was ridiculous...except she kept coming back to it. Something about Marble Cove was drawing her. It was more than wanting to be near her father as he aged. It was more, even, than being close to her three new friends, though that was part of it. It was almost as if the Orlean Point Light, that mysterious beacon, was calling her.

She carried her bag down the stairs and then collected her laptop and files for the presentation, taking everything out to her car and then returning to tell her father good-bye. He sat in his chair in the library again.

"Father?"

He didn't respond.

"Hey?"

He opened his eyes.

"Why don't you sit in the living room? Maybe watch the noon news program or something." She felt odd encouraging her father to watch TV, but it seemed better than sitting alone in the dim light.

"I have my book." He did. It was closed, clutched by his right hand.

"It's time for me to leave. I'll be back tomorrow by noon. Mrs. Peabody should be here any minute to start your lunch."

He nodded.

Beverly bent down and gave him a kiss on the forehead. He gave her a quick peck on the cheek. As she stood, she felt another pang of sadness. "Do you want to come with me?" she blurted out.

"To Augusta? Now?" His voice was one big question mark.

She nodded, knowing it was a silly idea.

"Oh no," he said. "I'll just wait here until you get back."

Five minutes later, as she left the city limits of Marble Cove, Beverly still had a lump in her throat. She wasn't used to feeling emotional, especially not about her father. She was usually pragmatic and even-keeled. She swallowed hard and tapped the CD button on her console, willing the classical music to distract her.

*   *   *

The budget meeting took place in the boardroom on the third floor. When it came time for Beverly to present her department's numbers, she popped in her thumb drive and clicked on the PowerPoint presentation. Even after doing countless presentations through the years, she always felt a wave of relief when the technology worked the way it was supposed to. She was also relieved to discover, as she strode to her place and picked up the remote control, that she felt like her old driven self again. Animated. Confident. In charge.

She began with the first slide, explaining the cuts that needed to be made due to the decline in property tax revenues because of the economy. As she clicked forward to the second slide, she became aware of her briefcase buzzing at her feet. She'd left her cell phone on vibrate, but she couldn't help but be distracted. Thankfully, no one else seemed to notice—or maybe they were just being polite.

She continued with the presentation, relieved when the buzzing stopped. Soon she found her groove again, sailing through the slides, ad-libbing a little here and there, even garnering a few laughs.

As she finished, her cell began to vibrate again. She flipped the briefcase onto its side with her foot so that the pocket her phone was in was now against the carpet. "Any questions?" she asked. Unable to hear the buzzing any longer, she answered her colleagues in peace for the next twenty minutes.

When she finished and the next presenter stood, she sat down in her chair and slipped the phone into her hand, sneaking a quick peek at the missed calls. Both were from her father, but he hadn't left a message either time. An uneasiness rose inside her, and for a moment she considered sneaking out in the hall to call him back. But she stopped herself. Surely he—or Mrs. Peabody, if she had been the caller—would have left a message if it were an emergency.

But after the meeting, in the hall on the way back to her office, she speed-dialed her father. Mrs. Peabody answered, and Beverly said she'd missed two calls.

"I didn't know the mister called," she said, sounding more annoyed than alarmed. "I'll check the library." Beverly heard a knocking sound and then Mrs. Peabody saying, "Did you call Beverly?"

There was a long pause, and Beverly imagined the worst as she opened the door to her office and hurried to her desk. What if her father had collapsed? Maybe he'd fallen out of his chair and had just happened to have the phone nearby.

The sound of a muffled voice came through the phone again, but Beverly couldn't understand what was being said.

Mrs. Peabody came back on. "Here he is."

Relieved, Beverly sank into her chair.

"I did call," he said, not bothering with *hello*. "Now let me see if I can remember why."

Beverly realized she was drumming her fingernails on her desk and stopped.

"Oh, I remember now," he said. "I was thinking about that photo, the one you showed me."

"Yes?"

"I think I recognize the boy—or maybe the man."

"Shelley found the photo—"

"In the lighthouse. I remember. You think he's a Marble Cove boy. But I knew him in Augusta, although he was older than me. He used to do yard work for my folks."

"What's his name?" Beverly asked, sure her father was confused.

"I'm not sure of that," her father said. "Teddy. Eddie. Something like that."

"Edward?" Beverly sat up straight. He hadn't seen the back of the photo.

"That's it!"

"How about a last name?"

"It hasn't come to me yet... Do you know where my old yearbooks are? That's why I called."

"I thought you said he was older?"

"Back then, the junior high and high school photos were all put in the same book," he said.

Beverly wasn't sure about that. There was a chance her father wasn't remembering correctly. "Aren't they in the library?"

"Couldn't find them," he said.

"Maybe in the attic?" She was doubtful. After her father had gone through all of his old boxes and left them undone and scattered all over the attic, she hadn't come across any yearbooks when she'd repacked everything. A new wave of panic gripped her. What if he tore through everything again? "Wait until I get home to look up there, please."

"I'll look in the library again." He sounded dejected.

"They'll show up."

Her father quickly said good-bye.

Beverly glanced at her watch. If she worked until nine o'clock, she could catch up on all of the work she'd neglected because she'd been doing the PowerPoint presentation. She could probably also get to the last questions her colleagues had raised in the presentation. That way, when she forwarded the report on to her new boss, all the issues would be covered.

Giving the presentation had given her a burst of energy for her work. She decided to get as much done as she could while she was feeling inspired.

CHAPTER FOUR

The ringing of her cell phone on the nightstand woke Beverly from a sound sleep. Alarmed, she grabbed for it, knocking it to the carpeted floor. Groaning, she flipped the lamp on and slipped out of bed to her knees, fishing under the bed. Thankfully, the phone was still ringing. It was 4:37 AM, and she was in her bedroom in Augusta. The number on the screen was her dad's.

"Father?" She collapsed back on the bed and rubbed her knees where the carpet had roughed them up. "What's wrong?"

"Nothing. I just thought of something. Were you sleeping?"

"Um, as a matter of fact, yes." She'd ended up staying at the office until ten and still hadn't finished her updates. She's climbed into bed after midnight.

"Oh, I'm sorry. I thought you got up early. For your morning run."

Five thirty was early. Four thirty-seven was inhumane. "What's up?" she asked, trying to calm the panic that had gripped her chest.

"I was thinking about that photo again," he said.

"Yes?" She turned the lamp off and pulled her pillow under her head.

"I couldn't find my yearbooks, but I remembered his name. I even wrote it down—" Pages rustled. "Here it is. I wrote it on the editorial page of the newspaper." He was in the library. She wondered how long he'd been awake. "His name is Edward Maker."

She sat up straight. "Maker? Are you sure?"

"Positive. He moved into our neighborhood when he was in elementary school. By the time he was eleven or so, my mom had hired him to help her with the yard and garden, which he did for several years. His family was poor, but not like the rest of us. They were really poor."

"Thanks," she said, her heart pounding. "That's great! The message we found was signed by an E. M., so this fits perfectly. This really helps."

"Are you coming home today?"

She smiled in the darkness. Home. "I'll be there by noon."

Beverly held the phone in her hand for a moment longer, wide awake now. Edward Maker. She had a name, first and last. But could she trust her father's memory?

She settled back into her bed, determined to get another hour of sleep.

But by five, light was sneaking in where the two panels of curtains didn't quite meet, and birds were starting to sing in the clematis vine outside her window. At 5:05, she got up, quickly made the bed, and stepped into the roomy master bath. Under the skylight, she changed out of her pajamas into her running shorts and a long-sleeved shirt.

Even though Will had been gone for five years, the house still didn't feel as if it was hers. Will had been an architect. He'd designed the house for them and had had it built before their wedding. Every detail was perfect, from the spacious kitchen to the great room to the outdoor patio and perfectly landscaped yard.

He'd designed the one-story modern craftsman for entertaining. The idea was to have a showcase where he could invite potential clients, while also offering a place for Beverly to entertain the people she rubbed elbows with at the State House. They'd thrown several sit-down dinners and garden parties in the four years before Will had died. She hadn't invited a soul over since.

She padded down the hallway over the thick carpet in her running shoes. The house was still practically brand-new. Will's children had been teenagers by the time their dad had married Beverly, and they were able to make their own decisions as far as visitations. They were busy in school and activities and usually declined to spend weekends with their dad. On the rare occasions when they had spent a night, they'd acted like guests, asking if they could eat the snacks and ice cream Beverly had bought especially for them. It should have been obvious—it wasn't food Beverly or Will would ever eat.

A dust bunny in the corner of the stone floor entryway caught Beverly's attention as she opened the front door, and she noted she needed to spend some time cleaning the place when she was back next week. Closing the door firmly, she started down the walkway. The lawn service she'd hired was doing a good job keeping the grass fertilized and trimmed, and the automatic sprinkler system was keeping everything green.

Beverly had inherited the house when Will died, but that was all. Everything else had gone to his children. Thankfully, her income was enough to cover the mortgage, but that didn't change the fact that it was much bigger than she needed, than she'd ever need.

People at work assumed she felt sentimental about the place, since Will designed it. But the truth was, it had never felt like hers. It had always—and still did—feel like his.

She turned right at the intersection, pushing her memories away, and jogged toward the Kennebec River. She had an extra half hour today, thanks to her dad. She'd be able to go a mile farther along the running path, at least.

★   ★   ★

Beverly spent two hours in her office, all the while thinking about the little boy in the photo, sure her father wasn't remembering things correctly. After she'd finally caught up with her work and not able to stand it any longer, she logged onto her laptop and entered "Edward Maker" into the white pages, adding "Maine" as the location.

Three entries popped up. One in Portland and two in Augusta. One of the entries for Augusta had only a phone number listed, while the second one had only an address. She jotted down both.

Collecting her things, she left her office, saying good-bye to the receptionist at the end of the hall.

"See you tomorrow," the young woman called out.

Beverly stopped. "No, not tomorrow. Next Monday."

"That's right." The woman sighed. "I'm having a hard time keeping track of everyone's schedules, what with vacations and telecommuting." She laughed uneasily.

"Remember, you can shoot me an e-mail or give me a call if anything comes up."

"I know, I know," the woman said. "Even if you're relaxing on the beach you'll get right back to me."

Beverly pursed her lips. She knew the receptionist was joking with her, but she didn't appreciate it. Not at all. Especially not if anyone else was eavesdropping. She waved and continued down the hall to the elevator.

When she got to her car, she took the slip of paper from her briefcase and called the number on her cell phone. It rang several times, and finally a woman answered. "Hello," Beverly said. "I'm looking for an Edward Maker."

"What has he done now?" The woman's voice was harsh.

"Nothing." Beverly spoke quickly. "There was a man by that name who went to school with my father."

"How old's your dad?" the woman said unnecessarily loudly.

"Seventy-nine."

The woman began to laugh. She continued to laugh until it sounded more like a howl coming through the phone. "Got the wrong number," she finally managed to stammer.

Beverly thanked her but before she could hit "End" the woman continued, "My Edward is my son. He's thirty-seven. Moved back in with me, the no-good louse—" She stopped. "Ha. I shouldn't say that!" The woman erupted in laughter again.

"Thank you," Beverly muttered again and hung up. Obviously that wasn't the man she was looking for.

She studied the piece of paper and read the address again. Duncan Road. She didn't remember where that was. She pulled her GPS from her purse. Will had bought it just before he'd died. She felt it was an extravagance, something they didn't need. But now it seemed like everyone had one, and, honestly, it came in handy now and then. She punched in the house number and then the street. She started the car and headed off in the direction it told her to go.

The GPS took her east of the State House, across the river, toward the part of town where her father had grown up. It wasn't until she'd passed the high school that she realized she was within a few blocks of where her father had lived.

When she stopped at the address, she realized with a shock that the house, with its double lot and towering hemlock tree in the back, was the very house in which her father had grown up. It was painted a sage green now instead of the white she remembered, but there was no doubt about it: it had once been the Wheeland family home.

As if in a daze, Beverly climbed from the car and headed up the flagstone walkway, noting how similar it was to the one at her father's home in Marble Cove. Had her grandfather put this one in all those years ago? Had her father chosen his home in Marble Cove because the walkways were so similar?

Both her grandparents had died when she was in elementary school, one after the other. They were in their late sixties. Her grandmother had died from complications from diabetes, and her grandfather had died the year after from, according to her dad, a broken heart. Her mother had told her once that it might have been so, but the death certificate listed the cause as coronary disease.

Her shoes made a hollow sound against the painted steps of the porch as she hurried up to the front door. Terra cotta planters of petunias stood on either side of the front door, and more petunias spilled over the sides of a window box. The house was a two-story, large bungalow, probably close to a hundred years old. She could hardly remember it from when her father drove her by it when she was little, but she felt sure it was better taken care of now than it had been back then. It couldn't be a coincidence that Edward Maker lived in the house.

She rang the bell.

After a minute, she rang the bell again and stepped closer to the door, hoping to hear someone inside but she couldn't hear a thing. She stepped down from the porch and looked over to the side yard. There was the driveway that led to a small, detached garage with a Chevy pickup parked inside. She wondered if Mr. Maker still drove it. He was most likely in his early eighties, which wasn't too old to drive, although the thought of what it would be like if her father were still driving made her nervous.

She turned toward the house again. The windows were all draped with curtains. More flowers filled pots along the steps to the back door. She scanned the whole property. A large, well-tended vegetable garden grew in the second lot, and behind it was an irrigation ditch. The property was well cared for, but there wasn't a soul in sight.

She walked slowly back to her car and drove away. Once she reached the highway, she wondered why she hadn't left a note. She sighed. She'd stop by next week when she was in town. Unless he was away on an extended vacation, she would find him home sooner or later.

Chapter Five

Diane opened one eye and turned her head toward the digital clock on her bedside table—ten thirty. It would be late except that she hadn't gone to bed until after eight. She closed her eyes again, determined to get at least three or four hours of sleep.

She tossed and turned. Her mind was stuck on the middle of her story, where the heroine couldn't start her car. That made her think of an episode of a car repair show she'd heard on the radio. A widow had called in saying she couldn't start the car her husband stored in their garage before he died. The hosts had asked, in very somber tones, if she'd checked to see if her husband had unhooked the battery. Of course the woman hadn't. The host told her how to check the battery and then how to rehook it.

Diane remembered the segment because she'd heard it not long after Eric had passed away, and she'd cried for the widow on the phone, knowing full well she was crying for herself too.

Perhaps someone had unhooked her heroine's battery in her story. But her character's father had been a mechanical engineer, so she would know what to look for. Diane opened her other eye and looked at the clock—10:40. It was no use. She might as well get back up and work on the story. The heroine was on her way to the lighthouse near where her family used to vacation when she was a child, looking for a clue to solve the mystery.

Rocky was at her side before her feet hit the floor. It made her smile how the dog anticipated her every move. Diane reached out and stroked his head, wondering if he was feeling out of sorts from her burning the candle at both ends. She wasn't usually such a night owl. She marveled at her energy the last week to write twenty hours a day. It wasn't as if she was on a real deadline, only a self-imposed one. But she was determined to get her manuscript sent off to the agent she'd met before the woman forgot who she was.

She showered and pulled on a pair of sweats, then poured herself a cup of coffee and settled down at her computer again, finding the scene where the car wouldn't start. This time, instead of flagging down help, her heroine would fix the problem herself.

Two hours later, her stomach rumbling, she stood and stretched. She'd changed the scene and read through the middle part of the story again. She'd once heard that the middle of a novel was often the hardest to write, that the story often lagged and sometimes even sagged. She was determined for that not to happen.

After devouring a granola bar, she was back at her computer again reworking the first three pages for the fifth time. If the beginning didn't catch the agent's attention, and then the editor's, the story would never sell. She had to nail the start.

It was sometime in the early afternoon when Diane began feeling she was ready to send the manuscript to the agent. The beginning and ending were strong. The middle moved along at a steady pace. She'd rewritten, revised, edited, copyedited, and line edited.

She was sure she could keep working on it for the rest of her life if she wanted, but it wouldn't necessarily make it any better. She decided to give herself until four o'clock and then send it off to Frieda Watley, of the prestigious Brewster Literary Agency in New York City.

As Diane clicked on Spell Check for the third time that day, she imagined Frieda in her Manhattan office overlooking Central Park. Or maybe she was taking one of her authors out to lunch at that very moment, eating at the Four Seasons or Le Cirque. The heat would be sweltering in New York, so they would have taken a taxi or a car service. Maybe even a limo. Ha! Diane couldn't help but laugh out loud at her fantasy. She directed her imagination back to her manuscript again.

By the time four o'clock rolled around, she felt she was finished. She knew the feeling from her days of working as a reporter. There came a time when one's brain screamed, "Done!" She just hoped Frieda Watley agreed that it was so.

She opened her e-mail account, clicked "new message," and typed in Ms. Watley's address. As she attached the document she said a little prayer and then wrote a quick accompanying note, reminding Frieda that they'd met at a writers' conference and that she had asked Diane to send her the finished manuscript.

As she hit Send, she exhaled dramatically. She pushed away from the desk and stood. But immediately she felt a little lost. Writing had been consuming all of her time. What would she do now?

Looking around her office, Diane knew what her next task had to be. Stacks of paper littered the floor, her desk, and the table under the window. Books were off their shelves and stacked around the room. Three coffee mugs were lined up to the left of her screen. She picked those up and shuffled down the hall, with Rocky trailing behind her.

She yawned as she stopped in the middle of the kitchen, the linoleum cool to her stocking feet. Dirty dishes filled the sink. The hot-cereal box from breakfast the day before still stood on the counter. A piece of forgotten bread waited in the toaster. She shook her head at herself. She wasn't usually so untidy.

She started in on the dishes, realizing that in the last days of intense writing it had felt as if she'd been away on a trip. Actually, she had been. A mental trip. An emotional trip. It was the same feeling she had when she was reading a good book. She hoped that meant her book would send readers on a fun trip too.

After she finished the last of her dishes, she dried her hands and thought about dinner. She hadn't done any grocery shopping for days. Maybe she should run to the store.

As she slipped her shoes on, the phone rang. The shrill noise startled her, and she had to laugh at herself again. She really had become a hermit. She cleared her throat before she said hello, hoping her voice still worked. It did, barely.

"It's Margaret," said the voice coming through the receiver. "I need a favor."

"Sure," Diane stammered, still trying to sound normal.

"It's these blasted colors. I can't seem to get them right."

"Pardon?" Was she talking about one of her paintings?

"You did such a good job in your cottage. Well, I thought maybe you could help me out."

"Sure!" Diane smiled to herself. Margaret was finishing up the repairs to her gallery. That's what she wanted help with. "When do you need to decide?"

"Three hours ago."

Diane chuckled. "I was just headed to the store. How about if I come by now?"

"Perfect," Margaret said, sounding relieved. "Beverly and Shelley are on their way too."

★   ★   ★

Diane decided to walk and to take Rocky with her. When she reached the gallery, she tied his leash to the bicycle stand on the sidewalk. The dog gave her a pathetic look, but as she said, "Stay," he settled down and put his head on his paws.

As Diane stepped into the gallery, a sense of peace settled over her. The paintings were back on the walls in the front gallery, but the stains from the water damage were definitely noticeable on the ceilings. Scaffolding from the repairs loomed in the middle of the room, and Diane had to walk around it to reach the next gallery. Last month's storms had damaged the roof of the building, which had caused extensive water damage to the gallery ceilings.

She heard Beverly's voice before she saw her, and patted her hair, trying to remember if she'd combed it before she ran out the door. She never felt self-conscious about her appearance with Margaret, but now that she knew perfectly put-together Beverly was here…

As she rounded the corner, Diane saw that Shelley was there too, standing next to Beverly. Sure enough, Beverly looked radiant. She was thin as a reed and strikingly beautiful with her dark shoulder-length hair. She was dressed in slacks, a white blouse, and low pumps, as if she'd come straight from work.

Happily, Shelley and Margaret were dressed casually. Shelley wore overall shorts with a sweatshirt tied around her waist.

"Oh good," Margaret said. "We're all here."

For a second, Diane wondered if she'd really been summoned about choosing paint colors. Maybe the women knew, somehow, that she'd sent off her manuscript, and they'd planned a celebratory gathering. But then Margaret waved a collection of paint chips, and it was obvious they'd been called together for that reason.

"I'm wondering if I should add some color to the ceilings," Margaret said. It was like her to be all business, right from the start. "Maybe blue. I'm even thinking about repainting the walls too."

Beverly reached out her hand, and Margaret split the chips into three groups, handing one to each of the women. "I want to get the painting done as soon as possible. First of all, so I can get my business back to normal, but also because I have a family reunion coming up and would like to be able to go to it without worrying about all of this."

Shelley nodded.

As Diane took her chips, she couldn't help but notice Margaret's hands were chapped and rough. She'd probably done the cleanup from the repairs to save money.

"I like the idea of color," Margaret said, "as long as I can make it work with the paintings."

Diane sorted through her chips. There was a periwinkle that she liked and a lemon yellow. "What if you go with the colors of the sunrise over the ocean?" she suggested. "Pale colors."

"That's an idea," Margaret said.

"Or," Diane said, "you could paint it haint blue."

"Huh?" Margaret's eyes grew large.

"It's the color that porch ceilings in the South are painted. It's supposed to represent the water and protect the house."

Margaret's eyes lit up. "That sounds interesting."

"But what if the painting you need to display clashes with the colors?" Beverly asked. "And blue can be bit of a downer, depending on the theme of an exhibit."

Diane mulled over that—how could the color of a sunlit sky and ocean be a downer? Someone might get the blues all right, but the color blue usually cheered her up.

Margaret sighed. "That's just it. I know some galleries repaint every time they change exhibits, but I can't do that. It takes too much time, plus the cost really adds up."

Diane shuffled back through the colors. "You could choose one color for the ceiling and then repaint the walls every time."

"There's this gallery in Augusta," Beverly said. "The walls are all black. At least for the exhibit I saw. Would that work for yours?"

"It's an idea," Margaret said. "Speaking of Augusta, there's an exhibit there now that I want to see. Jude LeBlanc. He paints seascapes. Anyone want to go with me this Friday?"

"Sure!" Diane said, almost before thinking. Getting out of Marble Cove would be good for her.

"We could do dinner," Margaret suggested.

"And stop by Edward Maker's house," Beverly added.

"Whose house?"

"E.M.'s." Beverly kept her eyes on her paint chips.

"E.M.? As in from the lighthouse?" Shelley sounded dumbfounded. "As in from 'Robert and Edward, 1933' on the back of the photo? You know for sure his name is Edward Maker? How did you find out?"

Beverly smiled and looked up. "I don't have conclusive proof. But my dad thinks he knew the boy in the photo way back when—Edward Maker. And there's an

Edward Maker who lives in Augusta. I stopped by his house this morning."

Diane felt her mouth drop open. "You found his house and went there? Girl, you should be a detective."

Beverly beamed. "And get this." She took a deep breath, and her eyes twinkled. "The house he lives in used to be my grandparents' house. This Edward Maker used to help my grandma with yard work."

The other three ladies looked at each other in amazement.

"What did he say?" Diane asked, her heart racing at Beverly's discovery.

"He wasn't home," Beverly said, and the women groaned. "That's my point: we could stop there on Friday."

The other women agreed.

"Oh, I don't know if I'll be able to join you on Friday," Shelley said, sounding as if she were about to miss out on Christmas. "I'll have to see about Dan's work schedule. It's more erratic than ever."

Diane nodded. "I've seen his truck coming and going at the oddest hours. I've been up fini—"

"Allan feels so bad he hasn't had any work for Dan lately," Margaret said to Shelley. "Things have slowed down..."

A sympathetic looked passed over Shelley's face. "Tell Allan not to give it a second thought. Dan's overtime seems to be making up for it."

"What time should we leave here on Friday?" Beverly brushed her hair away from her face in an impatient gesture as she spoke.

"Well," Margaret said, "traffic should be fine going toward Augusta. I'd say four o'clock would be plenty early enough."

"We'll need to take two cars," Beverly said. "I'll go ahead and spend the night in Augusta. The gardeners are coming Saturday morning, and I need to talk with them about the back hedge. I want to be there to show them in person. They've done it wrong the last two times."

Margaret shifted the discussion back to the colors, and the women threw out ideas, one after another, but after a half hour Margaret still hadn't decided.

★   ★   ★

That evening, as Diane washed her one plate, her one glass, her one fork, and her one knife, she felt an overwhelming sense of loneliness. Oh, how she wished she could let Eric know she'd sent her novel off to Frieda Watley! To take that huge step but not be able to tell anyone left her feeling empty.

She should have told her friends when they were at the gallery. She should have just forced herself to do it. It wasn't bragging—it was simply sharing information. But it felt a little arrogant, especially when there was absolutely no guarantee anything would come from it.

She could call her kids. Well, she could call Jessica and leave a message via Skype or send an e-mail to Justin. They should be the best options, next to Eric. But she wasn't sure they'd understand. She dried her plate, glass, fork, and knife and put them away one by one, deciding she would send Jessica and Justin each an e-mail saying she'd sent it off.

A minute later, she was back in her office, powering up her computer, and going online. She opened a new e-mail message and wrote, "Just had to share my excitement" in the subject line.

"Hi, kids," she wrote. "Wanted you to know I sent off my manuscript to the New York agent today." She had told both Jessica and Justin about the wonderful meeting with the agent, but they might have forgotten. "I'm excited— although it might be several weeks, even months, before I hear back from her. Love, Mom."

Weeks or months. She sighed as she hit Send. It didn't feel like she was any closer to being published than she'd been before.

Feeling exhausted, she climbed into bed at nine, accompanied by the sound of Dan Bauer's truck rumbling down the street outside her window. Maybe he needed a new muffler. She was sure the beast was growing louder with each passing day. His new work schedule certainly was full of odd hours. She felt for Shelley.

CHAPTER SIX

Friday afternoon Margaret got out the paint chips once more and fanned them across the counter of the shop. It wasn't that she thought another look would help her make up her mind; she just liked the way colors all looked, one after another. She was hoping the visit to the gallery in Augusta would help her make up her mind.

"We're here!" Adelaide's voice came trilling through the door of the gallery.

"I'm in the back," Margaret called out.

A moment later Adelaide had her arms wrapped around her mother's waist, hugging her tightly. Allan stood behind their daughter, his cap in his hand and his hair mussed up just a little.

Margaret hugged Adelaide back, waiting for the girl to release first. Finally, her daughter let go, stepped back, and brushed her honey-colored bangs away from her eyes. "Why can't I go with you?"

Even after all these years, Margaret still sometimes couldn't understand some of her daughter's words. But this time she had no trouble, since they'd had this very conversation at least five times in the last two days. "Not this time," Margaret said.

A hint of a pout passed over Adelaide's face, but then she spotted the new pad of fluorescent green stickies and skipped over to the counter.

"You may use ten of those," Margaret said. "To write notes."

Adelaide quickly began counting out the squares of paper, grinning as she did, while Margaret told Allan that she'd already swept the floors, but if he and Adelaide wanted to wash the insides of the windows that would be great. Allan wore a pair of cargo shorts and a long-sleeved T-shirt. Margaret thought, as she often did, that he grew more handsome every day.

Beverly, who always seemed to be punctual, arrived first with Diane right behind her. Adelaide greeted both of the women warmly but then focused on recounting her squares of paper.

"Is Shelley coming?" Margaret asked Diane as Allan and Beverly chatted about the Friday afternoon traffic inching through Marble Cove.

Diane shook her head. "I'm not sure."

Just then, Shelley hurried through the front door.

"Oh good!" Diane said. "Dan must have the day off."

Shelley grimaced. "It's good and not so good. I don't know how long our budget can make it on his erratic hours."

"That bad, huh?" Margaret asked.

Shelley nodded and then looked around the small group. "Sorry—I hope I'm not making you feel bad, you know, since Allan hasn't had extra work."

Margaret flapped her hand around, as if to tell Shelley not to worry about it. She knew Shelley hadn't mentioned it to hurt Margaret and Allan, but still she felt bad. She remembered what it was like to live paycheck to paycheck. "Let's get a wiggle on," she said to the other three women. "Time's a-wastin'."

★　　★　　★

Diane rode with Beverly, and Shelley rode in Margaret's van. Beverly led the way as the small caravan made its way out of town in the bumper-to-bumper traffic. By the time they turned toward Augusta, the traffic going their way had thinned while the traffic heading to the coast had gotten worse.

"We're timing the trip right, at least," Margaret said. "Can you imagine if we'd decided to come over Sunday afternoon?"

"Exactly," Shelley said.

Margaret steered clear of talking about Dan and his work situation, and instead asked Shelley about her kids. Margaret well remembered those early years with Adelaide. Her daughter had digestive problems as a little one and even had to be on a feeding tube at one time. Thankfully, as she matured, she'd outgrown those problems.

Of course, Shelley's children had none of the challenges that Adelaide had. Back then, Margaret had had to fight the school district tooth and nail to get every service she could, starting with early childhood intervention. She knew Adelaide wasn't the first child with Down syndrome in the school system, but sometimes the administrators acted like it.

"When will Aiden start school?" Margaret asked.

"Oh, not for a couple more years." Shelley leaned back against the seat. "We can't afford preschool, so he'll have to wait for kindergarten. Although it would make starting my business easier to have him in school this fall. The kids are *at it* all the time. Aiden teases Emma. She's started grabbing his Legos, which annoys him to no end. He retaliates by poking her. It's endless."

"Is Dan a help when he's home?"

Shelley sighed and looped her long, loose hair into a ponytail and wound a fastener around it, creating a sloppy but attractive bun. "It depends. Sometimes he is, but a lot of the time I have to tell him what to do, you know?"

Margaret nodded, but the truth was that she never had to tell Allan what to do. He was a better homemaker than she was. Even when they were first married, he had a knack for housekeeping. And he'd always been devoted to Adelaide.

"Plus, Dan seems out of sorts, which makes things tense around the house."

"Still?"

"Yeah." Shelley paused for a moment. "In fact, I think it's worse. He's been out super-late, like middle-of-the-night late, three out of the last four nights."

"And he never was before?"

"Not very often."

"What does he say?" Margaret kept her eyes on the road as she spoke.

"The usual. It's 'special work circumstances.' And temporary."

"Does he seem defensive or annoyed with your questions?"

Shelley didn't answer for a moment, and Margaret stole a look at the young woman. She was clearly deep in thought.

"Actually," Shelley said slowly, "no. He doesn't."

"That's a good sign," Margaret said. "I heard once that you've really got to worry if they get angry or defensive." Not that she would know. Allan never got defensive.

Shelley sighed. "Still, it's disconcerting. Some days I don't give it a thought, but other times, usually in the middle of the night, I worry."

Margaret couldn't help but admire the young woman's honesty. Maybe it was part of her personality or her generation's approach to life, but Margaret wasn't so sure that, forty years ago, if she'd been suspicious of Allan, she would have shared it the way Shelley had.

"It's not like I think he's having an—" Shelley paused, then shook her head as if to clear her mind of the thought. "Although I have to be honest—in the middle of the night, every scenario has entered my head."

Margaret couldn't help but wince. She certainly hoped that wasn't the case.

Shelley chuckled. "Don't tell anyone that, okay? I don't want to start any rumors."

"Of course I wouldn't. And surely he's not," she said. "It has to be work-related, don't you think?"

Shelley agreed and then went back to the topic of starting a small business.

Margaret told them that the contract from the greetings card company had helped the gallery, but the status of the shop seemed to fluctuate with each day. "It's the nature of the business. I'll go weeks with nothing to deposit, sure I'm not going to be able to make the rent, and then *voilà,* I'll make a sale and have just what I need. But I'll be honest: I never have more than I need. Just enough to pay the bills. Never enough for even a salary for me."

"Wow." Shelley's voice was low. "Why do you keep doing it?"

It was Margaret's turn to chuckle. "Either I'm a glutton for punishment or this is what I'm supposed to be doing." She glanced over at the young woman and smiled. "It keeps me praying. Although, I worry a ton too. I want to trust God, but it's scary to let go. I think you've got that down better than I do. You're so involved in your church and you seem to have such a strong faith."

Shelley nodded, though the gesture seemed a little noncommittal. "I'd definitely need to start making money from the get-go if I start a baking business. Especially if I have to hire a sitter. Our budget can't handle any more losses right now."

*   *   *

Forty-five minutes later, Margaret pulled her car in behind Beverly's, a block from the gallery. The women congregated on the sidewalk, deciding to go to the gallery first and then to get a bite to eat before stopping by the residence of Edward Maker.

Margaret led the way, excited to get a look at the new exhibit. She'd visited galleries all over the area when she'd been about to open her own, but she knew this one would have been customized for Jude LeBlanc's show and would therefore be very different from the last time she saw it. She wanted to see how they'd matched the changes in the decor to the famed artist's work.

As the women strolled down the sidewalk, Beverly pointed out a café across the street. "Their salads are good," she said. "And their pasta." They agreed that would be the perfect place for dinner.

Orange and yellow marigolds filled the planters in front of the shops they passed and little flags that advertised the downtown district of Augusta flapped from the lightposts in the early evening breeze. When they reached the gallery, Beverly swung open the door, motioning for the rest of them to enter.

Margaret pushed her sunglasses atop her head and stepped into the cavernous space, her eyes adjusting to the dimmer light as she led the way toward Jude LeBlanc's exhibit. Two of the interior walls of the building were brick, and the other two were Sheetrock and painted a pale green, as was the ceiling. The paintings were hung on clear wire and positioned in front of the walls, giving the illusion that they were floating. She scanned the paintings. All were seascapes, many with lighthouses.

Her hand went to her chest. Again, she marveled that Matt Beauregard, the CEO of the card company, chose her work for their new line. He could have chosen any artist, including Jude LeBlanc, but he'd picked her. She breathed a prayer of gratitude again.

She stopped in front of the first painting and soaked in the scene. It depicted a seascape with a fishing boat bobbing in a stormy sea with an island in the background. The artist's style was bolder than hers and the shapes were sharper, plus the colors were vibrant and nearly jumped off the canvas, even though the setting was a storm.

The emotions of the stormy sea reminded her of how she felt the day she'd almost drowned. Her hand went to her throat again. Suddenly, she had an urge to paint that scene. Would she paint herself on the water or on the beach? And what about the stranger who had saved her? Would he be pulling her out or running up the dune away from her?

Diane stepped closer to Margaret. "It's beautiful, but I like your work better."

"Oh no," Margaret said. "He's much better than I am."

"Not in my opinion." Diane was adamant.

As the women made their way through the Jude LeBlanc exhibit, Margaret thought more about the painting she wanted to do. A storm was blowing in quickly on the day she'd nearly drowned. It had turned out to be an apple shaker, strong enough to knock fruit off a tree.

Because she'd been swimming, she hadn't realized how fast it had arrived.

She looked back to the stormy sea scene, tilting her head, examining the colors and brushstrokes the artist had used. A few minutes later, she realized that the other women had all wandered into the next room, so she followed.

It was an interior room with no windows, so all of the illumination was from the track lights affixed to the ceiling. The walls here were painted a pale yellow. The color perfectly displayed the watercolor wildflower paintings by another artist.

Margaret was sure that the gallery had more than a one-person staff. Surely they had the manpower and the financial resources to paint between exhibits. Again the other women finished before she had. They'd already gone to the last gallery, a collection of paintings done by Maine artists in the mid-twentieth century. By the time Margaret arrived, they'd finished. "Go on to the restaurant," she said. "I'll be right there."

She turned back toward a painting of two children, a girl and a boy, on a beach in front of a 1952 blue Ford truck. Her uncle had had a rig just like it. The girl had a seashell in one hand and a bucket in another, and her twin braids hung down over her collarbone. She wore a plaid dress and smiled broadly, showing a gap where her front teeth hadn't grown in yet. Her feet were bare. The boy was older and had a shovel slung over his shoulder.

Margaret shivered even though the gallery had become stuffy. She had grown up in Vermont but came to Maine every summer because her mother's relatives all lived up and down the coast, from just south of Marble Cove, where her cousin Buddy's family lived, to the Bar Harbor area, about two hours north.

She remembered her uncle driving down to the beach in his pickup. She remembered playing in the sand, summer after summer. Sometimes they would come up to Marble Cove. She remembered because of the lighthouse. She shuddered to think of Buddy and the lighthouse at the same time. The lighthouse conjured up so many good thoughts, while remembering Buddy brought up only bad memories.

Before she left to join her friends, she asked the gallery attendant a few questions. But the woman was new and said she worked only on Fridays and didn't have any answers. Margaret wanted to ask, *Then what is the use of your working here?* but it wasn't the woman's fault she hadn't been adequately trained.

Margaret left the gallery feeling unsettled but not knowing why. She still didn't know what color to paint her ceilings. But it was more than that. She touched her short hair, remembering that she'd worn her hair in braids all through her years growing up. She crossed the street in a hurry.

The restaurant wasn't nearly as busy as she'd feared, and she found her friends at a table in the front window. As she settled into her chair, it registered that Diane was talking about her novel.

"I'm still trying to catch up on my sleep," Diane said.

Margaret pulled her chair up to the table. "Did you send it off?"

"Wednesday," Diane said, looking a little sheepish.

"And you didn't tell us?" If Shelley had been standing, she would have had her hands on her hips.

Margaret picked up her water glass. "Here's to Diane's novel." The other women raised their glasses in a toast and they all clinked in unison. "May it meet with fabulous success!" Margaret said.

"Hear, hear!" Beverly and Shelley said.

Diane blushed. "We'll see. These things take a long time, months at least."

"But you did it," Margaret said. "You sent it off. That's what counts." She looked around the table, from Diane to Beverly to Shelley. She liked it that they were all ambitious women, each in her own way.

The conversation turned toward Edward Maker.

"I'm getting a little worried," Beverly said.

"That it's not him?" Shelley plucked a slice of French bread from the basket.

"No, that isn't it." She paused. "I'm probably worrying about nothing. But what if he doesn't want to see us?"

"Why wouldn't he?" Diane leaned back in her chair.

Margaret almost laughed. Diane was so Pollyanna, she probably couldn't imagine anyone not wanting the past thrown up in his face. She raised her water glass again. "To Edward Maker. May he welcome us with open arms."

The other women joined her, although Beverly didn't look as enthusiastic as the other two.

CHAPTER SEVEN

As Beverly shut her car door, her heart began to race. Her bad feeling about Edward Maker was growing. First, it felt really odd that he lived in her grandparents' old house. Secondly, what if he was a recluse who would resent the intrusion? Or what if he was confused? She couldn't help but acknowledge that she would feel unsettled by four strange women knocking on her father's door. On any given day, he might be either thrilled or scared to death.

She took a deep breath. They were here—they might as well knock. Maybe he wouldn't be home again.

"How about if you and Diane go up to the door?" Margaret said. "Shelley and I can wait by the cars. We don't want to overwhelm him."

Beverly nodded, grateful for the older woman's wisdom. Maybe she was grasping the awkwardness of the situation too.

Diane marched alongside Beverly up the walkway, up the steps, and across the porch. Beverly felt for the photo in the pocket of her purse. Once she'd reassured herself it was there, she knocked quickly.

In no time, a voice called out, "Coming!"

She could hear footsteps across the room, and then the door swung open. A man with a full head of salt-and-pepper hair, wearing slacks and a short-sleeved shirt, greeted them with a smile.

"Mr. Maker?" Beverly said.

He nodded.

She introduced herself and Diane. She explained that they had a few questions for him, but first she wanted him to know that her father had grown up in Augusta and that, in fact, her grandparents had owned his house years ago.

He grinned. "Yes, I remember the Wheeland family well. They used to hire me to help out here. That was one of the reasons I bought it. Do you have questions about the house?"

"Actually, no." Beverly reached for the photo. "My father lives in Marble Cove now." She nodded toward Diane and back to Margaret and Shelley. "And so do my friends. And I spend a good deal of time there." As she extended the photo to the man, it registered that his smile was fading. "My father thinks this is of you and your dad."

"We found it in the lighthouse," Diane said.

The smile was now gone, replaced by a stony glare.

Beverly held the photo in midair. "It says 'Robert and Edward, 1933' on the back. Was your father's name Robert?"

He didn't answer.

"And on the lighthouse," Diane said, "we found the initials E.M. carved into the foundation. We're hoping—"

The man stepped back into the house before Diane could finish her sentence, and slammed the door in their faces.

The two women jumped backward.

"Oh dear," Diane said. "I think we offended him."

Beverly clutched the photo to her chest, alarmed. They stood in stunned silence for a long moment. Finally, Beverly started down the steps, with Diane right behind her. Tears stung her eyes. What had they done?

★　　★　　★

Shelley dozed in the backseat of the car as Margaret drove. Every once in a while she was aware of the two older women talking. Beverly had taken her own car home, and it was Diane and Shelley in Margaret's van now. Once, Diane laughed out loud at something Margaret said, but Shelley didn't wake up enough to figure out what they were discussing. Both women had a good sense of humor. If Shelley hadn't been so tired she would have enjoyed chatting with them.

Emma had been up every night this week, it seemed. She'd been teething, sure, but it seemed like something more than that was going on. She was out of sorts and cranky during the day and sleepless at night. Dan didn't get up with her, and most nights he wasn't around anyway. A couple of times, Shelley had been up with Emma, had finally gotten her settled, and had herself fallen back to sleep only to be awakened by Dan an hour later.

Then early this morning, after another choppy night of sleep, Aiden had come into their room at 5:30 saying he'd had a nightmare. Shelley had gone out on the couch and turned on the TV for Aiden, thinking she would get another hour of sleep. It wasn't something she wanted to do or even approved of; she was just that desperate for another hour of sleep. But she'd only dozed on and off and then got up a half hour later when Emma awoke.

She drifted off again in the middle seat of the van, and it wasn't until Margaret stopped her car between Diane and Shelley's house that the younger woman woke again.

"We're here." Margaret turned her head toward the backseat. "Have a good nap?"

Shelley nodded as she gathered her purse. "You have no idea how tired I am."

"Our memories aren't that shot," Margaret said.

"We were reminiscing," Diane said. "And then I was sharing how during my kids' teenage years I wished they were toddlers again."

Margaret grinned. "At least the wild teen years weren't something I've ever had to deal with with Adelaide. I'm counting my blessings."

Shelley grimaced. She didn't want to think about the teenage years. She remembered her own too clearly. Surely her own kids would make better choices than she had. She and Dan would raise them right. They wouldn't be sneaking around behind her back the way she'd done with her mother. She opened the car door. "Thanks for the ride," she said, aware that her voice sounded sleepy.

Diane got out too and told Margaret good-bye, and then Diane told Shelley that she'd be home the next day.

"Let me know if you want me to watch the kids. I'd be happy to."

Shelley nodded, waved, and started toward her house. Dan had forgotten to turn the porch light on, and the place looked forlorn without it. She climbed the four steps slowly, yawning again. She wouldn't ask Diane to watch the kids tomorrow. Sure, they made Shelley tired, but it wasn't like she didn't want them around. Sometimes she just wanted to be able to be tired and overwhelmed without everyone wanting to come to her rescue.

She reached for the doorknob, expecting it be locked, but it wasn't. She opened the door and stepped inside to a dark house. She squinted, thinking she'd see Dan on the couch watching his big TV, but he wasn't. It took a moment for her to register that the TV wasn't even on.

She yawned again and put her purse on the entryway bench, locked the door, and padded into the kitchen for a glass of water.

"Is that you, Shell?" Dan's voice came from down the hall.

She stepped quickly out of the kitchen so he would see her and not wake Emma with his calling.

"There you are." He was wearing a towel around his waist and had obviously just come from the shower. His sandy hair curled around his forehead, and his brow was furrowed. "Why didn't you answer any of my texts?"

"What texts?" She dug her phone out of her pocket. Sure enough, there were five new texts and a missed call from Dan.

"I was afraid you wouldn't make it back in time."

"Time for what?"

"I got called into work. I need to be there in fifteen minutes."

"Oh." All of the texts had been sent in the last twenty minutes.

"Gotta hurry," he said, and turned back down the hall toward their bedroom.

A phone vibrated—but it wasn't Shelley's. She turned around. Dan's phone was on the kitchen table. He'd missed a call. She picked it up and held it for a moment. He was going into work again?

Or was he?

The phone buzzed as the call went to voice mail. She'd read about wives checking their husband's phones, but she'd never done it. She'd never had any reason to—until now. Her heart sank. She put the phone down on the table. She trusted her husband. There was no need to check his phone.

It buzzed again.

On the other hand... She picked it up, and checked the incoming calls. Four, including the current one, from the same number, a number she didn't recognize. It wasn't his work number. It wasn't even a local number.

She clicked over to his text messages. All of them had been opened. The last three were from her. One telling him they'd arrived in Augusta, one reminding him to give Emma her fluoride after he brushed her teeth, and the third telling him when they'd started home.

"Shelley!"

She practically dropped the phone onto the table.

"Could you bring me my phone? I'm expecting a call about some work details."

She picked it back up as if it were radioactive, and headed down the hall.

Dan was digging through his side of the closet. "Do you know where my black sweatshirt is?"

She shook her head, handing him the phone.

He slipped it into his jeans' pocket. "I wore it the other night."

"It's probably still in the dirty clothes. I haven't done laundry for a few days."

He pulled a dark green sweatshirt from his stack. "This will have to do." He kissed her quickly. "I'll be home around 3:00 AM or so."

She nodded and walked behind him to the door, closing it and then firmly locking it behind him. By the time she'd reached the hallway, eager to get her pajamas on and crawl into bed, she could hear his truck pulling onto the street. It sounded like he had a hole in his muffler. She sighed, wondering how much that would cost to fix.

★　　★　　★

That night, Beverly tossed and turned. The truth was that she would have welcomed a middle-of-the-night phone call from her father about then. Her house seemed to be growing larger and more vacant with each minute of the night.

She finally arose at five, deciding to go on her morning run. But she found the sight of a summer rainstorm out the bathroom window daunting. Her usual mantra was that rain or shine, she ran, but she was tired and she had no desire to spend a Saturday morning sloshing through mud puddles.

Instead she slipped on the plush terrycloth bathrobe Will had given her for their first anniversary and curled up on the couch in the den, pulling the throw over her. She closed her eyes, thinking she'd rest for a few minutes and then get up and assess the yard work that needed to be done before the gardeners arrived.

The next thing she was aware of was a knocking coming from down the hall. She stirred. Sunlight streamed through the room. Thank goodness the rain had stopped. The knocking grew louder. She stood and stretched, turning toward the entertainment console. The little blue numbers on the cable box caught her attention—8:52! It was the gardener who was knocking.

She cinched the robe tight and hurried down the hall. She'd tell the workers to get started in the back, and she'd be right out.

★   ★   ★

By midafternoon, the gardeners had finished the yard work, including properly trimming the box hedge, and Beverly had done a thorough cleaning of the house. It was amazing how quickly a layer of dust could settle on an unlived-in home.

She carried her bag from the master suite and closed the door firmly. This was her week to stay in Augusta, but she'd decided to go to her dad's for two nights and come back Monday morning for work. She had no desire to spend any unnecessary time alone in her house. Plus, she thought she'd ask Mrs. Peabody if she could take her out to visit her sister the next afternoon. The mystery of Edward Maker was growing heavier on her heart with each passing hour.

CHAPTER EIGHT

Diane stood in the middle of her kitchen surveying the bare countertops. Now she needed to tackle the floor. A good mopping was what it needed. She filled a bucket with hot water and added a wood cleanser. Then she spread it around the pine floor with the mop, scrubbing gently to make it shine.

She came out of the kitchen and looked down the hall. She hadn't stepped inside her office all day. It wouldn't hurt to check her e-mail. She hadn't heard from either of her kids for a few days—in fact, neither had answered the e-mail about sending her book off. Surely they'd answered by now.

Or maybe Frieda Watley had e-mailed her back. Diane smiled at the thought. She'd checked her e-mail last night, hoping the agent had responded, thinking maybe she'd stayed late at the office, poring over Diane's book, soaking up every word. She quickened her step down the hall and settled into her chair as she pushed the button to turn on her desktop computer.

Her daughter Jessica worked so hard during the week that she usually slept in on Saturdays and then called Diane in the afternoon, and Justin sometimes called to Skype on Saturday evenings, which was his Sunday morning in Dubai. Usually he sent an e-mail first to set it up, but he also e-mailed at least once during the week, just to let her know how he was doing.

She sighed as she logged in. They usually didn't go this long without communicating. She would send another e-mail if she didn't have a response.

She skimmed her in-box. There was nothing from either of her kids. Nor anything from Frieda Watley. She leaned back in her chair, shaking her head. What had she expected—to have Frieda e-mail her on a Saturday? Really? She laughed at herself, recapping her fantasy: big New York agent loved her novel so much that she read through the night and then dashed off an e-mail on a Saturday to say she loved the book and had a long list of publishing houses she'd send it off to. That truly was a fictitious scenario.

Diane clicked out of her e-mail program. There was no harm in dreaming, and at least she could laugh at herself.

She trudged back down the hall and grabbed her mop, turning her attention to the floor. Years ago she'd read that Virginia Woolf had often cleaned her kitchen after receiving a rejection letter concerning one of her novels. Diane wasn't sure what it meant that she was cleaning now. But if she waited until she received the rejection, her kitchen might sprout moldy wings and fly away.

Speaking of mold, she'd forgotten to clean the inside of the fridge. Probably on purpose. It had to be her least favorite job.

As she ran the mop toward the back door, Rocky barked. She'd tied him up outside to keep him out of her way. He barked again. A squirrel had probably found the audacity to try to venture onto the lawn. Rocky's barking became frantic. Finally Diane realized that someone was knocking on the front door.

She abandoned the mop and tiptoed across the wet floor. "Coming." She swung the door open.

Shelley stood before her, holding Emma in her arms with Aiden clinging to her leg. "Could you watch the kids for about half an hour?"

Diane looked past the young mother across the street to her house. Dan stood in the doorway. "Sure." She focused on the little duo before her.

"Dan and I need to talk something through, and the kids keep interrupting. It won't take very long—if we can just concentrate."

Diane put out her hand to Aiden, but he pulled back. "How about if you help me fix a snack?" she said. "You can look in the cupboard to see what I have." Aiden let go of his mother and headed toward the kitchen.

Shelley stepped inside with Emma. "This one isn't going to be so easy."

"That's okay," Diane said.

Shelley must have caught sight of Diane's mop because she squealed Aiden's name. "Stop! You're going to mess up the floor."

"It's fine." Diane wanted to laugh because in that short amount of time she'd forgotten all about the mopping.

Aiden had a look of horror on his face as he spun around toward them, one hand on the cupboard door.

"It really is okay. I'll spot-mop later. Just don't slip." Diane put her hands out for the baby and whispered for Shelley to go quickly. She did, reaching the door before Emma began to wail.

Diane wanted to stand at the window and watch Shelley go. Instead, she stood in the kitchen doorway praying for her friend as she bounced the baby in her arms and instructed Aiden to check the third shelf for the new box of cookies.

After they each had two cookies, she spent the next forty-five minutes on the couch reading through the basket of favorite picture books Diane had salvaged from her children's childhood. *Where the Wild Things Are, The Runaway Bunny,* and *Brown Bear, Brown Bear, What Do You See?* seemed to be their favorites, although Emma got a little wild-eyed at the little bunny leaving home.

Aiden was starting to get restless and Diane was about ready to suggest they go outside and play in the backyard with Rocky when there was a quick knock on the door.

"It's me," Shelley called, letting herself in.

"We're right here," Diane said, scooting to the edge of the couch with Emma.

The baby began to cry at the sight of her mother. Shelley took her daughter quickly and told Aiden they needed to get back over to the house. "Daddy's going into work in about an hour."

Aiden dragged his heels.

"Come on, Aiden," she said. "He wants to play ball with you before he goes."

Aiden lit up and ran to the door. "Can Prize play too?"

"Ask Daddy." Shelley positioned the baby on her hip.

"Dan sure has been racking up the hours, hasn't he?" Diane asked.

Shelley nodded.

"Is everything okay?"

Shelley nodded again, but her face was pinched. "I'll talk to you later," she said, pulling her daughter close.

★   ★   ★

The last of the tourists left Margaret's gallery at 6:30, a half hour after it closed. As she surveyed the walls, she smiled. She'd sold three paintings and hadn't had time to hang their replacements. They weren't the three most expensive in the gallery by a long shot, but one was hers, plus she'd sold one of Allan's inlaid boxes. She did a little jig on the hardwood floor. Of course, after she deducted the frame and her gallery expenses—rent, electricity, taxes—it had actually *cost* her to sell the painting, but there was no reason to go there.

No matter. She was grateful anyway, and she took a moment to whisper a prayer of thanks. She thought of Shelley and whispered a prayer for her, for both her marriage and the business she wanted to start. Margaret needed to make sure to tell the young woman about her own successes as well as her failures.

Margaret stepped into the back room and examined the painting she'd started that morning. It was hard to paint at the gallery with all the interruptions, but she'd been compelled to begin this one anyway. She hadn't gotten much done on it besides penciling in the stormy sea and the figure on the beach. She'd work on it more tomorrow if she had time, but no more tonight.

She was definitely tired. A long weekend day at the gallery made her feel old. At sixty-seven, she knew she was in better shape than most people her age, but she still felt, especially in her knees, the stress of being on her feet all day.

She locked the front door of the gallery and exited through the alley door, locking it securely behind her. The evening was warm and a little muggy. Thankfully, it was only a few blocks to their house.

Her cotton skirt swished as she walked down the alley to the main street, her soft-soled shoes quiet on the bumpy pavement. The gallery didn't open until noon on Sundays, which Margaret appreciated more and more with each passing week of the summer.

The traffic through downtown was still bumper-to-bumper as she turned down Newport Avenue toward home. The breeze picked up and whipped her skirt around her legs. The tide must have been high, because the fishy smell of the sea greeted her.

Her feet hurt worse as she neared their house. She could hear Allan's saw buzzing in his workshop, but she headed toward the steps winding up to the front door. There was no need to disturb him. He'd come up when he was ready. She opened the front door, nudging Oreo farther into the house with her foot. Her comfy leather couch with a collection of colorful pillows looked extremely inviting, but Margaret walked passed it, picking up the purple throw she'd made years ago that had landed on the floor.

"Adelaide," she called out. "I'm home."

"I'm back here."

"Back here" was the office, which meant Adelaide was on the computer. She had a couple of games that she liked to play. So far, she knew nothing of surfing the Web and online perils. She was content playing her handful of games.

"What's for dinner?" Margaret asked.

"Salad. I helped Dad."

Margaret glanced into the kitchen. A loaf of Allan's homemade French bread was on the counter along with a bowl of lettuce. She opened the fridge and found small bowls of chicken, orange slices, and chopped onions. It looked like one of Allan's specialty dishes. All three of them were watching their weight. He probably had a low-cal vinaigrette to go with it.

She made her way back down the hall to the office. As she entered, Adelaide swung around in the chair with a bit of a frown on her face. "I just lost at *Angry Birds*."

Margaret gave her a sympathetic smile.

"And I'm hungry."

"Go tell Dad I'm home."

Her daughter gave her a warm hug and hurried out of the room.

Margaret decided to check her e-mail while she had a moment at the computer. She was having an ongoing discussion with an artist who was interested in exhibiting at Shearwater Gallery. She logged on to her account, but she had only one message—and it wasn't from the artist.

It was from her cousin Beth, and the subject was "Family Reunion." Beth was the cruise director in the family. She was the one who, every couple of years, put together a reunion and pulled people in to make all of her ideas work. This year the reunion was going to be at Acadia National Park.

At the last reunion, Margaret had ended up being in charge of the relay races. She'd had to bring burlap bags, dozens of eggs, spoons, water balloons, beach balls, watermelons, hobbyhorses, cans of whipped cream, and other paraphernalia. The theme had been "a day at the races." Then, even though Margaret was supposed to be in charge of the relays, Beth had ended up taking over because, it seemed, Margaret wasn't doing things right.

Nevertheless, the races had been a hit, and nearly everyone had gotten involved, laughing and joking with each other. Great-uncles teamed up with five-year-old fourth cousins. It had been a hoot.

As she opened the e-mail, Margaret chastised herself. She really was grateful that Beth was willing to do the coordinating. Even better: Margaret didn't see a single reply yet to Beth's message, which meant Margaret would have first dibs at the list of tasks.

She checked the list of e-mail addresses the message had been sent to. There had to be forty all together...including her cousin Buddy. She leaned back in her chair. He hadn't been on the list in years. She knew it was uncharitable to think it, but there was only one person in her life she hoped never to see again, and that was Buddy.

She exhaled loudly. Chances were that Buddy wouldn't show up anyway. He hadn't for over a decade. He'd had a drinking problem for years.

She scanned the tasks, listed in alphabetical order, stopping at "name tags." She hit "reply all," wrote her name in caps beside it, and pressed Send.

★   ★   ★

"Aiden, you already had a drink of water." Shelley stood in the doorway of her son's room, her hands on her hips.

"How about another kiss?" His face was tilted to the side, a pout on his face. Prize was in her kennel at the end of the bed, her head tilted a little too.

"You already had that too. Now go to sleep."

His chin began to quiver. "I want Daddy."

Shelley nearly said *I want Daddy too*, but bit her lower lip. "He's at work. You know that."

"He's always at work."

"That's what daddies do. That's how we buy food for us and dog food for Prize." Shelley started to close the door, but then crossed the room and kissed her son's forehead again. "Now, go to sleep."

As she positioned the door so it was open a crack, she counted the evenings Dan had worked in the last week. *Four.* Sure, they needed the money, but the weeks of erratic hours were taking a toll on all of them.

She paced in the living room for a few minutes. She could scrub the bathroom floor, run another load of wash, or sort the Legos out of the toy box. She wished she could go see if Dan's truck was truly parked at work. She plopped down on the overstuffed couch and took a deep breath.

What if his truck wasn't at work?

A heaviness settled in the pit of Shelley's stomach. She was being ridiculous. Dan was too sweet to lie to her. What was she afraid of? That he was having an—

She jumped from the couch. She dug in her purse on the entryway bench and pulled out her cell phone. She'd send him a quick text, asking how work was going. She keyed in her message, sitting back down on the couch as her thumbs flew over the buttons.

After no immediate answer, she turned on the TV, jumping from channel to channel. Fifteen minutes later, she called Dan's phone, but no one answered. She left a chatty message, "Just thinking about you. Hope your evening is going well!"

Next, she picked up a women's magazine from the stack her mother-in-law had passed down to her and started leafing through it, stopping at a recipe for a lemon cake, Dan's favorite. She hadn't made one for a while, probably since before Emma was born. She dog-eared the page and moved on to an article on squeezing more out of your food budget.

She could save money by not making the lemon cake, but beyond that Shelley couldn't imagine cutting any more from her grocery shopping. She was already making practically everything from scratch, which meant they were eating healthier than ever. She could stop buying vegetables at the farmer's market, which might save a little but wouldn't help their nutritional needs.

She flipped to the next article but was unable to concentrate, and she dropped the magazine onto the coffee table. She should try to go to bed to get some sleep before Emma woke for her nightly visit.

She stood. Who was she kidding? She wouldn't be able to fall asleep. She was too anxious. She decided to call Dan's cell phone again. Maybe he'd answer, and she'd hear the sounds of the wharf in the background. Then she'd know where he was for sure. She dialed the number, and it rang until it went to voice mail, again. She hit End, not bothering to leave another message.

Thinking she wouldn't be able to sleep anyway, she decided to mop the bathroom floor. She peeked in on Aiden first. He was sound asleep on his tummy, his head turned toward the door. Prize's tail thumped against the side of her kennel when she saw Shelley, but otherwise she kept quiet. Shelley decided not to check on Emma, not wanting to chance waking her.

She collected the bucket, mop, and cleanser from the hall closet and carried them into the bathroom, taking her phone from her pocket and putting it on the counter. As she ran hot water from the tub into the bucket, her phone vibrated. She grabbed it quickly. It was a text from Dan: *Busy. Text if emergency. Be home around 1.*

Shelley didn't bother to reply. It wasn't an emergency—at least not a physical one.

CHAPTER NINE

The next morning, Shelley carried Emma and held Aiden's hand as they made their way slowly down the steps of Light the Way Chapel.

"Shelley!" She turned to see Dana, whose husband John worked with Dan, waving her hand as she hurried toward them.

Shelley braced herself.

"It looks like you're here alone today too."

Shelley didn't respond, not wanting to engage in conversation.

"John's working today." She said it quietly, as if it were top secret. "He hasn't had much extra work lately, so he jumped at the chance. I've been so busy picking up extra shifts at the market that he's been feeling a little guilty."

Shelley nodded. Dana had told her once that they were putting off having kids until they had all their bills paid off and a decent savings account, but John liked to buy toys, like boats and pickups, so it could be awhile until they were ready to be parents. She thought toys were a sorry substitute for kids, but Shelley couldn't help admire their foresight. She and Dan hadn't had any idea how much raising a family would cost, so they'd decided to have kids right away.

Dana put her hands out for Emma, but the baby jerked her head the other way.

The woman looked disappointed for just a moment but then looked around. "So where's Dan?"

"Asleep!" Aiden grinned.

"Really?" Dana laughed. "Since when does he get to sleep in?"

"He worked last night," Aiden said, matter-of-factly.

Dana's eyes widened. "Last night? John didn't get called in. Last time we talked—at the grocery when I checked you out, remember?—you said he was getting extra hours then too. What's going on?"

Shelley shrugged. John had seniority over Dan and got more hours. Dana's reaction troubled her. It was one thing for Shelley to be suspicious of her husband, but it was entirely another for his co-worker's wife to be suspicious. She didn't want to add any fuel to the woman's ideas, though. As the other congregants streamed around them as if they were rocks in a brook, Aiden held up his Sunday school paper to Dana.

"Look!" The lesson had been on the healing of the man born blind. "Jesus made this man see." He'd colored the man purple and Jesus green, but he'd pretty much stayed inside the lines.

Shelley was relieved that Dana praised Aiden's work. She didn't have children of her own and could have pointed out that Jesus was a man of Middle Eastern descent and not a Martian. Thankfully she hadn't. Shelley took Aiden's hand and the foursome made their way the rest of the way down the stairs. Shelley kept going toward the parking lot.

Dana was right on her heels. "I'll ask John about Dan working last night and let you know what he says."

Shelley shook her head. "Please don't. I'll ask Dan about it."

"Oh." Dana's mouth stayed open even after the sound coming out of it had stopped. She seemed offended by Shelley's straightforwardness.

When she reached their station wagon, Shelley opened the back door, slipped Emma into her seat, and ducked her head into the car to fasten Emma's straps. "His schedule has been all over the place." She turned back to Dana, determined to make herself clear. "And I certainly don't want to burden you with keeping track of our schedule on top of your own." Shelley led Aiden over to his side of the car.

"Oh, it's no burden..." Dana's voice trailed off. Shelley's firm look must have convinced her otherwise. "Okay, well, tell Dan hello," Dana said. "Maybe the four of us can get together sometime."

"That would be fun." Shelley tried to smile but felt it fizzle. It wasn't just that she had little in common with Dana, it was that finding a sitter so she and Dan could go out was low on her priority list. Then again, a discussion out in the open about extra hours at work would be enlightening.

Shelley felt uneasy as she pulled out of the parking lot. On the one hand, she wondered if she'd been too curt with Dana. But on the other, the woman seemed to want to dig into their business, and that was the last thing Shelley needed right now.

She sighed as she waited for a car to pass before turning back onto the main road. She couldn't bear going back to a quiet house, knowing Dan was still asleep, so she headed through the drive-through of the Tastee Freez and bought chicken strips and fries for the kids. It wasn't in the budget, but she'd scrimp somewhere else to make up for it.

"Are we eating at home?" Aiden asked.

"No. The park."

"What about Daddy?"

"He's still asleep." She didn't know that for sure, but he hadn't sent her a text saying he wasn't.

As she pulled her station wagon up by the park, her phone rang. It was Dan asking where she was. She said they'd come home, but Dan suggested he stop by the deli and pick up sandwiches for the two of them.

"We'll have a family picnic," he said. "I'll throw in Aiden's plastic bat and Wiffle ball. I'll be there in twenty minutes."

Shelley hung up the phone feeling pretty sure Dan didn't sound like a man keeping a secret. She grabbed a blanket from the back of the car and then got Emma out of her car seat. Aiden carried the bag of food, holding it with both hands very carefully and leading the way to a spot between two fir trees, near the playground. They laid out the blanket and sat down.

"Mommy, how long until Daddy gets here?"

"A little while," Shelley answered. "But not too long."

Aiden beamed. "I can't wait. I wish Prize could come to the park too."

"I know, Aiden, but you know the rules. The city says no pets at the park."

Aiden sighed. "I don't like that rule."

By the time Dan showed up, Aiden was playing on the play equipment and Shelley was pushing Emma in one of the baby swings. Aiden spotted him as Dan hurried across the grass carrying a paper bag in one hand and the red plastic bat in the other, wearing his Boston Red Sox cap backward.

"Daddy!" Aiden shouted and scrambled down the ladder, nearly tripping over the concrete curb around the play area. He took off running at full speed. Emma watched him go, clapping her hands.

Dan pulled the Wiffle ball out of the pocket of his sweatshirt and tossed it into the air, and then lifted the bat up, connected with the ball, and sent it sailing toward Aiden. The little boy turned his head upward and reached up with his arms, staggering around a little. As the ball came toward him, he fell into a heap.

Shelley couldn't tell if Aiden caught the ball or not until he held it up in triumph. Dan ran toward their son, pulling him to his feet and giving him a hearty high-five. Emma clapped again. Shelley lifted her from the swing and carried her over to the others.

Dan met her with a kiss, which made Aiden cover his eyes. Emma giggled and stuck out her lips for a kiss too. Dan reached out his arms for her, but she clung to Shelley. Once they'd all sat down on the blanket, the little girl wouldn't leave her mother's lap. Soon Aiden was back at the play structure.

Shelley ate her sandwich, working around Emma's head, thinking that in another year Emma would be off playing with her brother. "How was work?"

"Fine."

"Are you going in tonight?"

"I don't think so," Dan said. "At least that's what the boss says."

"I saw Dana at church. She said John's working this morning."

Dan sighed. "Well, if I had more seniority I guess I would be too."

"She was surprised you were working last night. She said John didn't get called, which surprised her because he has more seniority than you do."

Dan's gaze fell off into the distance, past the play equipment. "It was a special project. No one offered it to John." He yawned.

Maybe Dan was more qualified for the job that needed to be done last night. If so, it would make sense that he'd been called in instead of John. "How'd you sleep?" She pulled a piece of cheese from her sandwich and gave it to Emma.

"Good." Dan kept eating his sandwich, devouring it in big bites. His eyes wandered to the play area where Aiden slid down the fireman pole. Shelley registered a buzzing sound and realized it was Dan's phone. He pulled it out of the pocket of his jeans and read the text. "Looks like I'll be going into work after all."

"Now?" Shelley choked on the word.

"Nah. Not until tonight." He took the last bite of his sandwich, wadded up his wrapper, and tossed it into the garbage can a few feet away. "It'll help pay the bills. And buy a new muffler for my truck."

Shelley hadn't even bothered pointing out how loud his pickup was getting. She knew they didn't have the extra money to fix it. But maybe they did now.

Dan jumped to his feet. "Hey, Aiden. Ready to play ball?"

Aiden's face glowed as he ran toward his father.

★   ★   ★

"So the name Edward Maker doesn't ring a bell?" Beverly tightened her grip on her steering wheel and glanced over at Mrs. Peabody. For the last half hour Beverly had been trying to talk about the photo, but the woman wanted to talk about everything else, mainly their neighbors in Marble Cove.

"Edward Maker," Mrs. Peabody said slowly and then cocked her head. "You know, my sister went to college with a boy with the last name of Maker. He was sweet on her. I think she liked him too, although she never confided much in me back then." The woman pulled her purse tight against her middle and seemed lost in thought for a moment.

The name Maker wasn't common. Perhaps the long-time-ago college friend was at least related to the boy in the photo. Beverly felt encouraged.

"Oh, it's the next right," Mrs. Peabody said suddenly. "No, wait. I'm not sure."

Beverly slowed the car, hoping Mrs. Peabody would remember the way to her sister's house. "Has it been a while since you've been out to visit?" She spoke slowly, hoping to have a calming effect on the older woman.

"It's been a couple of years. Let's see, maybe more than that. We'd had that bad windstorm. Do you remember that?"

Beverly shook her head. "Does your sister get into Marble Cove much?"

"Now and then. More often than I get out this way. But she does most of her shopping at Willow's Corner."

There was a market there and a post office. It would seem the woman would need to come into Marble Cove for any medical care though, and she asked Mrs. Peabody about that.

"Celia? She never has any need for medical care. She's as healthy as a horse and strong as an ox. Always has been."

Beverly mulled that over for a minute. She'd been expecting a frail old lady.

"Here's the turn!" Mrs. Peabody sounded so pleased with herself. "I remember this shed..."

Beverly made a sharp right onto a gravel road and slowed. The car bumped along at a near crawl along the narrow road tucked between the trees. "How old is your sister?" Beverly took off her sunglasses. The shade from the trees made it hard to see.

"Eighty-four."

Beverly wasn't sure exactly how old Mrs. Peabody was, but she knew the woman had to be in her early eighties at least. Beverly hadn't told her father about going to Edward Maker's house, and she wasn't about to tell Mrs. Peabody, not until she had more information.

After maneuvering around a slight turn, a home came into view. The wood was weathered, completely bare of paint, or so Beverly thought. As they grew nearer it became obvious that the wood had been stained and oiled. Three rocking chairs sat on the wide porch and each of the windows had a set of lace curtains. An old pickup truck was parked beside the house.

"Is your sister married?"

"No. Never has been," Mrs. Peabody said. "She had a beau—the one I told you about, that Maker boy—but he went off to the Korean War. It seems they had a misunderstanding when he returned, but she never told me exactly what happened."

"What does she do?" Beverly pulled her car to a stop behind the pickup.

"She's retired now, of course, but she taught school for years. She was a career girl, through and through."

Beverly wanted to laugh, realizing she not only expected the woman to be frail, but she also expected her to be uneducated and, as ridiculous as it sounded, a backwoods type. "Did she teach in Marble Cove?"

"No. North of here. Past Willow's Corner. In a three-room school."

"How'd she end up here?"

"This old place? It used to be our daddy's hunting cabin. For some reason she's always liked it out here."

Beverly climbed out of the car and hurried around to help Mrs. Peabody.

The woman brushed Beverly away as she eased herself out of the car, appearing to be mindful of her bad ankle. "I'm fine."

A dog barked and came running toward them, wagging its tail. It was a hunting dog, a Brittany, Beverly thought, white with auburn markings on its face and back, full of energy.

"Down, boy," Mrs. Peabody said and then muttered, "Celia always has to have some hound around, just like our daddy."

Beverly followed Mrs. Peabody up the porch. She could see through the closed screen door into a dimly lit interior.

"Coco, is that you?" came a voice from inside, followed by quick footsteps.

"It's me." Mrs. Peabody turned to Beverly. "No one besides Celia calls me that anymore."

Coco? Beverly was having a hard time imagining how that sort of nickname would come to be. She wracked her brain trying to figure out what Mrs. Peabody's first name was. She thought it started with a "C," so that at least made sense.

An old woman wearing jeans and a tailored shirt appeared. Her absolutely white hair was pulled back in a bun, and her dark eyes sparkled. She opened the screen and bounded across the porch, sweeping Mrs. Peabody into a full hug. She was of medium build, not slim but not overweight either, and she certainly seemed strong and sturdy.

Beverly stopped on the top step. Mrs. Peabody, with her practical shoes, summer dress, and gray sweater and her gray hair bobbed at her chin, looked older than her sunny sister, even though "Coco" was younger.

After a moment, Mrs. Peabody pulled away and introduced Beverly. "Beverly, this is my sister, Celia Patterson. Beverly is the daughter of Mr. Wheeland I told you about."

"You folk come in," Celia said. "I have iced tea and lemon bars."

The dog was on the porch now and tried to sneak through the screen door, but Celia shooed her away. "I'm assuming you still don't like dogs, eh?" she said to Mrs. Peabody, a lilt to her voice.

"Assumption correct." Mrs. Peabody was already through the door.

"Have a seat while I'm a-gettin' our refreshments," Celia said, motioning to the couch.

The interior of the house was knotty pine walls with old-growth fir floors. Enough light came through the lace-covered windows to cast a yellow glow across the room, which smelled of lemony wood polish. The furniture was simple—a camelback couch, a wingback chair, and a cherry wood coffee table and matching end tables. The room gave way to a dining room with a big oak table and six chairs. Beyond that, there was a kitchen with red countertops.

Beverly sat beside Mrs. Peabody on the couch, and in no time Celia returned with a tray that had obviously been prepared ahead of time.

There was a vase of daisies on the table and a black-and-white photo of two girls and a boy.

Beverly sat and turned her attention to the photo. "Is this the two of you?"

Celia nodded. "Cece and Coco. All those years ago."

"And our brother, in between us. He gave us each our nicknames." Mrs. Peabody's voice sounded far away.

"Where does he live?" Beverly picked up the photo to examine it more closely, expecting him to be somewhere in the vicinity.

"Heaven," Celia said softly. "For the last fifty-five years. Isn't that right, Coco?'

Mrs. Peabody nodded.

"Oh, I'm so sorry." Beverly put the photo down quickly, as if it had suddenly grown hot. She wanted to ask how he'd died, but from the look on the women's faces she felt the subject might still be too painful even after all this time. Their brother would be a few years older than her father, if he had lived.

"Speaking of photos," Celia said, "Coco said you had one you wanted me to look at."

Beverly nodded and pulled the snapshot out of the pocket of her purse. "A friend of mine found this at the Orlean Point lighthouse. My dad thinks it's a boy he knew in Augusta, who was older than he is. But the photo was clearly taken in Marble Cove. We think the background is the exterior wall of the lighthouse. The names on the back are 'Edward' and 'Robert.' My father thinks the boy is Edward Maker—"

Celia reached for the photo, a wild look in her eye. Beverly handed it over. As Celia's eyes fell on the image, her expression softened. "It's him."

"Who?" Mrs. Peabody asked.

Celia stared at the photo. "I'm sure it is."

"I don't know who you're talking about." Mrs. Peabody's voice was high.

"It's Edward. Edward Maker."

Beverly sat up straight. "That's the name my father gave me."

"Your college friend?" Mrs. Peabody's face bore a confused expression. "But he didn't grow up in Marble Cove. Maybe it's a relative."

"I know it's him." Celia looked from Beverly to her sister. "He went to first and second grade in Marble Cove. You were only a baby, so you wouldn't remember. I became reacquainted with him in college, my first year. By then he looked more like the man in the photo—his father, I'm guessing—than the boy." She held the photo away from her, examining it again.

"When was the last time you saw him?" Beverly was on the edge of the couch now.

"Oh, years ago. I think…1953? No, it was January of 1954."

Beverly's heart fell. "Oh." She was hoping Celia would be the key to getting Mr. Maker to talk. Surely he had some information about the lighthouse for her and her friends. "Can you tell me anything else about him?"

Celia shook her head. "No, nothing at all. He vanished from my life—just like that." She snapped her fingers.

"I think he lives in Augusta…" Beverly said.

Celia wrinkled her nose and focused on the picture again. After a moment she shut her eyes. "I don't want to talk about Edward Maker anymore. It's too hard." Her voice was low and shaky.

Beverly felt stunned. There was a short, uncomfortable silence during which she had no idea what to say, but then, thankfully, Mrs. Peabody asked her sister how her garden was coming along.

"Really well. Have a lemon bar, and then we'll go take a look." Celia's voice was back to normal, and she handed the photo back to Beverly. The moment of drama passed, and the woman reached for her glass of tea. "Beverly, do you garden?"

"Not much." She was sure confessing to hiring gardeners wouldn't go over very well. "But my father used to be an avid gardener."

After discussing gardening for a few minutes, Celia led the way through the dining room and kitchen, past an eating nook with a gray Formica table and four vinyl chairs, and out the back door.

"Oh, look at your hollyhocks!" Mrs. Peabody said. "And at your rhubarb."

A large garden filled most of the backyard, except for a patch of grass and a brick area where a single wooden rocking chair sat. The hollyhocks grew against a weathered shed, and there were also cosmos and zinnias. Pole beans, tomatoes, zucchini, and other vines grew in the garden, along with lettuce, chard, and spinach. On the far row were potatoes— at least Beverly thought that's what the plants were.

"I've already canned a few jars of tomatoes," Celia said, "although I think I'll freeze the rest. I haven't had a power outage in years."

"How long have you lived here?" Beverly stepped closer to the garden.

"I've always spent my summers here. But it's been, oh, seventeen or eighteen years since I retired, so full-time since then."

"How is it in the winter?"

"Depends. But I'm usually not snowbound for more than a few days at a time." She nodded toward a woodpile. "I still chop my own wood. That's what keeps me young."

Beverly couldn't imagine. Next to the shed was a huge woodpile. "You cut all that?"

Celia chuckled. "No, I chop it. I don't cut my own trees down anymore. But I used to, with Daddy's old chain saw. Now I have it delivered."

There was a field of grass beyond the garden, and beyond that lay the forest. But Celia's little place was definitely in a sunny spot, and the garden got plenty of light. Beverly couldn't imagine living alone so far away from friends and family. The three women chatted for a few more minutes, and then Mrs. Peabody said she was ready to go. Beverly was surprised, sure the woman would have wanted to stay longer to visit with her sister.

"Now it's your turn to come into Marble Cove." Mrs. Peabody's voice sounded as if she were chastising her sister. "And spend the night when you do. It's been too long."

Celia crossed her arms. "Don't get bossy with me."

"Bossy? Ha. That's something you've never put up with, is it?"

"That's right. And I'm not starting now." Celia smiled at her sister, and they hugged.

Beverly felt as if she were intruding, and she looked away. When she was little, she'd wanted a sister. She hadn't thought of that for years.

"I'll come in sometime soon," Celia said. "I need to do some shopping."

Beverly turned back toward the sisters. They'd pulled away but were still looking at each other intently.

"You take care of yourself." Celia pulled a piece of lint from Mrs. Peabody's sweater.

The younger woman snorted. "I'm not the one living out on the edge of nowhere."

★   ★   ★

Ten minutes later, Beverly pulled her car onto the highway. Driving on the gravel road had been too noisy to have a conversation, but as soon as they were on the smooth pavement Mrs. Peabody began talking about Celia's house.

"Daddy built it when we were little. We'd stay for weeks at a time in the summer. Funny, isn't it? To live right by the beach but go up into the mountains to a cabin for vacations? It's not like it was ever too hot or anything in Marble Cove, but it was fun to explore the forests. Then Daddy and his friends would come out in the fall to hunt." She stopped only long enough to take a breath. "I never liked the cabin the way Celia did, though. That's why I got the house, which she said she never wanted." She sighed. "My, the years certainly speed by."

Beverly tried to imagine herself in forty years. She'd have no father. No sister. No brother. No nieces or nephews. Would she have a husband? Children of her own? Would she have someone to share life with? That was the difference between herself and her three new friends: All of them had people in their lives who weren't pushing eighty. People who they could depend on. Sure, Diane was a widow too, but she had children. And Margaret had Allan—and Adelaide, although she would never be able to take care of her parents. Beverly sighed.

Celia didn't have children. She'd never had a husband either. But she seemed perfectly content to be living by herself even at her advanced age.

Beverly took a deep breath, working up her nerve. "Is there more to Celia's story than what she shared with me?" she finally asked.

"It's hard for me to remember, honestly," Mrs. Peabody said. "She didn't talk about it much, but I do remember that when Edward came back from the war he headed out to California."

"The Korean War?"

Mrs. Peabody nodded. "He served with our brother."

Beverly's vision blurred for just a second. "Your brother? They were friends?"

"No. They were in the same unit. But Celia put it together. Edward stopped writing to her halfway through his time over there, after our brother was killed. But then it sounds as if she saw him one last time after he came home. I didn't know about that."

"So Celia loved Edward Maker?"

Mrs. Peabody turned back toward Beverly. "She never said. I don't know that. But I will admit that she never dated again after that. I think it hit her pretty hard."

"Would she want to visit him in Augusta?"

It took awhile for Mrs. Peabody to answer. "Probably not. What would be the use now?"

Beverly could think of all sorts of reasons, but she kept quiet.

CHAPTER TEN

Shelley stood at the kitchen window, peering out into the darkness, listening as Dan's truck roared away down the street. It would seem that a wonderful afternoon at the park as a family should ease her fears, not magnify them, but she was feeling even more anxious than before.

She'd read one time that men who were unfaithful were sometimes extra nice to their wives, thinking they'd be less suspicious that way. Could that be what Dan was doing?

She focused on her reflection in the window, at her hair hanging around her shoulders, at her big eyes. She could go check on Dan at work. She exhaled loudly. But if she drove down and he really was on the docks, he might see her car. Turning away from the window, she crossed her arms and leaned against the counter. She could walk down and make sure to stay hidden so he didn't see her.

And leave the kids alone? What was she thinking? She was being obsessive, and it was making her crazy. She needed to stop.

She'd been in high school when her dad had left. Her parents hadn't fought—in fact they'd hardly interacted at all. They were like two ships passing in the night—on an icy sea. She still didn't know the whole story of how her parents' marriage had ended. They'd both remarried and seemed content. They remained amicable toward each other. They were both civil at Shelley and Dan's wedding. But Shelley didn't understand any better now than she had then why their marriage hadn't survived.

She shivered. What if her own marriage was falling apart, and she didn't see it coming? What if she didn't understand, just like she hadn't with her parents, what was coming?

Determined to distract herself, she pulled a cookbook from the shelf above the plates and took it into the living room, settling down on the couch. She didn't have the time or the energy to be suspicious. She flipped through the tart recipes. If she was going to open a business, she needed to be putting her energy into that. Until recently, she'd been thinking of doing a cookie business only. But now she was playing with the idea of broadening out to other kinds of dessert baking.

She read through a lemon tart recipe and then a hazelnut one. She liked the thought of tarts. She could sell them individually or as part of a catering package. The overhead was a little more than with a cupcake or cookie because of the tin, but she'd be able to charge enough to cover it. The work involved was more too. That might be a little harder to cover...

Her thoughts were interrupted by a soft knock on the door.

Shelley's heart raced, her anxiety returning. Maybe something had happened to Dan. Or maybe it was someone with some information about him. Something bad...

There was another knock, and Shelley jumped to her feet and hurried to the door, hoping the sound hadn't awakened Emma.

Diane stood on her stoop, a measuring cup in her hand. "Is it too late?" Her friend had a sheepish look on her face. "I saw your light."

"No. This is fine." Shelley wondered if she sounded as relieved as she felt. Diane didn't have any bad news—she just needed to borrow something.

"You're not going to believe this, but I ran out of flour."

Shelley motioned her in.

Diane continued talking, a joking tone to her voice. "I'm pretty sure you have some I can borrow."

"That you can *have*," Shelley said.

"Oh thanks. I had a bunch of bananas go bad while I was writing. I tossed them in the freezer last week and just now decided I should do something with them, but I'm a cup of flour short." Diane followed Shelley into the kitchen.

As she opened the canister, doubts swept over Shelley again.

Diane handed her the cup. "What's wrong?"

Shelley turned toward her friend. "Would you mind watching the kids for a few minutes? Maybe half an hour at the most."

"Right now?"

Shelley nodded and bit her lower lip. It was too much to ask her friend. Here it was almost ten on a Sunday evening.

"Sure." Diane watched as Shelley filled the measuring cup with the flour scoop. "Is everything okay?"

Shelley nodded but didn't look at her friend. "I just need to get out of the house. Thought a quick run would do me good." She had arrived, abruptly, at the conclusion that not knowing was worse than knowing, no matter how bad it might be.

"Want to take Rocky with you?"

She certainly didn't want to take Prize! Shelley took a deep breath and kept her expression even, but inside she chuckled. She could imagine, even with Rocky, how that would go over. Either the dog would get away from her and announce his presence to the whole wharf or else he'd bark his head off with the same result. "Thanks, but no thanks. Maybe next time."

Diane nodded slowly but didn't say anything more.

"I'll just put my running shoes on." Shelley placed the cup of flour on the counter and hurried down the hall. When she returned with her shoes on, Diane was sitting on the couch, leafing through one of the cookbooks. Shelley thanked her profusely, grabbed her sweatshirt from the hook by the door, and hurried out into the night, taking in a deep breath as she did.

She felt as if she were in a perpetual state of anxiety, between wondering about what Dan was up to, worrying about the kids, fretting over their finances, and always being sleep-deprived. She hurried down the walkway of her house, turned onto the sidewalk, and headed toward town, which felt much safer than walking down the beach.

She jogged slowly. She wasn't much of a runner—never had been—but watching Beverly fly by her house every morning she was in Marble Cove was starting to inspire her.

A cat leaped off a fence in front of her. She startled and then laughed. It ran before she could get a clear view of it in the dark, but it was most likely one of Adelaide's.

She increased her stride for half a block, then slowed down again, her heart racing. Ahead, a city police car turned down the street toward her. It slowed and stopped, and the officer rolled down his window.

Shelley came to a stop.

"Nice night," the officer said. It was that new guy— Crawley was his last name.

She nodded, catching her breath. "I'm just out for a run."

"Next time wear a reflective vest or something. You're a little hard to see."

She nodded again. "Good idea." *For next time, but not tonight.*

The policeman drove on, and she continued toward downtown, slowing to a walk by the time she reached the business district. She passed Margaret's gallery and made her way to the end of Main Street.

If Dan's truck wasn't in the wharf parking lot, she would assume he was having an affair, and she would confront him.

The breeze picked up as she neared the wharf. A fire burned somewhere nearby and the acrid scent of the smoke jolted her brain. There was a crescent moon high in the sky with a single strip of a cloud over it, and stars shining brightly in the summer sky. But low across the cove hovered a bank of fog.

As Shelley neared the wharf she squinted into the darkness toward Dan's workplace, realizing that there were no cars parked in the lot. Her heart lurched. He'd lied to her. She continued walking toward the wharf, to double-check the adjacent lot, just to be sure.

Should she confront him when he came home? She would be awake, that was for sure. Or wait until morning? Tonight, the kids would be asleep, at least Aiden would be. She didn't want him to hear what she had to say. He would understand too much. It wasn't something she wanted him to hear.

She turned north on Water Street, parallel to the ocean, and stopped in her tracks. There was Dan's truck, parked all alone in the far corner of the auxiliary lot. She turned back toward the warehouse. She couldn't tell from where she stood if there was a light on inside. Maybe Dan was working security for the business. But why wouldn't he tell her? And why the irregular hours?

Hurrying down toward the wharf, she spotted a light on the water coming out of the fog. She froze, thinking the boat was coming toward the dock, but in a minute she realized its trajectory was headed toward the beach to her left. She couldn't tell how big the boat was, but she couldn't imagine why it wasn't coming toward the dock.

She retraced her path, hurrying down the steps of the dock back to the street. There was no other activity going on anywhere along the oceanfront, which made her all the more suspicious of Dan's nighttime hours. She might as well see if she could find out what was going on with the boat.

The light on the water grew closer as she hurried back down the street the way she'd just come, then turned down a little trail to the beach, staying back in the brush. She was sure no one from the boat would be able to see her, but she didn't want to take a chance of being spotted.

She glanced down at the sand, picking her way through a rocky area, determined not to trip. When she looked back at the water, the light was gone. She squinted into the darkness, wondering for a moment if the boat was in distress. She could make out a smaller boat, a rowboat on the water, and then, finally, she could see the larger boat about two hundred yards out into the water. She hunched down behind a stand of grass to watch.

The rowboat reached the bigger boat. Two men handed down several boxes to the man in the rowboat and then one of the men in the bigger boat climbed down. She gasped, sure he was Dan. A wave of relief passed over her. He wasn't having an affair. He was at work!

Or was he? Why were they out in the cove and not the dock? Why was the light turned off on the boat?

As the rowboat came toward the shore, Shelley snuck back to the street, keeping hunched down. As soon as she reached the pavement, she started running.

The police car passed again, and she gave Officer Crawley a quick wave as she hurried past the gallery. Her stomach lurched. Was the policeman on his way to the beach? Was Dan doing something illegal? Not her Dan. He'd never done anything worse than exceed the speed limit, she was sure. He had a heart of gold.

In no time, she reached home, and as soon as she barged through the door she thanked Diane profusely, saying the run was just what she needed. "You can go home now."

Diane looked a little startled, as if she'd been dozing. She stumbled to her feet and headed to the door, but then stopped. "The flour."

"Oh right." Shelley hurried into the kitchen and picked up the measuring cup, spilling a little on the counter. "Here you go." She handed it to Diane, spilling a little more.

Diane cocked her head, her brown hair falling to the side a little. "Are you all right?"

"Yes. I'm fine."

"Shelley, what's going on?"

"We'll talk tomorrow." Shelley opened the door. "'Night."

It seemed like Diane was moving in slow motion, but finally she was out the door and going down the steps.

Shelley closed the door and locked it, then ran down the hall. She'd hop in the shower. That way, if Dan came home soon she wouldn't have to explain that she'd been out for a run.

Just as she was ready to turn on the water, she heard his truck in the driveway. She stepped into the shower and pressed her forehead against the cold tile as the water ran. She'd dispelled one fear—only to replace it with another.

★   ★   ★

By the time Shelley climbed into bed, Dan was already asleep. Amazingly, Emma didn't stir until six.

Shelley scooped her daughter up out of her crib and headed toward the kitchen, filling the coffeemaker with water and a scoop of coffee, all with one hand. Next she headed to the front door for the newspaper, but before she reached it she stumbled over Dan's shoe, which had been left in the entryway from the night before. She caught herself, clutching Emma even tighter, and kicked the shoe off to the side. It left a trail of sand.

She groaned. Last night really did happen.

She opened the door to a gray mist.

"*Owside?*" Emma grinned, showing off her two lower teeth as she said one of her few words.

"We'll go outside later." Shelley yawned as she picked up the *Press Herald,* turning it around so she could read the front page. The title of the lead article was "Pine Point Men Involved in Drug Ring." A spike of fear ran through her. She scanned the article. Three twenty-year-olds had been running drugs in one of their daddies' boats between Canada and Maine, all the way down to Pine Point, which was an hour south of Marble Cove.

Not her Dan. She dropped the newspaper on the table— front page up. She'd gauge Dan's reaction when he saw it.

But when Dan finally got up, Shelley was helping Aiden brush his teeth in the bathroom. By the time she'd made it back into the kitchen, he'd pulled the sports page out of the pile, and the front page was upside down on the table.

After his shower, Dan said he was going to the wrecking yard to look for a muffler for his truck. He asked Aiden if he wanted to go, and of course the boy was thrilled.

Shelley wasn't as sure. "Make sure and get his booster seat out of the car. And keep a close eye him. The place is probably teeming with tetanus."

Dan gave her an accommodating glance, which she actually thought was gracious. The nitpickiest things tended to jump out of her mouth when it came to her kids.

After Dan and Aiden had headed down the street, Shelley walked over to Diane's house with Emma in her arms, but her friend wasn't home. Her car was in the driveway, and Rocky wasn't barking from behind the door, so Diane was most likely on a walk. Shelley pulled her cell phone from her pocket and hit speed dial for Diane. Her friend picked up immediately. She wasn't on a walk—she was at Margaret's gallery.

"I have her in a vice grip, insisting she choose the paint colors." Diane laughed, and Shelley could hear Margaret's deep chuckle in the background. "Come on down," Diane said. "I could use some help."

Shelley hesitated for a second but then decided a walk would do both her and Emma good. "I'll be right there." She crossed the street and headed for her garage to grab the stroller.

By the time they reached the gallery, Emma was dozing. Shelley wrestled the door open and pushed the stroller through. In an instant she was greeted by both of the older women. Of course they both ignored her after saying hello, focusing their attention on Emma instead.

"Why is she sleeping?" Margaret asked with a smile. "Didn't you tell her we wanted to play?"

Shelley was tempted to wake her daughter up so she would nap later, but if she did, she might start screaming, and then she'd end up carrying Emma and pushing the stroller, which wasn't much fun to do. "Sorry," she said. "When it comes to Emma, sleep is a priority." She parked the stroller along the far wall of the first gallery room and followed the other women to the desk.

"We have it narrowed down," Diane said, "to white and white."

Margaret chuckled. "That's not entirely true."

"'Eggshell' doesn't qualify as a color," Diane said. "It doesn't have enough pigment."

"Diane thinks I'm going from one extreme to another." Margaret smiled. "I'm not used to working with such a big canvas, that's all."

Shelley stood back, feeling a little overwhelmed by the conversation. She felt she had nothing to contribute to a discussion between an artist and someone who had just beautifully redecorated her own cottage.

Diane must have sensed her discomfort because she turned toward Shelley and smiled gently. "How are you?" She had a searching look on her face, as if she wondered if Shelley wanted to talk in front of Margaret or wait. She didn't want to wait. She needed to talk now.

Shelley explained to Margaret that Diane had come over late last night to watch the kids, and then she told both of them about sneaking down to the dock and seeing the boat stop out in the cove and then the light going off. When she said Dan got off the boat into a rowboat, she noted the surprise on both women's faces.

"Are you sure?" Diane said. "You said it was dark."

"I'm pretty sure. Besides, there was sand on his shoes this morning."

"And on yours too." Margaret's eyes were lively. "What did you say when you asked him about it?"

Shelley's face grew warm. "I haven't asked him yet."

"Why ever not?" Margaret nearly choked on the words.

"I didn't want to start anything in front of Aiden."

"I can watch the kids so you and Dan can talk," Diane said. "This afternoon."

"Thanks," Shelley said. "But I'll ask him during nap time."

Margaret nodded. "Stop borrowing trouble. I'm sure, if it was Dan, he has a good explanation."

Shelley didn't say much more after that. She was certain she wasn't borrowing trouble. She listened in on the color conversation a little longer, but then Emma began to fuss, and she decided to leave.

"Oh, don't be all in a pucker to get home," Margaret said. "Let us play with the baby."

But Emma didn't want to play. She clung to Shelley and flicked her head away from Margaret over and over. Finally Shelley said her good-byes and headed out the door.

She felt discouraged as she pushed the stroller. Soon Emma began to cry, not just whimper, and Shelley increased her stride. A block from the house, she took the baby out of the stroller and carried her, doing the one-hand push with the stroller. As she neared their house, Dan's truck pulled into the driveway. By the time she reached him, he had Aiden out of his booster seat and the two were running in a circle around the front yard.

"Where've you been?" Dan asked.

"We went for a walk."

"Oh." He stood still now. The rim of his baseball cap shaded his eyes.

She left the stroller at the bottom of the steps.

Dan unlocked the front door, and Aiden led the way in. But as Shelley approached the doorway, Dan put his hand on her arm. "Is something going on?"

"What do you mean?"

"You've been acting weird lately."

She pulled away from him.

"You've been moody," he said.

"Sleep-deprived."

"And sneaking around."

She looked at him sharply. "What?"

"There was sand on your running shoes last night when I got home."

"I went for a run."

"Who watched the kids?"

"Diane."

His face clouded.

"There was sand on your shoes last night too." She watched his face closely as she spoke, but his expression didn't change.

"I was at work."

"You work on a dock, not a beach."

"I ended up piloting a boat into the cove. It was a special deal." He spoke with a totally straight face.

"You expect me to believe that?"

"Shell," he said, "it's the truth."

"Mommy!" Aiden's voice came from down the hall. "I need you."

Dan stepped into the house. "I'll help him."

Shelley watched her husband head toward the bathroom. He didn't look like he was lying. So why didn't she believe him?

CHAPTER ELEVEN

By the time Beverly got her briefcase packed she was running half a day behind schedule. She'd planned to leave Marble Cove around eight and get to the office before midmorning, but after responding to her e-mail and going on her morning run she spent the next three hours working back through her electronic files and documenting a series of interactions with a union representative.

"You might as well have some lunch before going." Her father stood in the dining room, looking into the little alcove.

"I have a granola bar in my bag." She stood and pushed in her chair. "If I wait any longer I won't make it into the office at all."

"I've been thinking…" her father said.

Beverly was ready to hightail it to her car. "About?"

"Edward Maker."

She stopped at the end of the table. "What about?" She hadn't told him about how the man, who most likely was Edward Maker, had slammed the door on her Friday evening. Nor had she told him what Celia had said.

"We used to play baseball in an empty lot. He'd join us, even though he was older. But he didn't have a glove."

"What would he do?"

Her father shrugged. "Sometimes he'd borrow one. I used to bring my old one. Sometimes he'd play without one."

"Ouch."

Her father winced. "Exactly. Tell him hello from me if you see him."

Beverly said she would and then hugged her father and kissed his forehead. "Mrs. Peabody will be here any minute. I'll be back Friday evening."

★   ★   ★

The drive to Augusta went quickly, and she was at the State House in just over an hour, parking in the back lot and hurrying up the steps to her office in the new wing.

The receptionist gave her a wistful smile when she arrived. "You're so lucky to be telecommuting."

Beverly smiled back. She'd called the receptionist early in the morning to explain her delay, but still she wondered if her co-workers really believed she was working when she wasn't there. Maybe they thought she was slacking during her weeks at Marble Cove, sailing over the ocean and hiking in the forest.

At her desk she ate her granola bar and checked her e-mail again. The office was quiet—a large percentage of her colleagues were on vacation. She probably could have gotten away with staying in Marble Cove this week too. She didn't have any meetings on her calendar for another two weeks.

As she worked, her mind wandered to Edward Maker. Maybe he would have responded differently if her father had showed up on the man's porch instead of her. Then she thought of the lighthouse, the image of the white exterior and tile roof clearly in her mind. She felt a little sad that her morning run wouldn't take her toward it tomorrow or for the next three days after that. No salty air to breathe. No birds diving for fish. No horns blaring on the bay.

Oh why had Edward Maker been so defensive? All they'd wanted was information on the lighthouse. It was incomprehensible that a town like Marble Cove didn't have an archive on the place. Sure, Augie had told them about the Coast Guard logs, and how they'd lost half of them. But someone in Marble Cove must have kept a list of the keepers and their families.

"Beverly?" The receptionist stood in her doorway. "Is your phone working? I just tried to put a call through."

She picked up her receiver, but it was dead. She followed the cord to the wall. It had been disconnected. "Oh dear," she said, quickly plugging it back in.

"I think it's your dad. He's on line three."

Beverly answered quickly, wondering why he hadn't called her cell phone. "Are you all right?"

"Sure, sure. I just wanted to make sure you arrived safely."

She relaxed and fell into her chair. "Made it fine. Thank you for asking. Did Mrs. Peabody get to the house?"

"Yes, she's here. I just finished my lunch."

Beverly felt a little impatient, wondering why her dad had really called.

"Did you stop by Edward Maker's house?"

"No," Beverly said. "I came straight to the office."

"Oh," her father said.

"I thought I might drive over to his house after work." She wasn't sure she'd stop in, though.

"Let me know what he says. I was just thinking about him. Mrs. Peabody said her sister used to date an Edward Maker. Do you think it's the same one?"

"It could be."

"All right," he said. "Well, that's all. Bye now."

"Bye, Father."

Beverly hung up and returned to work. On her computer desktop was the photo of the Marble Cove lighthouse. She minimized everything else from the monitor and stared at the image. It was a picture of her standing alone in front of it. Will had taken the photo when they were dating. It had been fall, early October, and already cold. In the picture she was bundled up in a parka with a scarf looped under her chin. Strands of hair blew around her face.

After she and Will had married they'd docked his sailboat at Marble Cove, but she'd sold the boat soon after the accident. She wasn't competent enough as a sailor to go out on her own, and she didn't have the desire to learn.

Also, it was too painful of a reminder of what had happened.

One day she might let her new friends in on that day. Right now she just wished she could fully play the part of a grieving widow.

★　　★　　★

After work, Beverly drove back to Mr. Maker's neighborhood, the air-conditioning turned on low against the August heat. That was another thing she missed about Marble Cove. Very rarely did the summer weather even grow hot, as it did in Augusta for a short time each summer. Winter in Maine, however, was equal opportunity: cold in both Augusta and Marble Cove.

As she neared the block Mr. Maker lived on, she slowed her car, trying to analyze her motivation. Sure, she wanted to talk with him and find out what his connection to the lighthouse was. But she also felt bad about barging in on him last Friday. How would barging in on him a second time make the first time less traumatic? Was she burning two lamps when there was no ship at sea? Was she being foolish, wasting her energy when there was no hope of any interaction with the man?

She passed his house and turned along the side street. She saw him in the backyard working in the garden. He looked up, hoe in hand, straw hat covering his head, neck, and ears. He wore jeans and a denim work shirt. He must have recognized her car because he started toward the back steps.

She sighed and thought at first not to stop. But if she didn't, he would never know about Celia—and he'd think she was stalking him. Beverly pulled to the curb. It wasn't exactly her business to let Mr. Maker know about an old friend. In fact, the woman hadn't said anything about wanting to even know where Mr. Maker was now. She hadn't even asked why Beverly was trying to find him. Then again, if Mr. Maker let her into his house she could tell him about whom she'd talked with and what was said.

She drove around the block again and parked across the street. The shades in the front window moved a little. Beverly took a deep breath. She would apologize, that's what she would do. Maybe now that he'd had a couple of days to think about things, Mr. Maker would be more open to talking.

Slinging her purse over her shoulder, Beverly climbed from the car and hurried across the street and up the walkway. When she reached the porch, the shades moved again.

"Mr. Maker," Beverly called, "I promise I'm not here to harass you. I wanted to say I'm sorry for barging in on Friday."

She heard footsteps, and the front door opened. Mr. Maker stood in front of her, his hat in his hand.

"I wanted to apologize," she sputtered. "My curiosity got the best of my manners."

Mr. Maker hesitated for a moment. "I'm afraid my alarm got the better of my manners too." He motioned for her to come inside.

The interior of the house was as immaculate as the exterior. There were no rugs or carpets, only honey-colored hardwood floors. There was a built-in hutch and fireplace, crown molding, and simple but sturdy furniture.

Now it was her turn to hesitate. She decided it was better not to bring up Marble Cove at all, not yet. She didn't want to take the chance of alarming him again. "My father drove me by here when I was little, but I haven't been back for years."

"It was in pretty bad shape when I bought it," he said, motioning toward the couch. "Did you notice the peony tree in the front flower bed?"

She shook her head. "I'm not much of a gardener."

"That's a shame." He smiled kindly. "Your grandmother is the one who got me interested. Anyway, she had a similar plant in that bed years ago. I put in the new peony in her honor."

Beverly held her purse in her lap as she sat.

"I remember your father well too," Mr. Maker said, sitting in the straight-back chair to the side. "He was younger than me by several years."

"He identified you in the photo," she said. "He remembers playing baseball with you in a vacant lot. He said you used to borrow his glove."

"He was very kind to me." Mr. Maker seemed much more settled than he had on Friday night.

Beverly decided to go for it. "Celia Patterson identified your photo too."

Mr. Maker's face clouded a little, but he maintained his composure. "Is that right?"

Beverly nodded. "I saw her just yesterday. Her sister helps care for my father."

Edward Maker stared straight ahead. At length, he stirred and took a deep breath. "I'm feeling a little dehydrated. Would you like some lemonade?"

Beverly gratefully accepted, thinking it would buy her a little more time. She watched as he walked through the dining room and pushed through a swinging door. She could hear him in the kitchen, the water running in the sink, a door closing, his footsteps back and forth. She wondered if he was making the lemonade.

She looked around at the sparsely furnished room and contrasted it to her father's Victorian house, full of china, serving dishes, and knickknacks. By the looks of this house, Beverly was pretty sure Mr. Maker hadn't married, or if he had, his wife had been gone a long time.

He returned a few minutes later with two glasses. She thanked him and took a drink. The lemonade was homemade, with pulp and all.

He took a drink. "What exactly do you want from me?"

Beverly held the glass carefully. "What I'd really like is information about the Orlean Point Light."

Again, it was as if a dark cloud cast a shadow over Mr. Maker's face.

She hurried on. "But I'm also curious about your house. And your connection to my father. He said to say hello to you, by the way." She should have said that earlier.

"Thank you. Please return the greeting."

Beverly wanted to ask him about his vocation, where he'd lived through the years, if he'd been married, all of that, but she was sure he wouldn't welcome her questions. "Could I bring my father to visit sometime?"

Mr. Maker finished his lemonade in a long gulp before he answered. "He'd probably like to see the old place, wouldn't he?"

"I think so." Beverly nearly held her breath.

"That would be fine." He stood and walked back into the dining room and opened a drawer in the hutch, pulling out a pen and notepad. He returned a moment later, handing her a folded piece of paper. "This is my phone number. Please call first." He didn't sit back down, and she had the feeling it was time for her to go.

She thanked him for the lemonade and said she would call soon. "And maybe, in time, you'd be willing to talk about the lighthouse."

From the sour look on his face, it was pretty clear he wouldn't be. He muttered good-bye.

As she rounded the corner of his lot in her car Beverly saw Mr. Maker back outside again working in his garden. He hadn't wasted a minute. Perhaps all of his yard work was what kept him young. She thought about Celia chopping wood in her backyard, and smiled. She was disappointed Mr. Maker wouldn't talk about Marble Cove and the lighthouse, but at least she'd be able to see him again.

When she reached her own home, she stood out on the patio before going in, gazing at her view of the Kennebec River in the distance. Her father would be pleased to know she'd visited with Edward Maker. She took out her cell, speed dialing the number.

Her father seemed a little flustered when he answered. "Mrs. Peabody is ready for me to eat," he practically whispered.

"No problem," Beverly said. "I'll call back later."

After she ended the call and was unlocking the kitchen door, it dawned on her that she probably missed her father more than he missed her when she was away. "Who needs whom?" she asked aloud, her voice swallowed by the empty house.

She'd never felt so lonely in her entire life.

CHAPTER TWELVE

As she loaded the last plate into the dishwasher, Shelley heard Aiden's voice coming from down the hall in his bedroom. He'd fallen asleep on the couch in the afternoon, which meant he might be up half the night.

"Dan," she called, "can you check on him?"

When she didn't hear an answer, she grabbed a towel, dried her hands, and headed toward the living room. Her husband was asleep on the couch, his stocking feet propped up on the coffee table.

"Mommy." Aiden probably wanted another drink of water. Or another kiss.

She pushed his door open a little. "What is it?"

"How come Miss Diane was over here last night?" Aiden sat cross-legged on his bed, his spaceship on his pillow. Prize was in the kennel at the foot of the bed.

"I went for a run."

"In the dark?"

She nodded, trying to appear matter-of-fact.

"But that doesn't sound safe." His eyes were big and full of worry.

"It's safe for parents," she said. "And you and Emma were safe too because Miss Diane was here."

He turned his attention to his spaceship. "Are you going running tonight?"

"No."

"But Daddy's here to keep us safe."

"Yes, he is. But I don't need to go for a run tonight."

He zoomed the spaceship in front of himself, keeping his eyes on it instead of her as he spoke. "Why did you need to last night?"

"I just needed the exercise, that's all."

"Does Daddy know you were out?"

"Yes, he does. I told him. Now it's time for you to go to sleep."

"I'm not tired," Aiden said, meeting her gaze and then flying the ship between the two of them.

"Then play quietly until you fall asleep, but stay in your bed. Prize is here with you." She pulled the door nearly shut again, leaving just a crack of light.

She was glad Aiden had asked about her being gone. She had no idea he'd gotten out of bed. Diane probably didn't either. She didn't want him to think she was keeping secrets from Dan—even though she was. She was suspicious of him but hadn't told him so, at least not straight out. She'd intended to at nap time, but he'd ended up working on his muffler, and she was so happy for the peace and quiet in the house that she hadn't wanted to interrupt it.

When she returned to the living room, Dan had his eyes open and seemed interested in the documentary on PBS about rising living expenses. It seemed like costs all over the world were rising. Food. Fuel. Repairs. Life.

"No work tonight?" She sat beside him, the dish towel still on her shoulder.

"That's right," he said, taking her hand.

She stroked his thumbnail, running her finger over the ridge left from when he'd smashed it unloading a ship a couple of years ago. "You know how I went for a run last night?"

He pulled his cap off his head and looked into her eyes. "Yes."

"I was checking up on you."

He smiled. "Actually, that was what I was hoping. Because if you weren't, that would mean you were up to something else."

She tilted her head, surprised. "Why would you think that?"

"You never go running. Especially not at night. You're usually too tired."

He had a point. "I saw you down by the beach. On that boat."

He nodded.

"But it doesn't add up. Why would your job have you pilot a boat to the beach and not the dock?"

Dan's face reddened. "Good point. I was doing some freelance work—for a buddy. He didn't want to pay the dock fee."

"Is your work okay with that?"

"It doesn't have anything to do with them."

"Except it's about taking from their profits."

Dan looked uncomfortable. "Except they'll never know."

"And if they found out?"

"They won't."

Shelley rolled her eyes. "Of course they will. This is Marble Cove."

"No one cares," Dan said. "People do it all the time. Besides, the extra cash paid for the muffler. And we should have extra to put on our bills too."

"Dan." She knew her voice had a bit of a whine to it. "Please don't do anything that will get you in trouble with work—"

"Yeah, yeah, yeah. Tell me how else to make some money around here, and I'll do it. In the meantime, I'll help my buddy when he has work for me."

★   ★   ★

Tuesday afternoon Diane surveyed her office. Everything was finally back in place. She needed to restock her supplies, and she would make a trip to Wal-Mart to do that. The thought made her smile. She enjoyed organizing her office almost as much as she enjoyed writing.

Next, she decided to tidy up outside. She had some zinnias to deadhead and a flowerbed to weed, although she'd be able to wait a couple of days until she had to mow. She slipped her feet into her gardening clogs by the back door and pulled her gloves out of the cupboard. Before she'd even opened the door, Rocky was beside her, wagging his tail.

"You'll have to stay on your leash," she said. It was distracting for him to have Prize across the street in Shelley's backyard. Rocky liked to take off to visit—and chase a squirrel or two on the way.

She deadheaded the flowers, starting in the back and working her way to the front, using a pair of short shears. She looked longingly over at Margaret's yard. It was immaculately designed and cared for. Diane had to remind herself that the Hoskinses had lived in that exact house for over thirty years and had been adding perennials and paths and rockeries to their garden ever since.

When Diane was working in the bed under the front window, she became aware of a car stopping. Usually such an encounter meant a tourist was lost, but when she heard a car door slam, she turned toward the street. Detective Little was walking toward her, coming from his house where his blue pickup was parked.

"I haven't heard from you in a while," he said, and then a smile spread across his face. He wore a short-sleeved shirt that was a little tight around his middle, and his gray hair was as short as ever in his signature buzz cut.

"You've missed me, right?" Diane asked. "And all my questions about the lighthouse."

"Nah," he said. "I figured maybe the whole subject was boring you by now."

"Are you kidding?" Diane clicked the shears shut so she wouldn't accidently clip herself. "I just decided to give you a bit of a rest."

He laughed. "Well, the timing is perfect. I've been swamped with"—he cleared his throat—"more important things."

"Do tell," Diane teased, knowing he couldn't.

"Looking for material for your novel?"

"Actually I finished it. Sent it off to an agent." She blushed as she said it, again wondering if she were sounding pretentious.

Fred Little's eyebrows shot up. "Good for you. What's next?"

"I wait. Until she gets back to me."

"But what's next as far as your writing?"

"Oh." Diane was touched that he asked. "I thought I'd start another one. Do you have any ideas?" She grinned from ear to ear.

He crossed his arms. "Let me think about it. I might have some cases from years ago that I might be able to share bits and pieces of. I've been at this long enough, that's for sure. Most of the people involved have hung up their boots by now." He chuckled and turned to go. "Can't wait to read your first one, hot off the press."

"You've got it." Diane waved even though his back was toward her. "I'll be in touch soon with more questions about the lighthouse, don't worry."

Even though he was across the street now his voice was loud and clear. "Follow my advice, and stick to your fiction!"

She laughed and unlocked the clippers. It was surprising to her how supportive of her writing some people were, including Fred Little. He was far more interested in her novel than her obsession with the lighthouse.

After another hour of yard work, she decided to take Rocky for a walk on the beach. The dog had been barking in the backyard for the last fifteen minutes, obviously at the end of his rope.

She put her tools away and grabbed Rocky's leash, then Diane went back into the house and slipped her cell phone into the pocket of her sweatshirt. If she saw something suspicious at the lighthouse again, she could call Detective Little right away. She smiled at the thought.

Rocky lurched ahead on his leash, and Diane pulled him back as they walked down the trail to the sand. There were a few families playing on the beach and two teenage boys tossing a football. Most of the tourists were probably getting cleaned up for dinner. In another hour or two they'd be back playing in the sand until darkness fell. Then a few would build bonfires and enjoy the night sky.

She liked the smell of the smoke that wafted up to her cottage and the sound of laughter that sometimes reached her if it was warm enough to leave a window open.

When she and Eric used to bring the kids to Marble Cove, they would try to do a bonfire one night during vacation, usually on the last night. They would bring willow sticks and marshmallows for the kids to roast. A few times they'd made a picnic of it, bringing hot dogs and buns, chips and soda too. A perfect meal for the kids. She smiled at the thought, sure she wouldn't be able to stomach that kind of food anymore. Fifteen years made a big difference when it came to diet.

She reached the sand and let Rocky off his leash. She knew that was why he liked the beach so much. He would run and run in circles, looping around her over and over. She was certain he ran ten times farther than she walked. Off he zipped in a flash, chasing a seagull. The bird squawked and took off in flight, three more following it. Rocky changed direction and veered toward the ocean's edge.

She followed Rocky but stayed on the firm sand, walking at a brisk pace and swinging the leash along in a circle. As the shoreline turned a little, the lighthouse came into view. Rocky was near the outcropping of rocks where she'd first found him. She often wondered if, in his doggy brain, he remembered the incident. But he never seemed hesitant around the area. She picked up her speed, aware once again of the activity around her. Ahead, far beyond the dog, a seagull dropped a mussel onto an outcropping of rocks, and out in the ocean a fishhawk dove into the water.

As she neared the rocks, her phone vibrated in her pocket. She pulled it out and checked the number. She didn't recognize it and nearly didn't answer, thinking the sound of the waves would make it hard to hear, but she decided she might as well give it a try.

"Hello, this is Diane," she said, the phone to one ear and her finger in the other in an attempt to block out the noise.

"Frieda Watley here."

For a minute Diane was sure someone was playing a joke on her, but then she couldn't think of a single soul she'd told the agent's name to.

"In New York," the woman added.

It was her! "Frieda! Hello." Diane's heart raced. "Can you hear me all right?"

"Just fine."

"Oh good. I'm on the beach, and it's a little noisy on my end."

"The beach? How lovely. Oh, that's right. You live in Maine, don't you?"

Diane managed a garbled affirmation. Her hand had gone sweaty, making the phone feel slippery, and her legs were growing weaker by the second.

Rocky ran toward her barking, and Diane realized she'd stopped walking. He liked it better when she was moving. She started up again, pressing her finger into her other ear more firmly. A ship horn blasted in the distance.

"Well, I wanted to let you know how much I'm enjoying your story."

"You already read it?"

"Most of it," Frieda said. "Not every word, but all the way through to the end. More than enough to know I want to represent you."

Now Diane almost fell face-first into the sand. "R-really?"

"I think the ending is very powerful. The middle sags a little…"

Diane wasn't sure what to say. She wanted to say how much she'd tried to keep her pace tight and that she was sure she could fix it. No words found their way to her mouth, though.

"But the writing and the proposal are definitely strong enough for me to pitch. I'd like to send it off to three different houses." She rattled off the names of the publishing houses, and every one of them was familiar to Diane. This was unreal. "But first I'll send a contract from my agency off to you. I'll overnight it in tomorrow's mail...if you're interested."

"I'm definitely interested." The words tumbled over each other.

"Good. Sign the contract, and send it back. Then I'll begin pitching. And, Diane, congratulations on a story well written."

Chills traveled up Diane's arms, and she stopped walking again. "Thank you!"

"Call me if you have any questions. And I mean that."

Diane assured her she would, racking her brain as to what questions she might have. "I can't think of any now."

"Oh, you will," Frieda said. "Believe me." Then she said a quick good-bye and hung up.

Diane threw her head back and laughed. Rocky bounded toward her again. Diane slipped her phone into her pocket and clapped her hands, inviting the dog to jump up. He did, his front paws landing on her chest. She grabbed them and danced around, laughing. He cooperated for a moment but then struggled away from her and bounded on down the beach, turning and lunging forward, begging her to follow. She began jogging, swinging the leash around again.

"Dear God," she said aloud, "an agent is interested in my novel. Can You believe it?" She cast her eyes up into the cloudless blue sky. Of course He could! He already knew.

Eric. She felt his loss for the millionth time. He would be so proud of her. "Tell him, would You, please, God? Tell him how happy I am about this. Tell him I know how happy he would be for me too..." Tears stung her eyes. She stopped again.

Rocky returned, but, perhaps sensing her sadness, he didn't bark. Instead he nuzzled her free hand.

She patted his head and looked down at him. "Thank you," she whispered, her voice catching in her throat.

Tell someone. It was a thought inside her head. A prodding. *Someone human. Not just Rocky.*

She looked up toward the lighthouse. The evening rays bounced off the white exterior, and the roof looked barn red in the declining light. She could call her kids, but neither of them had even responded to her e-mail telling them that she'd sent the novel to the agent. Maybe it wasn't a big deal to them. Maybe they thought every middle-aged woman was working on a novel.

It would be easier to tell someone in person, but it was dinnertime. Shelley would be feeding her family. Maybe Margaret was still at her gallery. She could stop by there.

She turned around. Rocky, still at her side, followed. He walked near her all the way back to the boardwalk and waited patiently as she put the leash back on him. A few minutes later, she tied him to the bike rack outside of the Shearwater Gallery.

"Hello," she called out.

"Back here!" came her friend's voice.

Diane noticed that someone, probably Allan, had done some sanding on the ceiling, readying it for a coat of primer. That was hard, overhead work for anyone, but especially a man of seventy.

Margaret was in the back room, standing in front of an easel with a half-finished painting on it. Her reading glasses were perched on her nose, and a small brush was in her hand. "Did you come to harass me about colors again?" Her voice was full of fun.

"It's your lucky day," Diane said. "That's not on my list of topics today."

"The lighthouse then?" Margaret gazed over the top of her colorful glasses, which were studded with rhinestones.

"Strike two."

"What then?" Margaret pulled the glasses from her face.

Diane noticed Margaret's painting. It was a seascape with the lighthouse far off in the distance, a figure on the sand, and another person running up the sand dune toward town. "Tell me about your painting." Diane stepped closer.

Margaret stepped back and stared at her work too. "This has practically painted itself," Margaret said, but then she sighed. "How about it if I talk about it after it's all done?"

That was fair enough. If anyone could sympathize, it was Diane. It was hard to talk about one's art when it was still in-process.

"So what's up?" Margaret asked, turning her gaze back to Diane.

"I have good news about my novel."

"Already!"

Diane nodded. "The agent wants to represent me. She's sending a contract tomorrow."

Margaret jumped up and down in glee, and in half a second she'd propelled herself around the counter and into Diane's arms, the paintbrush flying over their heads. They jumped together—two women, one in her sixties and the other in her fifties—acting as if they were in kindergarten.

"That is so fantastic!" Margaret spoke and laughed and giggled all at the same time. She came to a stop. "Congratulations!"

"It doesn't mean anything for sure." Diane held onto her friend's arm.

"Sure, it does. It means a professional in your industry sees the value of your work! It's a huge step toward being published."

Diane agreed. It was significant. She was so glad she'd shared the news with Margaret. As an artist, she understood all the work that went into a piece. And the risk. There was no guarantee that any of the time would ever pay off beyond the intrinsic satisfaction of doing it. And Diane had to admit that, for the first couple of novels, it would be enough to write them solely for herself because she was just learning. But she couldn't imagine making it a permanent part of her life if she never had any hope of getting published.

She shivered a little. She had an agent! She did have hope of getting published, at least until she got a rejection.

"We should celebrate!" Margaret was a little out of breath.

"Not yet."

"You're going to tell Shelley and Beverly, though, right?"

"I think so."

"Tell them right away. Otherwise I'll let it slip." Margaret grinned. "By accident, of course." It was clear that wouldn't be the case.

"I'll tell them as soon as I see them."

"Diane." Margaret had her hands on her hips, and she said the word the way Eric used to when he was exasperated with her, somehow turning it into three syllables.

That made her smile. "Are you ready to head home?" she asked her friend, changing the subject.

"Not yet. I'm going to paint a little longer. You go on ahead."

Five minutes later, Diane was on their block. Rocky was tuckered out and following like a well-behaved dog. Ahead, Aiden was hunched over on the strip of grass between the sidewalk and the street, overturning the stones around the birch tree. He had a plastic bug-catcher in his hand. He must've spotted one because he plucked something out of the dirt and plopped it in the container. Prize was on a chain by the porch, and she barked out a welcome. Rocky lumbered over to say hello.

"What did you find?" Diane asked Aiden.

"A roly-poly. Want to see?"

Diane increased her speed, tugging Rocky away from Prize. As she reached the Bauers' house, she noted that Dan's truck wasn't in the driveway. She spotted Shelley sitting on her stoop, staring off toward the ocean with Emma in her arms.

Shelley turned her head slowly, and it seemed to take her a minute to notice Diane was with Aiden.

"Hello," Diane said.

"Oh, hi." Shelley looked a little more alert.

Diane stopped a minute to examine Aiden's bug. He had a single roly-poly, or pill bug as her kids called them, and it had curled up into a ball, all alone. "Don't keep it too long," Diane said. "Or he won't make it back home."

"I'll let him go back under his rock," Aiden said. "That's what Mama said I'm supposed to do."

"Good thinking," Diane answered, tousling his sandy hair. She started up the walkway to Shelley. Emma grinned at her and then hid her face against her mother's shoulder. "What's up?" Diane asked.

"You first," Shelley answered. "You're smiling."

Diane wasn't sure if her friend was being sincere. She sat down on the second step, below the mother and child.

"I'm serious." Shelley scrunched her nose. "I could use some good news."

Diane took a deep breath. "I had a call from the literary agent in New York. She wants to represent me."

"Oh, that's wonderful!" Shelley's response was immediate and heartfelt. "I'm so excited for you!" She leaned forward with a half hug, bumping the little girl against Diane's face. Emma pulled back and clung to her mother more tightly.

"Thanks." A congratulations from someone in the midst of her own struggles seemed like an extra gift. "Now it's your turn."

"I talked with Dan. Twice. First he said he was working Sunday night. Then when he brought it up again he said he was doing freelance"—she made a quote gesture with her free hand—"work for an old buddy, piloting his boat into the cove and unloading on the beach because the guy didn't want to pay a docking fee."

"Is that legal?"

Shelley shrugged. "I'm more worried about what the guy was hauling."

"Oh dear," Diane said. "What are you thinking?"

"Actually I'm trying not to."

"What did Dan say?"

"He said it was the guy's personal items, and that he was moving. He's convinced his buddy's on the up-and-up."

Diane's mind started whirring. The whole scenario sounded like a great premise for a novel. She forced herself back to the present. "What are you going to do?"

Shelley sighed and started to say something, but stopped and tensed up.

Diane followed her gaze. Detective Little and his wife Cindy were strolling by, headed toward the beach.

Aiden held up his bug-catcher. The Littles called out a greeting to Diane and Shelley and then examined Aiden's find. A minute later they continued on their walk.

Shelley groaned. "I don't know what to do."

*   *   *

Diane sat with Shelley for another half hour. She had no idea how to advise her young friend, so she listened and then played with Aiden while Shelley went into the house and gave Emma a quick bath. When she came out to call Aiden inside, a squeaky-clean and pajama-clad Emma in her arms, Diane told them all good-bye and took Rocky home.

Diane fixed herself a peanut butter sandwich for dinner. Then she called Beverly's cell phone. She didn't want her to hear her news from one of the other two women and feel left out. The phone rang several times before Beverly answered. When she realized it was Diane, she sounded alarmed. "Is everything all right? Is it about my dad? Is he hurt?"

"No, no. Everything's fine, Beverly." Now Diane felt a little silly for calling. "I just wanted to share my good news." She explained about the agent wanting to represent her.

"That's fantastic," Beverly said. "I'm so happy for you."

The chatted for another moment, and Diane said she'd visit Beverly's dad tomorrow to talk about what he was reading and check in with him. "I'll see you Saturday then."

"Maybe not," Beverly said. "I may bring Father back to Augusta to visit Mr. Maker."

"Oh?" Diane said. "How did that come to be?"

"I talked with him on Monday and apologized for barging in on him like that."

"And he was cordial?" Diane was surprised Beverly had gone back.

"Very. Although he wouldn't talk about the lighthouse. But I thought if I took Father to see him, and the two of them started reminiscing about growing up in Augusta, maybe he'd talk about his days in Marble Cove."

"Let me know how that goes," Diane said.

Beverly assured her she would, but her tone seemed a little funny, as if she were holding back some information.

After they hung up, Diane chuckled at her reaction. What more could there be to say? Edward Maker hadn't wanted to talk about the lighthouse, and that was all Diane was interested in. If Mr. Wheeland and Mr. Maker had known each other as boys, then they had lots of things to talk about that didn't have any bearing on the lighthouse or Diane at all, except that she was always interested in a good story. And two old friends coming together after so many years was one of the best kinds of stories.

Her mind started whirring again, but soon it landed back on Beverly. Maybe she wasn't holding back any information. Maybe she was just lonely. That, Diane could relate to, with all her heart.

Chapter Thirteen

Thursday morning before heading into the gallery, Margaret checked her e-mail. Her relatives had been slow to sign up for the tasks Beth had outlined for the reunion. Margaret wondered if maybe she should sign up for a couple more. She could make signs pointing the way to the park site Beth had reserved. That would be an easy task to take on and something she would enjoy.

There was a new message under the subject "family reunion." From Buddy. She clicked on the message.

Can't wait to see everyone. I'll do the games and
relays. Will also bring drinks.

Margaret groaned out loud, imagining coolers filled with adult beverages.

I can also do the signs to direct family to the site. Let
me know what isn't covered when it gets closer to the
date, and I'll pick up a few more tasks.
Thanks so much, Beth, for all of your hard work.
Love, Buddy

Margaret closed her e-mail program, dumbfounded. What was Buddy up to? Wanting to distract herself, she clicked onto the Internet and Googled, "ceiling paint." Up popped a site on "haint blue." She laughed. That Diane really did know what she was talking about. As she scrolled down, Adelaide came into the room, coming to a stop behind Margaret. "I'm still trying to decide what to paint the gallery ceilings."

"I like that blue," her daughter said.

Margaret wasn't sure. She'd been thinking of a lemon yellow and pale orange to look like sunset. She needed to decide soon and order it from the hardware store. Of course, having it done by the reunion was just an arbitrary deadline she'd set. It really had nothing to do with finishing it. It was just that it was at the end of August, and she really wanted the painting completed before September.

★   ★   ★

Diane read the return address on the large white envelope a second time. She took her letter opener out of her desk drawer and carefully slipped it under the seal, pulling it along slowly. She didn't want to risk damaging the contract. She pulled it out carefully and read the cover letter, her eyes lingering on Frieda's signature and the New York address.

She flipped to the actual contract and read over it. It was only two pages long and seemed pretty straightforward. There were several "Whereas" clauses and a cancellation clause. There was also a clause affirming that the story was not libelous in any way and was the sole creation and property of Diane Spencer.

She read on. If Frieda couldn't place the book within six months, the contract said, Diane was free to contact another agent. If the initial book was placed, Diane could suspend her association with the agency for the next book or choose to submit another one.

It all seemed legit, but she felt she should have someone else look at it. Beverly would be a good person for that, but Diane didn't want to wait until Sunday to sign the contract and send it back. She could hire a lawyer, but that would be expensive, and it would need to be an entertainment lawyer. She was pretty sure there weren't any of those in Marble Cove. Margaret would be a good person to ask. She had a ton of experience with contracts and artists, but Diane didn't want to disturb her at work.

Diane remembered she'd told Beverly she would check in on her dad. She'd meant to do it yesterday and then had gotten busy with more yard work and then an extralong walk with Rocky, and by the time she'd gotten cleaned up it was dinnertime, and she didn't want to interrupt him.

Later, she wondered if perhaps he was an early-to-bed sort of person and decided not to disturb him then too. She slipped the contract and cover letter back into the envelope. It wouldn't hurt to have him take a look. If nothing else, he would be happy to hear her good news.

Five minutes later, she was knocking on Mr. Wheeland's door. She was surprised when a woman she didn't recognize greeted her. She wore her snow-white hair back in a bun and had on a blue skirt and blouse.

"Is Mr. Wheeland in?" Diane asked hesitantly. She knew Mrs. Peabody helped Beverly's dad with light housework and meals, but she'd never seen this woman before.

"Coral," the woman called down the hall, "someone's here."

A moment later Mrs. Peabody appeared, barely limping. Diane was pleased to see that the older woman's ankle was nearly healed.

Mrs. Peabody dried her hands on a dishtowel as she said, "Well, ask her in, for Pete's sake." As Diane stepped into the entryway, Mrs. Peabody introduced her big sister Celia, whom she said was visiting for the day. The two women didn't look much alike, and even though Celia was older she actually looked younger.

"What brings you to Marble Cove?" Diane asked.

"My little sister insisted." Celia laughed. "She came out to my home on Sunday with Mr. Wheeland's daughter. That got me thinking about some things."

"Really?" Diane didn't know Beverly had gone anywhere with Mrs. Peabody.

Celia nodded. "She showed me a photo that stirred up a lot of memories."

Diane's hand went to her throat. "Of Edward Maker?"

"Do you know him too?"

"No. Well, I met him, kind of. Actually, I didn't. He slammed the door in our faces."

"When?" Celia's face went nearly as white as her hair.

"Last Friday."

"Where?"

"Augusta. Well, I wasn't sure it was the Edward Maker we were looking for then, but I talked with Beverly a couple of days ago, and she confirmed it was. In fact, she's thinking of taking her father to see him on Saturday."

"I need to sit down." Celia stepped into the living room. The other two women followed her. She plopped down into one of the wingback chairs by the fireplace. "Why is Mr. Wheeland going to go visit Edward?"

Diane sat in the other wingback. "They knew each other in Augusta while they were growing up, or so it seems."

"Why didn't Beverly tell me that on Sunday?"

Mrs. Peabody let out a groan. "Because you didn't act like you were interested at all in talking about Edward Maker. You hushed Beverly up."

"Why didn't you say anything?" Celia glared at her younger sister.

"I was having a hard time remembering the details of your friend Mr. Maker, because the truth is, you didn't talk about him much back then either." Mrs. Peabody snapped the towel off her shoulder.

Celia waved her hand dismissively in her sister's general direction and turned her attention to Diane. "Coco's always sticking her nose in where it doesn't belong—and then she gets the details wrong." She gave her sister a woeful look. "But I love you, you know that, right?"

Mrs. Peabody gave a little nod and crossed her arms.

Celia addressed Diane again. "How is Edward?"

"Fine, I think. Health-wise, anyway. He has a beautiful home and garden, which used to be Mr. Wheeland's parents' place. It seems like Mr. Maker is able to keep up with everything."

Celia was quiet for a moment. "I guess I'd better speak with Beverly, hadn't I?" She was looking at her sister now.

Mrs. Peabody nodded, but she didn't look very pleased. She turned toward Diane. "Mr. Wheeland's in the library. I'll tell the mister you're here."

Diane followed the woman down the hall, leaving Celia alone in the living room. There was definitely a long story behind Celia's interest in Mr. Maker, and Diane was as curious as could be, but she didn't feel right prying for details. Hopefully she'd hear more about it from Beverly.

"You have a visitor." Mrs. Peabody pushed open the door.

Mr. Wheeland sat in his chair, a book in his lap. He looked up quickly and smiled, but Diane wondered if perhaps he'd been dozing. "Diane," he said. "How nice to see you. Come on in and sit down."

She did, placing the envelope on her lap.

"What do you have there?"

She glanced toward the door. She couldn't see Mrs. Peabody but wondered if she was still in the hall. No matter if she was. Diane pressed forward, explaining about the phone call from the agent. "I was wondering if you would take a look at the contract."

"I'm afraid I don't know anything about literary contracts. Now if it was a teachers' union contract, I could help." He put on his reading glasses and reached for the document. "But I'd be happy to read it."

Diane pulled the contract from the envelope and handed it to him. As he read, she scanned his library.

The room was one of her favorite places in all of Marble Cove. The floor-to-ceiling bookcases were filled with hardbound classics. The shelves and molding were all dark cherry wood, and the furniture was old-fashioned and comfortable. The morning paper was strewn across the coffee table, open to the crossword puzzle, and several books were stacked next to Mr. Wheeland's chair. She wondered if he was still adding to his collection or if he was content to reread his old favorites.

"Well," he said after a couple of minutes of silence, "it certainly looks like it's on the up-and-up and professional." He handed the contract back. "I don't see anything suspicious." He looked over the rims of his glasses at her. "Congratulations." His voice was as even as ever, but she could tell he was happy for her.

They chatted for a few more minutes, then Diane let herself out of the house without seeing Celia or Mrs. Peabody again.

She'd decided to stop by the gallery and interrupt Margaret's work after all. She'd know better than anyone what to look for when it came to representing and selling art. Diane went straight to the gallery instead of going home to get Rocky. Every once in a while it was nice to go on a walk alone.

Margaret was with a customer when she arrived. Diane kept busy looking at the artwork, even though she'd seen it quite a few times before. She examined a painting of Margaret's a little closer. It was the one she'd been working on. And now it looked finished.

The lighthouse stood at the bottom of the painting, and she'd changed the figure on the dune so that he was running toward the water, not away from it. And the other figure wasn't on the beach anymore, it was in the water. The sky was dark and ominous with clouds billowing on the horizon. The lighthouse had a subtle glow to it from the light emanating from the stormy sky.

Diane heard the customer say she would look around a little longer before she made her choice.

"So what's up?" Margaret asked, approaching Diane.

Diane patted the envelope under her arm. "I got the contract from the agent. I wondered if you would take a look at it for me, if you're not too busy."

Margaret rubbed her hands together. "I'd love to."

The customer wandered into the second gallery room as Margaret read, and Diane examined the painting with the two figures in it again.

It looked as if the first figure was going out into the water and the second figure was keeping watch. Purple and red flowers bloomed in the grass. Diane didn't remember ever seeing flowers like that on the edge of the sand. Margaret must have added them, which meant they were symbolic in some way, as were the stormy sky and the glowing lighthouse.

Every element in one of Margaret's paintings had some sort of meaning.

"What percentage does the agent get if a publisher buys your book?" Margaret was looking over her glasses.

"It's in the last paragraph."

Margaret nodded as she found the information. "Okay. I see. Fifteen percent. That's fair. And she receives no payment from you if she doesn't get you a contract with a publisher?"

"That's my understanding," Diane said.

"Mine too, from reading this." Margaret handed it back. "I think it looks good. I can't see any holes in it. I think she has your interests balanced with hers."

"Thanks," Diane said.

Margaret pulled a pen from the drawer under the counter. "Want to sign now?"

"And then I could get it out in today's mail." Diane took the pen from her friend.

"You should make a copy," Margaret said.

"I'll stop by the library and use their machine before I mail it."

"I even have a stamp." Margaret rummaged in the drawer again. "And an envelope."

As Diane signed on the line with a flourish, the customer said she'd decided which painting she wanted to buy. She pointed to the new one, the one with the two figures on the beach. Diane's heart fell a little as she watched the woman, and she wondered if Margaret was a little sad to have the painting going so soon.

"Can you tell me about the artist?" the woman asked.

"Actually, that's one of my pieces."

"Oh, how wonderful!" The woman looked at Margaret with admiration. "Tell me about the painting."

"That's me in the water." Margaret's voice was serious, not her usual jovial self.

"And who's on the shore?"

"I don't know who it is."

Diane's hand went to her mouth. It was the scene of Margaret's near-death experience. A stranger, who to this day hadn't been identified, had rescued Margaret from death and then disappeared before Margaret could thank him.

"Any idea who it is?"

Margaret shook her head, and her eyes twinkled. "You get to decide that. It can be whoever you want."

The woman stepped back as Margaret lifted the painting from the wall. "I think it's an angel," the woman said. "Keeping watch."

Margaret didn't respond. She headed straight to the desk and began tearing brown butcher paper from the big roll to wrap the painting. Diane said a quick good-bye and slipped out the door, a shiver running down her back as she hurried on down the sidewalk.

Ten minutes later, she pushed the envelope through the letter slot inside the post office, grinning as she did. "Thank You, God," she whispered, watching as the contract disappeared.

It would be in New York and on Frieda Watley's desk by Monday. Diane had read online that August was a slow month to pitch manuscripts because so many people at the publishing companies went on vacation then. But maybe that would work to her advantage. Maybe the editors Frieda was pitching to weren't on vacation. Maybe they'd have a little extra time to look at Diane's proposal.

Or maybe not. She turned and hurried out through the glass doors of the post office. She'd have to leave it up to God—it was entirely out of her control.

*   *   *

Shelley wheeled the shopping cart through the Wal-Mart just outside of Tussacusset. Deciding where to shop was never easy for her. Was it worth it to spend more money on gas to save money on groceries? Plus, when she had to haul both kids along, she hardly had any room for anything else in her cart. She pulled a box of crackers off the shelf and wedged them between Aiden and a gallon of milk.

"You'll have to get out in a minute," she said. "I'm running out of room."

He made a face. "I'm too little to walk."

"You?" she responded in mock horror. "Not Aiden, my big boy?"

He smiled a little and ducked his head.

Dan was home working on his truck some more. He hadn't worked at the docks at all for the last couple of days—which was both a relief and a concern. At least he wasn't involving himself in something potentially shady. On the other hand, the lack of hours at his job meant they would be digging deeper into their minuscule savings to pay the bills.

"Can we get cupcakes?" Aiden asked.

"No, but you could help me make some from scratch."

He crossed his arms. "But yours don't have enough frosting."

Emma pointed to the cupcakes too. "Pweeze?"

Shelley kissed the top of her daughter's head. "I like your 'please,' but no."

Emma's chin quivered. "Pweeze!" She was getting to that stage where she thought anytime she said 'please' she should get what she wanted. It *was* a magic word—but not in the way Emma thought.

Shelley pushed the cart quickly past the cake section and into the bread aisle. It was a really bad idea to bring the kids to the store. She should have asked Diane if she would watch them. Or waited until Dan was done with his truck. She pulled a loaf of dark whole-wheat bread from the shelf.

But Aiden pointed to a loaf of white balloon bread. "I like that."

"When have you ever had that?" She was dumbfounded. She only fed her kids whole-wheat bread.

"At Grandma's. She buys cupcakes too."

That figured. Shelley put the loaf in the cart, and Aiden leaned against the bread. "Okay, time to get out, buddy."

She stepped around to the side of the cart and began to lift him, but he resisted. "Aiden. Cooperate, now."

"Only if you'll buy me a toy."

She lifted him abruptly, but he hooked one foot on the edge of the cart, pulling it toward her and upsetting Emma, who began to cry. She held onto Aiden with one hand and grabbed his foot with the other, sweeping him down to the floor. She knelt beside him.

"That wasn't safe at all. You could have pulled the cart over—with Emma in it. It could've fallen on top of you. Both you and Emma could have been hurt badly."

He began to whimper, and Emma escalated her cries.

"Walk beside me," Shelley said to Aiden.

She put a few more things in the cart but didn't get everything on her list. So much for saving money, but at least they hadn't had a horrible accident. She shuddered at the thought of what would have happened if Aiden had pulled the cart over.

She felt entirely tense as the checker, a middle-aged woman, bagged the groceries. Finances. Dan's work. His friend's suspicious activities. The kids. Her hope to start a business. It was all so overwhelming.

"Will you buy us a treat?" Aiden was standing to the side, looking forlornly at the candy rack.

"No, sweetie. We'll have a snack when we get home."

He stuffed his hands in his pockets and kept staring at the goodies.

"Mama, *pweeze*?" Emma pointed to the rack.

Shelley turned toward the register, ignoring both of her children. She wondered if her anxiety increased theirs, if it made them more on edge and more demanding. Did they sense when her mind was somewhere else and try to bring her back by vying for her attention?

She bent down and kissed the top of Emma's head and then reached for Aiden's hand. "I'll need you to help put the grocery bags in the car, okay? And once we're on our way home, we'll talk about what we'll fix for a snack when we get there."

He nodded solemnly.

The middle-aged checker bagged the last item. "Your kids are adorable, and I can tell you're a really good mom."

"Th-thank you," Shelley stammered, taken by surprise.

"Just know that you will never in all you life do anything more important than mothering them."

Shelley nodded as she handed over her debit card. She knew that, in her heart—but it was nice to be reminded.

CHAPTER FOURTEEN

Beverly sat at the desk in her alcove at her father's house and dialed Edward Maker's number. It was only 8:30 AM, but she felt sure the man had been up for hours. He seemed like the kind of person who was probably out of bed before the sun peeked over the horizon. He picked up on the second ring. She explained who she was—unnecessarily, it turned out. It seemed he'd been anticipating her call.

"I know I said this morning would be a good time to bring your father, but I'm not so sure it is now. I have a lot of yard work to do, and then I have some business I need to attend to this afternoon."

"What if we come by at lunchtime? I could bring sandwiches."

"No, I have food from last night. Some other time—"

"Who is it, Beverly?" Her father stood in the dining room.

"Edward Maker," she mouthed.

"Are we leaving soon?"

She shook her head.

"Is that your father?" Mr. Maker asked.

"Yes," Beverly answered.

"Wanting to come see me?"

"Yes."

"Let me think about it," Mr. Maker said. "Could you call me back in a few minutes?"

Beverly said she could, and she hung up, telling her father she wasn't sure what their plans were yet. "I'll let you know in a few minutes."

He turned around without saying anything and retreated back to his library.

Beverly imagined Edward Maker in his spotless kitchen washing his breakfast dishes by hand and then drying each item and putting them away. He probably wiped down the counters and stove after each meal.

Maybe he'd been a career military man. That would explain the discipline and order. And why he didn't come back to Maine until after he'd retired. Maybe Celia was opposed to him making a career out of the military. Maybe she'd wanted him to come home after Korea while he'd wanted her to join him in California. If Celia loved her daddy's hunting cabin so much that she wanted to live there the rest of her life, she probably wouldn't have wanted to leave Maine at all way back when.

Beverly stood and stretched. She'd already had her run, shower, and breakfast. She was anxious to get on with her day. If she wasn't going back into Augusta today, she needed to get some yard work done for her father.

She dialed Edward Maker's number again. He didn't bother saying hello. "You can visit for a few minutes," he said. "But come now. The longer it takes you to get here, the more likely I'll be to change my mind."

Beverly found her father back in the library, looking as if he were settling down for a morning nap. "He said we could come," she said. "But we need to go now."

He struggled to his feet. "I haven't been to Augusta in years."

She nodded and took his arm, wondering if he remembered the last time. It had been for Will's funeral.

★   ★   ★

Her father got his morning nap after all. He fell asleep in Beverly's car not too far outside of Marble Cove. A few times he let out a gentle snore.

When they reached the outskirts of Augusta, a red Jeep pulled out in front of them, and Beverly had to slam on the brakes.

As she did her father lurched forward, and instinctively her hand flew out to stop him, even though he wore a seat belt. His chest hit her arm, and she pushed him back as gently as she could. He startled awake as she released her brakes, gripping the steering wheel with only one hand.

"You okay?" he asked as the Jeep pulled ahead of them.

"I'm good. How about you?" She pulled her hand back, placing it on the wheel too, trying to slow her racing heart.

"I think I'm okay. What happened?"

"We seem to have been invisible to the Jeep ahead of us." It was speeding on down the highway.

"Well, well." Her father settled back against the seat.

Beverly thought for a moment that he might fall back asleep, but he didn't. Her heart was still pounding. What if she hadn't been able to stop? What would have happened to her dad? Her knuckles were practically white on the steering wheel. All those years he had protected her, and now it was her turn. A decade ago she would have thought he would have mourned their roles reversing, but she realized it was a perfectly natural occurrence for both of them.

"Can we drive through downtown after we visit with Edward? I always like crossing the river and seeing the capitol."

"Sure." It always thrilled her, seeing the brick buildings across the river and then driving over the bridge. The park in front of the capitol was beautiful too, and the dome of the State House always caught her attention, even though she worked there and saw it all the time.

She turned off the highway toward their old neighborhood, passing the high school.

"There's the ball field," her father said, craning his neck as they drove by.

When she stopped in front of Mr. Maker's house, her father didn't undo his seat belt or open his door. Instead, statue still, he stared at the house.

"What do you think?" Beverly finally said.

"Mother kept a perfect house and yard," he said quietly, "but it looks even better than I remember. I never would have expected Edward Maker to take such good care of a place. You should have seen the shack he grew up in."

Beverly was surprised at her father's use of the word *shack*. He wasn't usually one to exaggerate or be overly dramatic.

"I think he'll show you around."

Her father harrumphed.

Beverly got out and walked around to open his door, sensing that he needed a little encouragement. He climbed out of the car slowly and then took his time straightening up. But once he was upright, he led the way up the walk, up the steps, and onto the porch, ringing the bell firmly.

Beverly couldn't hear a thing inside. Not a television or radio. Nor any footsteps coming toward the door. "I'll check in the backyard," she said. "You stay here."

She hurried down the steps and around the side of the house. Maybe Mr. Maker had changed his mind and decided to run errands or go visit someone. She peeked into the backyard but didn't see anyone. There was a box with tomatoes and peppers in it, but she didn't see any tools. She headed back out to the porch, but when she arrived her father wasn't there. She glanced toward the car, but he wasn't there either. Bounding up the steps, she realized the door was open a little and that she could hear muffled voices from inside.

She knocked on the screen door.

"Come in." Mr. Maker's voice was loud and clear.

Beverly pushed the door open and went in. Her dad and Mr. Maker were standing in the middle of the living room looking up at the ceiling.

Mr. Maker greeted her and said he was showing her father the work he'd done on the crown molding. They spent the next half hour looking at the house. They went upstairs to where her father's room had been. It was now absolutely vacant. The other room upstairs had exercise equipment in it. Mr. Maker's room was on the first floor, but he didn't open his door to it. Next he took them on a tour of the yard.

Beverly's father remembered that his mother had grown raspberries and blueberries in the same spot. "And look, rhubarb," he said. "Was it growing here when you moved in?"

Mr. Maker said it was. He'd expanded the garden since he didn't have any need for a lawn, but the berries and rhubarb were already established.

Beverly's father shaded his eyes from the midmorning sun. "How often did you help out around here? I was trying to remember."

"I started by the time I was twelve," Mr. Maker replied. "And helped out until I got a job mucking stalls at a dairy farm when I was fifteen."

Beverly's father nodded slowly. "That would have been about the time I started mowing the lawn. I must have been about ten."

"Your mom was more than good to me. Besides paying me, she always sent something home with me. A container of berries. Or a head of lettuce. Tomatoes. Zucchini. Every bit of it helped my mom out. Some of my best memories from growing up were from this place."

"Do you have any family around?" Beverly asked.

Mr. Maker's gaze fell beyond the garden. "My parents are long gone, of course, and so are all of my siblings. I have one grandson, but that's all."

Beverly felt uncomfortable asking about a wife and children. Obviously he'd had at least one child—how sad that he was now mostly alone.

"But there are others in my life I can share with. I give away quite a bit of produce. And I preserve what I can, for me and for others." He dropped his head and toed the dirt along the berry bushes with his boot.

"We should probably get going." Beverly turned toward Mr. Maker. "Thank you for showing us around." She wasn't sure why she felt so uncomfortable.

"We can't go yet." Her father had his arms crossed. "You haven't told me what you've been up to for the last sixty years."

Mr. Maker grimaced. "Not much. How about you?"

"I taught for forty years. Social studies."

Mr. Maker's eyes clouded over, and he shoved his hands into the pockets of his jeans.

Sensing Mr. Maker's discomfort, Beverly changed the subject. "How long have you owned Grandma and Grandpa's old place?"

His face softened. "Over ten years. I was feeling ambitious when I bought it. I was still in my early seventies. That's young enough to take on a project like this."

"Well, you're doing great," Beverly said. "I'd say you have another decade at least before you start to slow down."

"We'll see." Mr. Maker motioned to the lone lawn chair for Beverly's father to sit in, and he stepped over by the porch and retrieved two more folding chairs, popping them open and forming a circle with the other one. The hemlock tree offered both shade and a cool breeze.

Beverly sat. "Father was telling me about the baseball games the neighborhood kids used to play in a vacant lot."

Mr. Maker smiled.

"Those games were never organized," Beverly's father said, sitting up straight, his eyes bright. "They just happened. And no one's parents were ever involved. If we had a problem, we worked it out."

"There's a convenience store there now," Mr. Maker said. "And you know, I never see kids playing the way we used to."

"It's a shame, isn't it?" Beverly's father said.

"On the other hand, having parents more involved is a good thing…" Mr. Maker sounded as if he might have more to say but his voice trailed off.

"I don't remember ever seeing your parents." Beverly's dad leaned forward a little. "I do remember a rumor about some problems—"

Beverly was pretty sure her father didn't realize he was being rude. "Mr. Maker," she said brightly, "how much time do you spend working in your yard each day?"

He looked relieved. "Six hours every day, at least in the summer."

They chatted more about gardening and the yard. After a while Mr. Maker stood and said he needed to get back to work.

Her father stood too, and Beverly thought he seemed to be standing a little taller next to his old acquaintance.

Mr. Maker started walking around the house, and they followed. "Thanks for stopping by," he said, glancing over his shoulder.

"Could I come back?" Beverly hurried her steps so she was walking beside him. "Would you mind?'

He didn't answer for a moment. "Why?"

"To visit. That's all."

"Because you didn't get the information you were fishing for?"

She shrugged. "Sure, I'd still like to hear about your time in Marble Cove."

"No," he said, his voice firm. But then it softened. "I won't talk about that. But if you did come back, you could tell me about Celia Patterson."

So there was still something there in him too. "I could tell you today." She was bluffing, since she really didn't know much about Celia. But she was still hoping he'd open up about the lighthouse if she gave him what he wanted.

He glanced back at her father, who was stepping carefully through the grass. "Not today," he said. "This has been enough. Call me next week."

After she and her father had settled into her car and she'd started the ignition, she realized that Mr. Maker hadn't revealed a single thing about himself except that he had bought the place over ten years ago and had at least one child, who was deceased, and a grandchild. She didn't know where he'd lived for the fifty years before that. Or what he'd done. The man was still a complete mystery—except that he had an interest in Celia Patterson.

"It was good to see Edward again," her father said as she pulled away from the curb. "Funny, though: he remembers a whole lot more about my family than I remember about him and his family."

"He was older," Beverly said, but she knew that wasn't it. Her grandmother's kindness had affected Mr. Maker, but her father had been too young to understand what a hard life the older boy had.

Beverly was pretty sure she wasn't having an impact on anyone in her life. She thought of the way Diane helped Shelley out, and Adelaide too. She thought of Diane's concern for their elderly neighbors. Even Mrs. Peabody, in her gossipy way, was concerned about others. In Augusta, Beverly could hide, but Marble Cove was too small for that.

So why, exactly, was she attracted to living in Marble Cove?

"Remember to drive through downtown," her father said.

"Right." She flipped her blinker from the right to the left. "How about if we stop for lunch at the deli not too far from the State House? The one that overlooks the river."

Her father agreed, a smile spreading across his face.

CHAPTER FIFTEEN

Diane spent a couple of hours on Monday morning with a yellow legal pad, jotting down notes longhand for a new cozy mystery. She played with the idea of someone running some sort of illegal substance from Canada to Maine by boat. She could set the story during Prohibition and have it be whiskey or rum.

Her first book, the one Frieda was now representing, was a contemporary novel, and all the advice she'd read said to stick with one genre. However, if no one bought her first novel, she could pitch a second one that was historical.

She tapped her pen against her desk. She could have a boy in the story, a boy wearing knickers and a cap. Maybe his dad was on the run for some reason. Her mind jumped to Mr. Maker and Celia Patterson. Their relationship, even though she had no idea exactly what it had been, fascinated her. Maybe her next story should be an epic novel instead of a cozy mystery.

She mulled over her ideas during the rest of the day and on Tuesday morning too. Finally, her curiosity getting the best of her, she wandered up to Mr. Wheeland's house around noontime. It was Beverly's week to stay in Marble Cove and telecommute.

Diane had chatted with Beverly on Sunday about their visit with Mr. Maker the day before. Beverly had said that Mr. Maker had talked about the house, the yard, and playing baseball but had refused to talk about Marble Cove. Beverly had added that he'd seemed to want more information about Celia, just not that day.

Diane couldn't imagine such restraint. Maybe Beverly had heard more since the visit. After all, Mrs. Peabody was Celia's sister. Diane decided to stop by the Wheeland place just to check in. She started up the slight incline of the street. As she neared the Victorian home, she heard voices in the side yard.

Beverly and Mr. Wheeland were out trimming the hedge with hand clippers, a half-full wheelbarrow between them. Diane had noticed in the last few weeks that the hedge needed to be trimmed, but she'd thought Beverly would hire it out.

"You two are ambitious," Diane said as she approached.

"Or crazy." Beverly turned her head toward her friend and gave her a woeful smile.

"I've been neglecting my yard," Mr. Wheeland said. "My little piece of paradise. I used to enjoy gardening. I'm trying to see if I can recapture that."

"And I decided to help out while I was on my lunch break." Beverly had on slacks and a blouse, even though she was wearing tennis shoes and gloves. "So someone didn't end up collapsing out here all alone."

Mr. Wheeland either didn't hear Beverly or else chose to ignore her.

"What's up?" Beverly scooped up an armful of debris and dumped it in the wheelbarrow.

"Oh, I was just thinking about Mr. Maker and Celia. Wondering, you know, if you have any news."

Beverly shook her head. "I thought I'd stop by next week though." She scooped up another armful. "Why do you ask?"

"No reason. I've just been thinking about them." Diane turned toward Mr. Wheeland. "Did you know Celia—way back when?"

He shook his head as he wiped his forehead. "It seems the two met at college. Isn't that right, Beverly?"

"Something like that. It's still a bit of a mystery, along with Mr. Maker's connection to Marble Cove." Beverly looked serious, and Diane decided her friend really didn't have any more information.

They visited for a few more minutes. Finally Mr. Wheeland stood tall, stretching his back, and said he was going to take a break.

"Why don't I have Mrs. Peabody ask Belinda to finish this up?" Beverly suggested. Belinda was Mrs. Peabody's granddaughter, who sometimes did the heavy lifting around the place.

"No, I can do it." Mr. Wheeland, clippers in hand, headed toward the back door. "I'm not as old as you think."

Beverly turned to Diane once he'd gone inside. "Mr. Maker inspired him to take up gardening again."

Diane raised her eyebrows.

"Seriously. I think Father's jealous of the man's youthfulness." Beverly put her clippers on top of the wheelbarrow. "I guess this means I can get back to work, at least until Father decides to do more out here."

"Oh, of course," Diane said. "See you later."

Beverly waved and grasped the wheelbarrow with both hands and pushed it back toward the garage, which was really an old-fashioned carriage house.

Diane stood for a minute, watching her friend go, as loneliness swept over her. She turned toward home, hoping Shelley and the kids would be outside, but they weren't, of course. It was nap time. And Margaret would be busy in the gallery.

Below, on the beach, an orange and purple kite soared high in the blue sky. Diane decided to go home and write, or at least try to. The words hadn't been coming very easily lately, probably because she didn't have a clear story in mind.

*   *   *

The next few days were the same for Diane. She struggled to write. She took Rocky for a walk on the beach. She stopped by the gallery and chatted with Margaret, but that would last only until a customer came in. She stopped to tell Shelley and the kiddos hello when they were in the yard. She wished, especially now, that Shelley would ask her to watch the kids more.

She tried not to think about Frieda Watley sending her story out. She tried not to wonder when the agent would get back to her. It could be weeks or months and months.

On the third morning, she noticed Mr. Wheeland and Beverly working on the hedge again, and she hurried over, offering to relieve her friend so she could get back to work. Fortunately Beverly accepted.

As Diane and Mr. Wheeland worked, they talked about books for a little while, and then he started talking about his childhood in Augusta. The more he talked, the more she liked the idea of writing a story set in the last years of the Depression and the beginning of World War II. A few minutes later she chided herself. She'd been off in her own little world working her idea instead of listening to Mr. Wheeland's story.

"It seems Edward Maker remembers a lot more about my family than I remember about him," Mr. Wheeland said. "Although I do remember his father had a drinking problem. I overheard my parents talking one night." The old man stopped for a minute, his clippers frozen in midair. "That's probably why my mother went out of her way to be kind to Edward, don't you think?"

Diane nodded. She didn't doubt that Mr. Wheeland's mother was a kind person. It had been passed down to both her son and her granddaughter. When Mr. Wheeland was ready to go inside, Diane pushed the wheelbarrow up against the garage and watched him on the steps until he opened the screen and stepped onto the porch.

The peal of children's laughter and the bark of a puppy caught her attention, and she guessed that Shelley, the children, and Prize were outside. In a minute she was walking across the street to their house.

"Miss Diane!" Aiden called out. "We're making a fort."

A beach blanket was spread over two lawn chairs. Shelley was on the porch, without Emma. Diane felt alarmed for a moment. Where was the baby? But then the little girl tottered out from under the blanket, laughing. Aiden slipped back into the fort, and his sister followed.

"Well, well, well," Diane said as she approached Shelley. "It looks as if your life may be getting a little easier."

"Shh," Shelley said with a smile. "Don't let them hear you."

"It was bound to happen sometime, them playing together." Diane thought of her own children, who were just two years apart, and all the hours they'd spent together, even when they were teenagers.

"I'm the captain!" Aiden's voice was loud and firm.

Emma giggled.

"You sit here," Aiden commanded.

Diane was fascinated by the play of children. "Are they pretending it's a ship?" It made sense that children who lived a stone's throw from the Atlantic would come up with a nautical theme.

"A spaceship." Shelley smiled. "Aiden's really into his space Legos right now."

The beach blanket rippled, and there was a brief whooshing sound from Emma's diapered bottom hitting the grass.

Enthralled, Diane put her hands together just as her cell phone began to buzz. At first she thought she would let it go into voice mail but then she decided to at least see who was calling. She fished the phone out of the pocket of her shorts. She didn't recognize the number.

"Go ahead and answer it," Shelley said. "You know I would." She smiled.

Diane stepped away from her friend as she said hello.

"Frieda Watley calling."

"Frieda!" Even in her excitement Diane made a mental note to register Frieda's number into her phone so the woman's name, and not just some number, would show up when she called. "Is everything all right?"

"Are you kidding? You are not going to believe this, but I already have a publishing house interested in your novel."

Once again, Diane's knees went weak. She knelt in the grass. "You...what?"

"It's the strangest thing," Frieda said. "I've seen this kind of thing happen only once before in my career. The perfect set of variables aligning to make a book shoot through the process like a meteor."

Diane tried to hold the phone steady, but her whole body was quivering. "Oh...?"

"Funny thing. The editor just happened to get back from vacation and was working through her e-mails backward. Your proposal was the first thing she saw—and because she's under pressure to find a replacement for a book that fell through, and yours is in the genre she's looking for, she sat down then and there and read it. Diane, she loved it!"

"That's..." Diane felt like a fool, but words were failing her right then. Not a good thing for a writer.

"And get this: because they were in the lurch about the book falling through, the publishing committee had an emergency meeting this morning—and they loved it too! Diane, your book is going to be published!"

All Diane could manage to say was, "Uh..."

"I know!" Then Frieda's voice turned serious. "Now, they've made us an offer. The advance isn't great—but it's very solid for a first novel. I'll send you the main points in an e-mail. And I see some things in the contract that will need to be changed. Don't worry: I go through this with this publisher for every book. They know to expect it. It's all good. Still, if you'd rather not jump on this offer, we could always wait and see what responses we get from the other publishers."

"Um..."

"Or you can think about it, and take this one if you want."

"When do you need know?" Diane realized as she spoke she was missing a word.

"A few days. Longer, if you want to see what other offers come in. Of course it could take months for those."

Diane took a deep breath. "What exactly is the offer?" She made a writing motion to Shelley as Frieda started talking, and her friend hurried into her house and returned in record time with a notepad and pen.

Diane sat on the stoop and jotted down notes about the advance, the deadline, and royalties.

"Any questions?" Frieda asked.

"So just because they've made me this offer, it doesn't mean I've agreed, right?"

"Of course! Nothing is official until you've signed their contract. And I'm going to have them send me a new draft of their contract first anyway. Maybe more than one revision. These things can drag on for months, though of course we don't want that. And sometimes, if a publisher really likes a first book, they may want to contract you for three."

Diane's head spun at all the things she didn't know.

"Any other questions?"

"Not right now," she answered. "But I'll call or e-mail if I have any. And I'll let you know my decision ASAP."

"Give it a few days, at least," Frieda said. "I want you to make sure you're not being rash. And we've still got to see where they'll give on the contract revisions."

After saying good-bye, Diane hung up and flipped her phone closed.

"Was that your agent?" Shelley asked.

Diane nodded in disbelief as she struggled to her feet.

"I thought you said it would take months?" Shelley's eyes were big.

"That's what I thought. But she already has an offer from a publisher." Diane's voice came out a little high-pitched, but at least all the words made it out of her mouth this time.

"Diane!" Shelley's arms encircled her in a hug and she did a little happy dance. "That is so cool!"

"It's so unbelievable," Diane said, moving with her friend. "Pinch me, would you?"

"That's not allowed."

Diane looked down at a somber Aiden, Emma at his side.

"It was a joke," Diane said.

"She's going to have a book published!" Shelley let go of Diane and reached out to her children, taking their hands. They smiled and laughed, and the three started moving in a circle. Shelley reached for Diane's hand, and they were going around together. Suddenly Emma plopped down on her diaper, and Diane realized the little girl thought they were playing Ring Around the Rosie.

And so they did, the four of them in the front yard, going around and around, chanting the rhyme, until Shelley suggested they go tell Margaret the good news.

"She's probably busy," Diane said. It seemed like every time she stopped in, the place was hopping, which was good for Margaret.

"Honestly." Shelley rolled her eyes. "She would be hurt if we didn't let her know right away."

Shelley convinced the kids that the wagon was the spaceship capsule and that they'd been selected for a special mission. Emma insisted on bringing the beach blanket along, and she pulled it over her head.

"I hope she isn't planning on falling asleep again," Shelley said. "Or she'll be up half the night."

Aiden stuck his head under the blanket and told Emma he needed her help. "You're the copilot," he said. "You have to look around and see if any other spaceships are out to get us."

Emma slowly pulled the blanket off her head, greeting Diane with a wide grin. She looked from side to side as Shelley pulled the wagon toward downtown.

★   ★   ★

The gallery was absolutely empty when they entered, and Margaret seemed thrilled to see them. "It's been the slowest day in weeks," she said.

"It would be better if we were buying customers," Diane said.

Margaret's round face lit up in a grin. "But you're the next best things."

The three of them chatted for a few minutes, but then Emma began to fuss.

"You'd better spill the beans," Shelley said to Diane. "Or I will, 'cuz I'm on a timer and probably only have another thirty seconds or so."

"My agent called." Diane's face flushed as she spoke. "A publishing house already made an offer."

"What?" Margaret's hands flew up in the air.

"A publishing company made an offer to publish my novel!"

"So soon? Oh, that's wicked good!"

Diane laughed at the Mainer phrase.

"Unbelievable," Margaret said. "But I knew from the get-go you had it in you." She broke out into a wide grin and wrapped her arms around Diane in a quick bear hug. "Can I sell the book here? Do you think they'd use one of my paintings for the cover? Oh, probably not. When will it come out? What kind of marketing will they do? Do they do e-books? We could have a book signing here! Shelley, you could cater!"

Diane laughed and took out the paper from her pocket. "Got a pen? I need to write all this down."

★   ★   ★

Shelley took the kids outside while Diane jotted down Margaret's knowledgeable comments. But when three customers wandered in, Diane hugged her friend and dashed out the door.

"How about if we walk down the boardwalk on the way home?" Shelley had the wagon already pointed in that direction. "Maybe the stiff breeze will keep Emma awake."

Shelley led the way, pulling the wagon, and Diane walked alongside Emma, pointing out different things along the way: a basket of flowers, a black Lab puppy, a red bicycle. The little girl's eyes were heavy, but she took it all in.

When they reached the boardwalk, Shelley turned south. Diane recognized Detective Little's blue pickup in the parking lot next to Dan's truck. She scanned the dock but didn't see anyone. But after another few steps she saw both men at the very end of the dock locked in serious conversation next to a stack of pallets that were as tall as Dan.

Shelley must have seen them too because she stopped dead in her tracks.

"Hey!" Aiden shouted. "What happened to the capsule?'

Shelley started walking again, slowly, her eyes still on the dock.

"So Dan's working today," Diane said nonchalantly.

"Yep." Shelley kept walking at a steady but slow pace. "What do you think Detective Little is doing?"

"I'm sure I have no idea."

"Dan hasn't worked for his friend since last week."

That was probably a good thing, Diane thought. As they watched, another man walked toward them on the dock. "Who's that?" Diane asked.

"One of his co-workers, John. His wife is Dana—she's the one who goes to our church and works at the market."

"Got it." Diane hesitated a moment. "Don't you think that's a positive thing that John is in on the conversation? Maybe something happened on the dock today. Maybe a boat was damaged or something. It could be anything."

Shelley nodded. "You're right. I shouldn't jump to conclusions." But then Dan glanced their way. Diane was sure he'd seen them, but he didn't wave or even smile. He turned his head away quickly, back toward Detective Little.

Shelley groaned. Diane patted her shoulder and turned her attention to the children. They hadn't seen their father or noticed their mother's reaction.

"Blast off!" Aiden called out. "Hyperspeed!"

Shelley began to jog, and Emma lurched backward a little. Diane pressed her hand against the back of the little girl's head, steadying her, and jogged along. She couldn't help but worry about Shelley and her children.

*   *   *

That evening, Diane sat in her backyard, Rocky at her side, gazing out at the waves crashing against the shore. It was high tide, and the water had completely covered the outcropping of rocks and the tide pools. Strips of fog had settled in the distance, waiting to roll in.

A family with a boy and girl, probably nine and seven, made their way up through the loose sand to the trail. The boy carried a soccer ball tucked under one arm and a pail and shovel in his other hand. He wore swim trunks and a wet towel over one shoulder, and he was shivering. The girl wore a sweatshirt. Sand dollars and seashells filled her cupped hands. Their parents followed with beach chairs and a blanket.

"Can we come back down after dinner?" the girl asked.

"We'll see." The mother looked tired.

The girl stomped her foot a little as she stepped forward. "But tonight's our last night. You said we could have a bonfire."

The mother was lagging behind a little. "I didn't realize the tide would be in so high."

"We should have done it last night."

Neither parent answered, and the girl charged ahead, passing her brother.

The father took a lawn chair from his wife and walked beside her. "Are you feeling all right?"

The woman nodded but didn't speak. Diane looked away, embarrassed for having eavesdropped. She couldn't help but wonder if the mother was ill and perhaps her children didn't know it. Or maybe they did and that was why the daughter was acting out a little. Or maybe the mother was just tired from a day at the beach.

Diane couldn't help but think about when she'd had cancer. Surviving, when all of her doctors had given up hope, was her miracle. Her children were much older then than this girl and boy, and it had been Jessica who was two years younger than Justin. She smiled at the thought of her daughter. Long before Diane had faith of her own, Jessica had prayed tirelessly for her, believing, absolutely, that Diane would be healed.

Sometimes, like now as she watched the husband take something else from his wife's hands, she wondered if the stress of her illness had somehow contributed to Eric's cardiac arrest. Her doctor had told her that it was a ridiculous idea.

A seagull flew low, just above her backyard, and Rocky sat up and barked. Diane glanced back toward the trail. The parents, now arm in arm, the lawn chairs propped against a post, had stopped and turned back toward the waves.

"Would you hurry!" the girl wailed.

The father rubbed the woman's belly, and she smiled wryly up at him.

She wasn't deathly ill—she was pregnant! That was the secret between them. And, judging by the expression on their faces, they were happy to be expecting another child. She barely had a bump, so the children wouldn't have noticed yet.

Diane smiled at the story she'd invented based on a simple action of the people in front of her. She thought how thrilled her daughter Jessica would have been if Diane had given her a baby sister. But if that had happened, Diane would have a teenager right now. God knew what He was doing when He'd planned their family.

Suddenly a wave of grief and loneliness swept over her again. It was as powerful as the waves against the shore in the waning light. As the couple walked the rest of the way up the trail, Diane pulled her cell phone out of her pocket and dialed her daughter's number.

The call went straight into voice mail. She left a message, saying she was just checking in to see how everything was going. She thought about calling Justin, but it would be early morning in Dubai. If Justin was asleep, she didn't want to wake him.

She petted Rocky's head and looked back out onto the sea. Lingering light from the day illuminated the foamy water as it rolled in, wave after pounding wave. She didn't think she'd ever grow immune to the sound of the surf and the endless movement of the water. It was mighty and mesmerizing and soothing and serene all at the same time.

She stood and stepped to the far edge of her lawn and looked to her right—south, toward the lighthouse out on the point. The last of the light bounced off the white walls and illuminated it for just a moment. Beyond it, the fog was creeping closer to shore.

The ocean was many things, but it could never fill the void left in her from Eric's passing or from her children growing up. Neither did the mystery of the lighthouse. She turned back toward her bungalow, whistled for Rocky, and then folded the lawn chair and put it under the eaves.

Chances were that she'd have the patter of rain along with the roar of the surf to keep her company through the night. But at that moment the fog was coming in thick, so thick, as the old timers would say, "You can hardly spit." Diane smiled. She was starting to think like a Mainer even though she would forever be a "from away."

CHAPTER SIXTEEN

Shelley sat down on the couch beside Dan with a pad of paper, a pen, and a pastry cookbook in her hands. He was watching the ten o'clock news. The sports, to be exact. The topic was the Boston Red Sox, and their game the next day against the Seattle Mariners. It had taken Shelley the first five years of their marriage to realize that it was futile to talk to him about anything important during the sports broadcast.

She flipped through the recipes. She wasn't going to tackle éclairs or cream puffs or anything like that. But tarts, *pains au chocolat,* and Danishes sounded manageable. She liked the idea of scones and turnovers too.

The sports ended, and a commercial for consolidating credit cards came on. Shelley picked up the remote control on the coffee table and muted the sound. "So, what was Detective Little asking you about today?"

Dan leaned his head back on the couch. "I knew you were going to ask about that."

"So you did see us."

He nodded. "But I couldn't talk." He sighed. "According to Detective Little, there's some sort of smuggling ring going on."

"And he thought your buddy might be involved?"

Dan shook his head. "No. My friend's on the level. The detective just wanted to know if I'd noticed anything suspicious."

"Just you?"

"And the other guys on the dock."

Shelley wrinkled her nose.

"Ask Detective Little, if you don't believe me." Dan reached for the remote, unmuted the TV, and turned his attention back to the next story on the sportscast, which was about the new recruits on the University of Maine's hockey team. But then his phone beeped and he read a text, glancing at Shelley.

"What's up?"

"My buddy wants to know if I'm available tonight. He said he'd pay me time and a half."

"Half of what?"

Dan shrugged. "He's generous. It's definitely worth my time. It'll help pay down the bills—and maybe even put a little in savings."

They needed that, especially if Shelley wanted to start her business. She might need a line of credit for her start-up expenses. She thought through their existing budget—their utilities, gas, and food had all gone up monthly for the last year.

"I guess it would be okay for you to take the job," she said at last. "What's your schedule like tomorrow?"

"I report first thing in the morning. We have a couple of freighters to unload." The port didn't handle the supersized ships, but small freighters did use the docks.

"You won't be too tired?"

"I'll be fine." He squeezed her knee. "I need to go now, though."

"Okay." She retrieved the remote from the coffee table and turned the TV off. She lifted her head for his kiss. "Be careful, okay?"

He shook his head slightly. "Shell, I'm serious: there's nothing to worry about. Your suspicions are totally unfounded."

A few minutes later, the rumble of Dan's truck faded away. It sounded as if he needed to do more work on the muffler. She hoped that wouldn't cost more too.

Shelley turned her attention back to the cookbook. If she could start making money from her business, that would take the pressure off Dan to work overtime—at least for his friend. Overtime on the docks with his real job was fine, but there hadn't been much of that available for months. In fact, even his normal hours had consistently been reduced.

Taking notes as she read, she contemplated ingredients. Maybe she could work with one of the local distributors to get a better price on butter and eggs. It wasn't as if she'd be buying enough for bulk rate, but maybe they'd take pity on a young mom trying to launch a business to help her family. Even if they didn't give her a deal, using local ingredients would be great for both the taste of her baked goods and for marketing them.

There was a place that sold honey and local produce not too far out of town too. Maybe she should stop and talk with the owner. In fact, she could ask if he would be interested in carrying some of her pastries in his shop. Although then she would need to distribute and rotate her goods. She wasn't sure if she could do that with the kids tagging along.

She yawned and closed the cookbook, deciding to go to bed. Just as she started down the hall, Emma began to fuss. Shelley froze, hoping her little one would go back to sleep, but her whimpering turned into crying.

"Mommy!" It was Aiden. Shelley didn't move. Aiden called her name again, and the sound was getting closer. By the time he was in the doorway of his room, Emma was screaming.

"I had a bad dream." Aiden's eyes were wide with terror.

"Go get in my bed, Sweetie," Shelley said. "I'll be there in a minute."

Emma was hysterical now, so Shelley quickly changed into her nightgown and pulled Emma from her crib. A moment later, with a child on either side, Shelley melted into her bed, already lulled by the crashing of the waves. Dan would have to put the children back in their rooms when he came home—she was too far gone to get back up.

By the time he did, she barely woke. But she could hear the falling rain on the roof and against the window, drowning out the sound of the sea.

*   *   *

Friday morning, Diane woke to rain and a chilly house. She climbed out from under her warm quilt, wedged her feet into her slippers, and quickly put on her robe, cinching it tight. It was only August, too soon to turn on the heat—or maybe not.

She stood at the living room window. The rain was coming down in sheets. Across the street, Dan ran to his truck, wearing a sweatshirt and his baseball cap and holding a yellow rain slicker in his arms. He jumped inside and slammed the door.

Diane stepped back from the gray morning and retreated to her kitchen to start a pot of coffee. She hadn't decided whether to call her agent back today or make a few other phone calls first and call on Monday. There were a couple of Eric's colleagues whom she was tempted to contact, although she thought it might be hard to reach them. Summer school would have ended by now, and fall term wouldn't begin for a while yet. Most of them were probably on vacation, and she wasn't sure if a publishing question was worth interrupting their time off.

She'd researched novel contracts and had come across a wide range of what was normal. According to the e-mail Frieda had sent giving the high points of the publisher's initial offer, Diane's contract offer was well within that range, which wasn't hard, considering the wide parameters. She'd think about it more after she'd had her first cup of coffee.

As the machine dripped, she stood at the window again. Shelley and the kids wouldn't be out today. The curtain at her neighbors' house swayed a little, and then Emma's head popped up, her nose pressed against the glass. Aiden appeared next. Diane waved, but the kids weren't looking her way. A minute later, Shelley appeared and pointed past Diane's house. Diane stepped away from the window, not wanting it to look as if she were spying.

In a moment, Adelaide appeared, crossing the street, a ladybug umbrella over her head. The young woman wore a pair of red and black polka dot rubber boots, black capris, a red jacket, and her hair in a high ponytail. She was smiling, clearly enjoying the rain, and she began to skip, splashing water with each step. When she was halfway across the street, the wind caught the umbrella, yanking it away from her and sending it tumbling up the street.

"Oh dear!" Diane raced toward her front door, thankful she had on her slippers. She was outside before she realized what she was doing. The umbrella twirled away from Adelaide. Diane began to run after it, her slippers slapping against the pavement. "I'll get it!" she yelled to Adelaide, who stood on Shelley's side of the street with both hands flat on top of her head.

A gust of wind propelled the umbrella farther up the hill. Diane ran after it. Out of the corner of her eye she saw Margaret coming toward her. She was wearing a shirt and sweatpants and looked as if she'd just rolled out of bed too. Diane laughed at how comical the two of them must look, and with each burst of giggles it was harder to run. Margaret began laughing too.

The umbrella was nearly to Mr. Wheeland's house when a figure stepped out of the driveway and took a couple of leaps into the street, snatching it up in a quick motion and lifting it gracefully over her head. It was Beverly, soaking wet and in her running tights and a long-sleeve Lycra shirt. She jogged toward them effortlessly.

Diane stopped laughing and put her hands on her knees, trying to catch her breath, and Margaret slung her arm around Diane.

Beverly's dark hair was plastered on her head and barely visible under the ladybug umbrella. She waved and gave them a sassy look as she strolled past them, straight to Adelaide. Diane and Margaret turned, still linked together.

Shelley stood on the sidewalk laughing, Emma in her arms and Aiden running in circles around her, dancing in the rain, his slicker unzipped and blowing around him. "I just took a pan of scones out of the oven. Can all of you come down?"

"More like *row* down," Margaret muttered, sending Diane into another fit of laughter. They were absolutely soaking wet. "That's a splendid idea," Margaret shouted. "Us two old ladies will try to make it before we drown." The wind was plastering the rain against their faces now.

Beverly handed the umbrella to Adelaide.

"I have coffee!" Shelley called out.

"I'll grab my coffee too," Diane shouted into the wind, pulling away from Margaret.

"Now, no fair getting dressed," the older woman said, glancing down at her sweats and then pointing at Diane's pajamas and robe. Both women grinned.

Diane was just thankful she hadn't worn a summer nightgown to bed. She did grab a bath towel, along with the coffeepot and her rain slicker for her trip across the street. When she entered Shelley's house she kicked off her slippers and wiped her face and neck with the towel and tousled her hair.

The women were all gathered in the kitchen around Emma, Aiden, and Adelaide, and Diane caught them in the middle of a conversation that quickly ended, although Diane didn't catch even the last word.

"How's your telecommuting going?" Margaret quickly asked Beverly.

"Good, but nearly everyone in the office has been on vacation, so no one's really missing me. We'll see if I can still pull this off in September."

Diane flipped the towel, intending it to go over her shoulder, but Margaret caught it in midair and wiped her face with it.

"Have you talked to Mr. Maker again?" Diane put her pot of coffee on top of Shelley's stove.

Beverly shook her head. "Hopefully I will soon, though."

Shelley pulled a stack of small plates from her cupboard, and the women helped themselves to the scones and coffee. Adelaide carefully lifted Emma into her high chair, and Aiden scooted onto his chair, visibly excited to have so much company so early in the morning.

Diane leaned against the counter with her mug in her hand and her plate on the Formica, wondering what the women had been talking about when she'd arrived.

"Did you say yes to the publishing house?" Beverly asked her.

"How did you know about the offer?"

Beverly cleared her throat. "Someone told Father." She grinned.

Margaret waved her hand. "I didn't think you'd mind."

"Not at all." She should have told him herself, especially after she'd shown him the contract with the agent, and she should have told Beverly. But she was flattered that Mr. Wheeland had remembered to tell his daughter.

"I think I'll call today, later this morning." The longer she thought about it, the less likely she thought Eric's colleagues would have any advice to offer her. This was a decision for her to make on her own.

Adelaide sat in a chair between Emma and Aiden and broke a scone in half. Shelley had obviously engaged her as a mother's helper today, which probably meant Shelley intended to spend the morning baking.

"Can we go outside and play?" Aiden asked. Emma pointed out the window as if she were echoing her brother's words.

"Too cold," Adelaide said, wrapping her arms around herself and shivering dramatically. "Maybe after the rain stops." She smiled at the little boy and then added, "Let's play inside. You, me, and Emma." Her finger pointed to each one of the children, and then herself. "We can play fort. And with Legos. Trucks. Whatever you want to do."

Aiden put his finger to the side of his mouth as he thought, and then he broke out into a smile. Finally he said, "Not a fort. A spaceship."

Adelaide put out her fist and bumped Aiden's, although it wasn't quite on target. Emma put her fist out, and although it took Adelaide a moment to realize what the little girl was doing, she responded in kind, this time hitting her target spot-on, although with care.

"What are you baking this morning?" Diane asked Shelley as she poured creamer into her coffee.

"A cranberry-orange torte and a pecan roll-up."

"Yum." Diane took a sip of coffee.

"*Ooh*," Margaret said. "What time should we come back?"

"Actually, I'll deliver samples to all of you as long as you give me your honest opinions."

"Shelley, you're going to be the end of me." Beverly patted her stomach, which, Diane noted, was absolutely flat.

"Ah, baloney," Margaret said, standing and grabbing another scone off the counter. "Careful, or we'll force you to take seconds."

Beverly shook her head. "You have no idea…"

"Of what the next decade will bring? As a matter of fact I do," Margaret said and then laughed. "And the decade after that too. But then again, you'll probably be one of those rare women who sail through menopause without gaining an ounce."

Diane thought Beverly was taking Margaret's teasing in stride, but still Diane, ever the peacemaker, changed the subject. She looked down at her pajama-clad body and laughed. "And I doubt if even another decade will find you running down the street in your pajamas." They all laughed at that, even Emma.

Soon the little party broke up, and Diane, Margaret, and Beverly said their good-byes.

"Don't forget to send samples our way," Margaret called out to Shelley as she tossed the bath towel back to Diane.

"Oh I won't," Shelley said. "I won't."

Diane couldn't help but feel as if she'd missed something, but she couldn't imagine what. She veered off toward her house, dodging mud puddles, as Margaret and Beverly continued up the street, their heads practically touching as they talked.

★   ★   ★

An hour later, sitting at her computer, Diane found the resource she needed to make her decision: an online critique group for professional novelists who were looking for a new member. She sent an inquiry, saying she wasn't sure if she qualified as a professional but she had an offer from a publishing house that she was considering, which was part of the reason she wanted to join the group because she could really use some sound advice.

Within fifteen minutes she had responses from two of the members. Within forty-five minutes she had five responses, which meant every member of the group had answered her inquiry. They welcomed her with open arms, and she quickly shot off her questions about advances and royalties.

By noon, she was sure the offer from the publishing house was probably as good as she would get.

She sent off a round of thank-yous to her new critique group, and within a few minutes she had a couple of e-mails back, saying they looked forward to reading her work and that now the fun part of writing would begin for her. The editorial letter! Revisions! Rewrites of revisions! Line editing! Copyediting! There were lots of smiley faces thrown into the messages.

Diane felt perplexed. Could the editing process be that complicated? She'd sent off a polished manuscript. She'd gone over it and over it. Surely the editor wouldn't have many changes. Well, there was the sagging middle Frieda had mentioned. But she couldn't imagine even that would be too hard to fix.

She turned away from her in-box and phoned Frieda. She was almost relieved the call went into voice mail because she was afraid that her voice might have started quivering and she'd forget her words if her agent had actually answered. As it was, she left a quick and concise message, saying that, after thoughtfully considering the publishing house's offer, she would like to accept.

As she placed the phone in its cradle, a wave of joy swept over her. She was on her way to selling a novel. Her dream was coming true!

Diane knew that it wasn't as simple as all that. She'd expressed her willingness to accept the publisher's offer, but Frieda was still working on hashing out exactly what that offer would be. The publisher was dealing with delays on their end—vacations, Frieda had guessed. And anyway, as Frieda had told her, nothing was official until she'd signed a contract, and Diane still hadn't seen a contract from the publisher.

So even though it wasn't a done deal yet, she felt relieved that she'd made a decision to go forward with it when Frieda was happy with the deal.

She stood, stretched her back, padded down the hall to the living room, and looked out the window. The rain had stopped, and Adelaide was out front with Emma, who was in a playpen, and Aiden, who was tossing grass on Emma's head. The front door to Shelley's house was wide open. Diane knew her friend was probably keeping an ear out in case the kids became too much for Adelaide.

Diane decided to pop over, so she grabbed her sweatshirt. Rocky gave her his inquiring look, asking if he could come along, but Diane shook her head. Aiden might get too rambunctious for Adelaide at the sight of the dog, plus Prize would get all excited in the backyard.

As she stepped outside, she tilted her head toward the sun. The day was cool but warming. She paused for a moment, enjoying the warmth of the sun, and thought of the family she'd seen the evening before. She wondered what adventures they were having today. Maybe exploring a tide pool somewhere—the tide was out. Or off on a hike. Or maybe playing miniature golf.

That had always been a highlight of her own family's vacation week in Marble Cove, although Diane truly was a failure at the game. One time, her club had gone flying and had barely missed Eric, and nearly every time they golfed, she hit multiple balls into the fountain, which for some reason embarrassed the kids more and more as they got older.

When it rained on vacation, they stayed in their condo and played Uno or Scrabble. Those were her kids' favorite games when they were little, keeping them happy as little clams at high tide for about an hour. After that, they usually went out even if the rain hadn't stopped. She sighed. Who would have thought the years would go by so quickly?

She crossed the street, and Adelaide spotted her with a wave. Aiden saw her, and his hand froze in midair and then opened, making blades of grass rain down on his sister's hair. Emma blinked a few times but besides that didn't seem to notice or at least didn't care.

"I'm just going to tell Shelley hello," she said to Adelaide as she gave Aiden and Emma a wave. Aiden grinned, although with a look of guilt, and Emma squealed in delight. Diane was sure the little one was feeling much more grown up out in the yard with her brother and Adelaide.

Diane knocked on the open door and stepped in. "Shelley?"

"In the kitchen."

Diane stepped around a baby doll and a dump truck in the middle of the entryway and veered to the right.

Shelley stood at the stove, stirring something in a saucepan with a wooden spoon. "I decided to make a batch of cinnamon rolls too." By the smell of the kitchen, she was stirring the caramel sauce.

Diane breathed deeply, thinking the sweet confection had to be one of the most comforting smells in the world. "I just left a message with my agent. I told her to accept the offer."

Shelley looked a little confused. "Oh, that's right. You were deciding what to tell her. I kind of forgot that part—all along, I was just thinking you'd accept it for sure."

Diane could see this step seemed a little anticlimactic to Shelley, although it didn't to her. No matter.

"Have a pecan roll-up." Shelley pointed with the spoon to the counter.

Diane popped one in her mouth. It was a rolled pastry with a cream cheese, nut, and caramel filling. "Oh my," she said and then swallowed. "That was delicious."

"Are you sure?" Shelley had a concerned look on her face.

"Positive. It was amazing."

"Oh good." Shelley left the spoon in the pan and consulted a piece of paper on the counter. It didn't appear to be a recipe—it was more like a list. She seemed a little distracted. Diane guessed she was just feeling hurried because she had only a little bit of time left until the kids would need lunch and Adelaide would go home.

"Why all the baked goods?" Diane asked.

"Oh, I just want to see how many reliable recipes I have for when I open my business." Shelley's face reddened. "You know, in case I can get up and running soon."

Diane thought of all the time Shelley was putting into her baking. It wasn't unlike all the time Diane invested in her writing, with no guarantee of success—until now. "I'll get going so you can concentrate."

Shelley nodded. "Thanks for stopping by."

Diane strolled down the front steps and told Adelaide and the children good-bye. Aiden was playing pat-a-cake with his sister now over the edge of the playpen. He hit her hands with the palms of his, hard, and sent her backward onto her bottom. She looked startled but didn't cry.

Deciding to capitalize on Margaret's knowledge of the arts, Diane hurried on toward downtown. But when she stepped into the gallery, Margaret was standing at her desk talking with two young men. When she noticed Diane, she shuffled a few papers on her desk. It soon became obvious that these were the painters she'd hired for the repairs to the gallery, and Diane decided the papers were probably notes about the work she needed done.

"We can't do it this Sunday," the taller one said. "We have an obligation."

"What about Monday?" Margaret sounded frustrated.

The two men exchanged a glance. "You could do it," the taller one said to the other.

"I'll need some help," the shorter one said. "I can't do it all in a day by myself."

Diane bit her tongue. It was just the ceilings. She couldn't imagine it would take that long. She wanted to barge in, but she controlled herself.

"How about if you call me in a couple of hours?" Margaret said. "Once you know what you can do."

The men nodded and headed toward the door, yanking their white caps from their back pockets and onto their heads.

Diane stepped around to the front of the counter that Margaret stood behind. "I know this is totally unsolicited, but have you thought about hiring Dan to do your painting?"

"No. I hadn't thought about him."

"He did a great job on the inside of my house."

Margaret nodded. "I know. He really did. And all the work he did for Allan was superb too."

"He might be able to work Saturday and Sunday night. You might not have to lose any business days."

Margaret cocked her head. "Good idea. I'll talk with him this evening."

Diane hoped that would help the young family out, and maybe keep Dan from doing the extra work that was stressing Shelley.

Margaret shuffled her papers again. "So what's up?"

Diane took a deep breath. "I did it. I called my agent and told her to accept the offer."

"Oh, that's right," Margaret said, crossing her arms. "You hadn't decided for sure, had you? I guess we all just assumed you would…"

Diane nearly let out a wry chuckle. This truly was anticlimactic. Or maybe she'd been milking the whole publishing thing a little too much. In fact, maybe her friends were growing tired of hearing about the whole process.

A few minutes later, after she'd bowed out of the gallery as gracefully as she could, Diane decided to cut over to the boardwalk. She peered out at the dock but couldn't see Dan. His truck was in the parking lot though, which meant he was around somewhere.

Clouds filled the sky, but it was warm out, so Diane slipped out of her sweatshirt and draped it over her shoulders. She stayed on the boardwalk for a block and then cut down to the beach, feeling a little guilty for going on a walk without Rocky. She'd take him out later in the day and bring a tennis ball. There was nothing he liked more than a game of catch.

The tide was still out, and since Rocky wasn't with her, she decided to keep going down to the rocky outcropping. She loved looking at the sea anemones and starfish. It was such an otherworldly feeling to try to comprehend all that went on in the sea. She could stare at a grouping of barnacles for hours if she had the time. And she certainly had the time today.

Ahead, there were several people already at the tide pool, including some children. The wind had died down to a slight breeze, and the sun peeked out from behind the clouds, casting a ray of actual heat. Diane hurried down to the packed sand and jogged along it, breathing in the cool, salty air.

When she reached the rocks, she stepped onto the first one and hopped along from rock to rock, out farther and farther. She stopped at one of the deeper pools and squatted down. Sage green sea anemones lined one side, and a starfish hovered at the very bottom. The pool was surrounded by barnacles. She trailed her finger in the water, stirring it up a little.

"I'll beat you to the edge!" came a girl's voice from behind her.

"No fair—you have a head start."

Diane turned. The children from the night before were coming toward her, hopscotching across the rocks.

"Watch out for waves!" their mother called out. She and the father were still in the soft sand, just down from the boardwalk.

Diane stayed at the pool but turned her head to watch the children. The boy had given up catching the girl and was poking at something about twenty yards to the south of Diane. The girl had reached the outer rock and had her arms spread out. Then she turned and pointed to the lighthouse, looking back toward her brother. "Race you to the point!"

He shook his head adamantly. "I want to stay here."

The parents were coming across the rocks now, slowly.

Diane felt invisible as she took it all in. She wanted to warn the parents—not about the waves or sharp rocks, but that the next ten years would fly by. She wanted to tell them to treasure every moment with each other and with their children. She wanted to tell them how life could change in a moment, how one of them could pass away, just like that.

She turned her head into the breeze. The wind blew her hair back and stung her eyes. She wouldn't say a thing to the young family. They probably did treasure every day. And she and Eric had too, in their way. Especially after her cancer scare. But a family couldn't live in fear of the future. Each day had to be lived for itself.

She stood and made her way off the rocks and back to the sand. She would walk to the lighthouse.

A figure ran toward her. At first she guessed it was Beverly, but then she remembered her friend had already been out for a run that day. But as the person grew closer it was obvious it was Beverly. Diane waved.

The two met and Beverly slowed to jogging in place.

"You already ran," Diane said.

Beverly shrugged. "But not far the first time. I decided to fit in a second workout, hoping it would make me stop feeling so antsy."

"About?"

"Oh, nothing in particular. Commuting. Father. The future. The past."

"Mr. Maker?"

"Some." She jogged around in a circle. "They say exercise is the healthiest of addictions, right? It's what I do when I'm feeling unsettled."

Diane told her she'd decided to accept the publishing house's offer.

Beverly wrinkled her nose. "That's so funny. I told Father this morning that you had. I guess I just assumed."

Diane didn't let her disappointment show. Either her three new friends were pretty well able to anticipate what she'd decide or she hadn't made it clear that she'd still had a decision to make. Or maybe it just wasn't that big of a deal to them anymore. Just like it was pretty clear that it wasn't that big of a deal to her kids either.

Oh, how she missed Eric.

"I'll let you keep running," she said.

Beverly waved and took off at a fast clip. Diane turned back toward the lighthouse, heeding its call, feeling a measure of peace wash over her.

CHAPTER SEVENTEEN

This is how Adelaide did it," Aiden said to Shelley, directing her to place the blanket over the playpen. "It makes a better spaceship that way."

Shelley had insisted that Emma stay in the playpen while Adelaide was watching the kids, because she was afraid that if Emma toddled out toward the street the young woman wouldn't get to her in time. "I'd better lift you in, huh, buddy?" Shelley swung her son over the side and landed him a few feet from his sister. They both sank to their knees, and Shelley draped the blanket over the top.

Shelley was headed toward the steps to sit for a moment as Aiden shouted, "Three, two, one! Blastoff!" A second later the slam of a car door caught her attention. Detective Little was walking away from his pickup and toward her. Her heart skipped a beat.

"To infinity and beyond!" Aiden bellowed.

Shelley could imagine the wild expression on his face, but she was frozen in place, her feet planted on the lawn, watching Detective Little. Once she was sure he was coming to talk to her, she made her feet move, determined to distance herself from her children, not wanting them to overhear the conversation that was coming, whatever it might be.

"Hello," she managed to say. The sun was finally poking through the clouds, and steam was rising off the pavement. Out of the corner of her eye, she saw Diane pop over the little hill from the beach, and for a moment Shelley wished her friend would come over, but she turned toward her own house.

"Shelley," the detective said, nodding his head slightly. "Do you have a couple of minutes?"

"The kids are playing." She pointed toward the playpen that was bouncing around a little, both the sides and the blanket over the top.

"It won't take long," he said. "And I only have general questions at this point, nothing specific."

"All right." That sounded a little better than what she'd feared.

"Have you noticed anything unusual about Dan lately?"

Boy, had she. "Like?"

"Extra money. New, unexplained electronic equipment. Laptops. Flat-screen TVs. Smart phones."

She shook her head. "He's been picking up some extra work for a buddy of his."

The detective took a notebook from his pocket. "What kind of work?"

"He navigated a boat for him into the cove. Other than that...dock work, I think. Unloading, mostly."

"What's the friend's name?"

Shelley wrinkled her nose. "You know, I don't think Dan's said. He went to high school with him."

A look of realization crossed his face. "Oh, that's right. You didn't go to school here, did you?"

"That's correct."

"And it's not anyone you know?"

"I'm sure I've never met him. I think Dan would have said. I got the impression the guy lived north of here. In fact, the time Dan piloted the boat into the cove, the guy was moving."

Detective Little raised his eyebrows like he was having a hard time believing what she'd said, which made Shelley grow more nervous. She reminded herself she had nothing to hide.

"Tell me about Dan," he said. She must have looked bewildered because he added, "What's he really like? What's he good at? Anything I should know as an officer that I don't as his neighbor."

"Well, he knows the cove really well. He's been running boats in and out of it since he was a kid." Not that they could afford a boat for him, but he'd learned on other people's boats. "And he has a good heart."

"I don't recall him ever being in trouble before," Detective Little said. "Is there anything I'm missing?"

"No." Shelley felt her face grow warm. "He's never been in trouble."

"How are things financially for the two of you? Does he have the motivation to"—he paused—"seek another source of income?"

"Sure, things are really tight. He bought a new muffler for his truck with the money he made last week. Well, he got it at the junkyard. Every little bit helps."

The detective jotted down a few things in his notebook and then pulled out his business card and handed it to Shelley. "Call me if you see or hear anything suspicious."

She took the card and curled her hand around it tightly.

"Thank you." The detective nodded again and started to walk away.

Shelley hesitated and then called after him. "We might be broke, but Dan isn't a crook. I know he's not."

The detective turned and gave her a look like he'd heard that line before.

"Sometimes he has too good of a heart, but he'd never knowingly do something illegal."

"Just give me a call. That's all I'm asking." With that he turned again and increased his stride. Shelley stood frozen until he drove away.

When she turned back toward her children, both had their faces pressed against the netting of the playpen, side by side, staring at her.

★   ★   ★

Diane stood on her porch, unsure whether to go to Shelley or not. She saw her friend kneel down on the grass in front of her kids. She leaned into them, but then, just for a second, she glanced toward Diane's house.

That was all the invitation she needed. Diane opened the door and called for Rocky, grabbing his leash from the hook on the porch. The dog came quickly, and she clipped the leash onto his collar. He would be a nice distraction for the kids. Prize had been banished to the backyard again.

In less than a minute Diane was at Shelley's side, kneeling down, putting her arm around her friend. "You okay?"

"You came." Shelley turned toward her.

"Look, we have a space dog," Aiden announced to Emma, who clapped her hands together. "Since our space puppy has to stay in the backyard—I mean, on another planet."

Diane dropped the leash. Rocky would stay beside the children, feeling as if he needed to protect them. "Come over to the steps," she said to Shelley.

Aiden began counting down, "Three, two, one! Blastoff!"

The two women settled on the stoop.

"You saw?" Shelley managed to say.

"Detective Little, yes. I didn't hear a word, though."

"He just had questions. If Dan had any new electronics. Extra money. Asked what his friend's name is—but I don't have any idea."

"You can only tell him what you know."

"But then he asked me what I thought. If Dan is"—she paused and then whispered—"crooked."

Diane shook her head. She couldn't believe that about Dan.

"I said I can't imagine him doing something illegal, at least not on purpose."

"Of course not," Diane said.

"But it sounds like he's part of the investigation too."

"He'll be cleared," Diane said. "Once Detective Little figures out what's going on." She had the utmost confidence in the officer—and in Dan. There was no way that sweet young man could be doing anything illegal.

"I sure hope—" Shelley stopped. Dan's truck came down the street.

Diane stood. "How about if I take the kids over to my house?"

"Good idea."

Diane approached the playpen. "Hey, astronauts, we have a special mission, and space dog is going to lead the way." She lifted Aiden out first and handed him Rocky's leash. Next she lifted Emma, swinging the little girl's face away from the driveway where Shelley was approaching Dan's truck, which had just turned in from the street.

Surprised that Emma hadn't started to scream yet, Diane hurried Aiden and Rocky across the street. The baby's pigtails bounced up and down, but her eyes were glued to the dog, and she seemed uncertain whether to like the creature the way her brother did or be afraid of him. By the time they reached Diane's porch, the little girl was starting to look around.

"How about a cookie?" Diane turned the knob and pushed the door open.

"And some milk?" Aiden followed Rocky into the house.

"You've got it," Diane said, thankful she'd stopped by the store the day before. She led the way into the house and quickly closed the door. When they reached the kitchen, Emma wanted to be put down. Thankfully Rocky only sniffed her and didn't knock her over.

As Diane opened the cupboard door, her cell phone rang. She checked it. It was Jessica. She answered it quickly.

"I got your message, Mom. So sorry I haven't called sooner. That's cool that you have an agent." Jessica sounded matter-of-fact.

"Actually, I have a publisher now too."

"Wow, Mom. That was fast. Are you sure these people are legit?"

Diane put the cookies on the counter and opened the fridge, tucking her phone under her chin. "Frieda Watley is one of the most influential agents in New York." She rattled off some of Frieda's well-known clients.

"I'm impressed, Mom. When will your book come out?"

"I'm not sure." Diane picked up the milk carton and closed the door with her foot. "The agent sent me the main points of the contract, but that part wasn't in the note. I'm assuming I'll get the contract soon, but my agent says that could take months. Hopefully it will say."

A frantic look crossed Emma's face, and then she began to fuss.

"Who's that crying?"

"The neighbor kids are over," Diane said.

"Oh." Jessica sounded surprised.

"Can I call back later?"

"Not tonight. I'm going out. How about tomorrow?"

"Sure," Diane said. "I'll call in the early afternoon."

"Perfect! Talk to you then."

A wave of loneliness swept over Diane. She would have liked to talk more about her novel. Jessica's faint skepticism had dampened some of her enthusiasm. She wanted to talk about their trips to Marble Cove all those years ago too. She thought she might even tell Jessica about the children she saw and how they made her think of Jessica and Justin when they were young.

She scooped Emma into her arms and settled her on one hip, opening the package of cookies with her right hand. The little girl started making a grabbing motion.

Maybe no one was going to truly share in her excitement about her novel. Maybe everyone was going to get tired of hearing about it. Maybe she'd already said too much. And maybe it wouldn't seem real to them until they held a copy of the book in their hands.

She looked around for Aiden. He wasn't anywhere in the kitchen or at the table either. She stepped into the living room. There he was, on the couch, on his knees, looking out the window. Diane sat down beside him, holding Emma. "Whatcha looking at?" she asked.

"Mama and Daddy."

Diane turned her head. Shelley and Dan were still by his truck. Shelley's hands were waving around as she spoke. Dan's were shoved into his pockets.

"*Mama!*" Emma wailed, her chin quivering.

"Let's go have some cookies," Diane said, struggling to her feet, her arms wrapped around the distressed baby. "Aiden, you lead the way."

★   ★   ★

"Shell, just because Detective Little asked you some questions doesn't mean I'm doing anything wrong." Dan's eyes were heavy, but he didn't look like he was lying.

"Then tell me the name of the guy you've been working with." Shelley knew her voice was shrill, but she couldn't seem to tone it down.

"His name is Brett Leburt. He was in my class in school."

"And he has an import business? Or is it exports?"

Dan shrugged. "One time, we were moving his stuff. Another time, he was working with a small manufacturer. It varies."

"And you really believe he's on the up-and-up?" Shelley crossed her arms.

"Yeah. I don't have any reason not to."

She gazed intently into her husband's eyes. He didn't seem defensive. He didn't seem annoyed. But he did look a little sheepish.

"Speaking of," he said. "Brett has another job for me—right now. I just came home to grab a quick bite to eat. He's paying the dock fee this time. He just wants me to help unload."

Shelley felt her eyes grow wide.

"It'd be one hundred dollars toward me not working this afternoon. And it will only take an hour or so." The official work for the day had only lasted five hours, which meant his paycheck would be short again.

She hesitated a moment. "Fine. I just want it clear: I'd rather we all eat beans and rice than have you involved in anything illegal." She almost made herself laugh, regardless of how serious the situation was, because rice had grown so expensive she could hardly afford it. Now it was more like beans and pasta. "I don't want extra money if it's not honestly earned."

Dan turned toward her and wrapped his arms around her. "I know, Shell. I don't either. You know I'm not like that."

She relaxed against her husband for a minute. How crooked could Brett Leburt be if he was unloading at the dock in front of everyone? Including Detective Little. She took a deep breath. She had the name of Dan's friend. Should she pass it on to the detective? Should she tell him Dan was heading to the dock this afternoon to work for the man? She whispered a prayer, asking God for guidance as she followed Dan into the house.

Thirty minutes later, Dan had left again and Shelley was crossing the street as Detective Little's Toyota pickup turned down the lane. She paused on the other side, waiting for him to reach her. He stopped his pickup and opened the window.

"Is Dan around?" he asked.

"You just missed him. He's headed back to the docks." She took a deep breath. She was sure Detective Little showing up was a sign. "He's doing some unloading for his buddy. But the guy, Brett Leburt is his name, is paying to use the dock."

"Brett Leburt?"

Shelley nodded. "Do you know him?"

"I'm familiar with him. Nice guy. Fast talker." He pulled down on his mustache a little and then said, "Thanks. I think I'll go pay him a visit." Then he turned his pickup around and took off.

Shelley's legs felt shaky, and she waited on the sidewalk a minute, trying to collect herself. When she reached Diane's door, she could hear Emma crying. She knocked quickly and walked in, finding her friend standing in the archway between her living room and kitchen bouncing the baby up and down.

Emma's wail grew louder at the sight of her mother, and she stretched out her arms, falling into Shelley's hands as she approached.

"How are you?" Diane asked, relinquishing the baby.

"Okay." But she wasn't, and she began to cry. A couple of weeks ago she'd been afraid Dan was having an affair. Clearly that wasn't the case, for which she was thankful. She dabbed at her eyes with one hand, the other grasping Emma. She just needed to know the truth, and the sooner the better.

CHAPTER EIGHTEEN

Saturday morning, Beverly was in her room, still in her running clothes, tidying up when she heard a knocking on the back door. She opened her window farther and poked her head out to where she could see the side of the house. Mrs. Peabody and her sister Celia stood on the stoop.

"I'll be right there." Her father was most likely in the library and hadn't heard the knocking.

She hurried down the stairs, surprised they would be visiting. Mrs. Peabody wasn't scheduled to work today, and just after nine in the morning was pretty early for a social call. But considering that Mrs. Peabody got up at five, it was hours into her day. Actually, it was hours into Beverly's day too. She'd awakened at four thirty thinking about Mr. Maker and Celia Patterson. She reached the first floor and then walked quickly down the hall. How funny that the woman was now on her stoop.

She opened the door and welcomed the women in. "I was just thinking about you this morning, Miss Patterson."

"Really?" The woman's white bun was slightly askew. "Because I was thinking about you too. That's why I decided to come into town. You can call me Celia."

Beverly led the women through the house to the living room and then poked her head into the library and told her father they had company. When she said it was Mrs. Peabody and her sister, he perked up. "Celia's here?"

"You know Celia?"

"She stopped by..." He raised one eyebrow. "When was it? Sometime, anyway. You must have been in Augusta."

Beverly wondered what else her father and Mrs. Peabody had forgotten to tell her.

He stood quickly, almost too quickly. She hurried to his side and helped steady him. He paused a moment. "Diane came by when Celia was here. I guess I had it in my head that you were here too."

"Did Diane and Celia talk?"

He thought for a moment and then shook his head. "I don't think so."

Beverly led the way to the living room. She knew Diane was fascinated by Mr. Maker's story. As it was, Beverly felt she was holding out on her friend by not telling her everything she knew about the man and Celia, although to be honest, it wasn't much.

Her father practically glowed when he said hello to Celia.

The woman shook his hand politely and then sat on the couch beside her sister. Beverly's father sat in the wingback closest to her, and Mrs. Peabody settled next to Celia. Beverly pulled out the piano bench for herself.

"Since this is Celia's second trip to Marble Cove in as many weeks, I know your visit with her really stirred up the past," Mrs. Peabody said to Beverly. "She can't stop thinking about Edward Maker."

Celia let out an exasperated sigh. "Honestly, Coco. Do you mind? I can speak for myself."

Mrs. Peabody folded her hands primly. "I was just trying to help."

"Coco said you visited Edward." Celia looked straight at Beverly.

"Yes, Father and I did."

"I knew Edward in Augusta," her father said.

Celia nodded. "His family moved there after they left Marble Cove."

"Do you know what year they moved away from here?" Beverly asked.

Celia shook her head.

"His dad had a drinking problem." Beverly's father sat up straight and spoke quietly. "I do remember that."

"That would explain a few things." Celia glanced down at her lap. "Edward seemed to be ashamed of something. I could never figure it out, though. I always had the feeling that something tragic had happened to him sometime. I just couldn't get him to tell me." There was a hint of regret in her voice.

"That was part of the reason I broke things off," she said. "He wanted to marry and move to California. It seemed like too much of a risk to do with someone who had some sort of secret. Plus I didn't want to leave Maine... And we were still mourning our brother, weren't we?" She patted

Mrs. Peabody's hand. "I couldn't make a decision like that at the time."

Beverly felt even more sympathy for Mr. Maker than she had before. He had loved Celia. He'd wanted to marry her.

"I'd like to go see him," the woman said, looking at Beverly again. "Would you talk to him for me? I thought maybe I could go visit with you. Thought that might make it easier for him."

Beverly's father cleared his throat. "We'd like to have you join us, if you'd like."

Standing, Beverly kept her eyes on Celia. Her father seemed to have missed the woman's request. It wasn't to go with him to visit Edward Maker. It was to go with Beverly. She couldn't help but notice her dad seemed a little smitten with Celia, and she was sure he was missing all the clues that Celia was still interested in Edward.

"What have you found out about him?" Celia's eyes shone a little. "As far as what he's been doing all these years."

"Actually, we didn't learn much. He had a child, but we don't know if it was a son or a daughter, and anyway that child is deceased. He has a grandson."

Celia stammered a little. "W-what about a wife?"

"She's deceased too."

"Oh." Celia sank back against the couch. No matter her intentions, she seemed genuinely grieved for the man's loss.

"He likes to garden," Beverly said. "And shares his produce with neighbors and a local assisted-living home."

Celia's eyes lit up again.

"He's in good shape," Beverly continued. "His mobility is great, and his house and yard are well cared for."

"Would you call him?" Celia asked. "Or give me his number so I can... Although if that's the case, you should ask him first if it would be all right."

"I'll call him," Beverly said. "Right now. I'll be right back."

She decided to use the house line instead of her cell phone since her signal there was questionable. She used the kitchen phone because she didn't want the others to hear.

The phone rang several times before Mr. Maker finally picked up. He sounded a little out of breath, and she imagined he'd been outside working. She greeted him and explained the reason for her call. He didn't respond.

Beverly waited a moment before restating the request. "She would like to see you. Father and I can bring her to Augusta. Would tomorrow work for you?"

"No. Wait. I don't know. Can I call you back?"

She gave her number again in case he'd lost it, which was hard to imagine considering how organized he was, and asked if she could call back tomorrow if she hadn't heard from him.

"I'll get back to you by this afternoon." He hung up without saying good-bye.

When Beverly returned to the living room, Celia was standing in front of the mantel examining a photo of Beverly's parents. She turned around quickly, an expectant look on her face.

"He's going to call me back this afternoon," Beverly said. Celia's face fell.

"I'll let you know as soon as I hear anything."

Mrs. Peabody stood. "We'll leave you two alone on this fine Saturday morning."

"Oh, don't leave yet," Beverly's father said. "Can't you stay for a cup of coffee?"

Beverly was embarrassed she hadn't offered them some sooner. Her mother never would have overlooked such a basic detail of hospitality.

Celia glanced at Mrs. Peabody, who responded. "Maybe just a cup. And how about one of those scones Shelley dropped by yesterday? Those need to be used up before they go bad." The sisters sat back down.

A few minutes later, as Beverly served the others, Mrs. Peabody said, "Did you notice Detective Little questioning Shelley yesterday around noon? Then that husband of hers came home. They were having quite a row. Why, I think—"

"I'll take cream in my coffee," Celia said curtly. "Coco, come show me where it is."

"In the refrigerator, of course. Even a country bumpkin like you knows that."

"Show me." Celia tugged on her sister's arm and then had her on her feet and on her way out of the room. "Forgive her," Celia whispered as they walked by.

Beverly nodded. Part of her was relieved that Celia had put an end to Mrs. Peabody's gossip, but the rest of her wondered what was going on with Shelley and Dan.

She remembered Shelley was worried about him working overtime, but Beverly was sure the young woman didn't suspect her husband was doing anything illegal.

Her father took a sip from his mug and glanced at her over the rim. "I have no idea what she's talking about."

"Neither do I," Beverly said, moving the scones away from her father.

★ ★ ★

Mrs. Peabody and Celia left a half hour later. "Cece's spending the day in Marble Cove," Mrs. Peabody said, "so just call my home when you hear back from Edward."

Beverly assured them she would. She watched the sisters make their way up the flagstone walkway to the street. She felt a flash of jealousy. She would have no one like that when she was old. No one who remembered her as a girl. No one to visit. No one to reminisce with. No one to grieve with. No one to call—and be called—by an endearing, decades-old nickname.

"What's the matter, Beverly?" Her father had joined her.

"Oh, nothing," she said. "Just intrigued by the two sisters."

Her father patted her back. "I'm thankful you've found such good friends here."

Beverly nodded, frankly surprised her father had noticed.

★ ★ ★

It was after three before Edward Maker called back. Beverly's father was dozing in the library, and Beverly was scrubbing out the tub. Mrs. Peabody and her granddaughter cleaned, and cleaned well, but sometimes Beverly just wanted to feel like she was doing her bit to keep the house clean.

She rinsed and dried her hands and hurried into the kitchen, snatching up the phone. "Hello?"

"Edward Maker here. I've decided I'd welcome a visit from Celia. Could you bring her?"

"Yes," Beverly said. "Will tomorrow work?" She didn't want him having time to change his mind.

"I suppose."

"And my father would like to come again too."

The man hesitated but finally agreed. "Two in the afternoon would be preferable."

"That would be fine," Beverly said, relieved that it was her week to be in Marble Cove and that she wouldn't have to turn around and drive back to Augusta Sunday evening or Monday morning. "We'll see you then."

As it turned out, Mrs. Peabody decided she wanted to go too. Beverly didn't have the nerve to call Mr. Maker back and ask if it was okay, afraid he'd call the whole thing off if given another chance. Celia didn't seem thrilled about her sister going, but she also didn't tell her she couldn't, so Beverly acquiesced.

Later that evening, she wandered down to Diane's house and told her what was going on.

"Can I go?" Diane begged.

Beverly must have looked as overwhelmed as she felt.

"Just joking," Diane said. "Kind of. What a story, though. Promise me you'll remember every detail. What everyone says. Mr. Maker's reaction when he first sees Celia. All of that."

Beverly promised she would. As she said good-bye, she gave Diane a quick hug. "Thanks."

"Whatever for?"

"For being my friend."

Diane's eyes grew a little misty. "Being your friend is about the easiest thing in the world. You need to get a little more demanding. Make me work a little harder." She laughed.

"Give me time," Beverly said.

"That, we have." Diane swiped her fingers under her eyes. "God willing."

They both knew how precarious life could be.

CHAPTER NINETEEN

Saturday evening, Margaret sat at her computer searching her e-mails. The reunion was only a week and a half away, and Buddy was the only cousin who had responded besides her. He'd sent a second e-mail that morning saying that he would also bring extra folding tables and chairs and paper plates and cups.

Margaret pushed back her chair, sure she didn't want to go to the reunion at all. Annoyed, she headed to the kitchen for a cup of herbal tea but stopped in the middle of the living room. Adelaide was sprawled out on the couch watching a reality TV program.

"Look." She pointed to the screen. "That big lady lost a hundred pounds."

Margaret winced. "Turn the TV off," she said. "Remember, you're the leading lady in your own show. Don't get sucked into other people's stories instead of living your own."

Adelaide groaned. "Oh Mom."

"Actually, I need to go talk to Dan, Aiden and Emma's dad." The professional painters had decided it would be mid-September before they could fit the gallery repair project in, and it was definitely too much work for Allan. She'd decided to ask Dan, as Diane had suggested.

Adelaide sat up straight, clicking off the TV. "Can I come?"

"As soon as you're off the couch."

Adelaide jumped to her feet, a wide smile spreading across her face.

★　　★　　★

The young family was in their front yard. The day had grown warm and muggy, and a thunderstorm was brewing. Thankfully, so far Maine had avoided all the hurricanes that had formed in the Atlantic this year.

Emma squealed with delight when she saw Adelaide, and Aiden started chattering away, asking if they could play spaceships.

"They adore Adelaide," Shelley said.

"Obviously." Margaret laughed.

"Are you two out for an evening stroll on the beach?" Shelley asked.

"Actually, I wanted to ask Dan some questions."

Shelley balked a little but then turned to her husband. "Honey, Margaret wants to interrogate you too."

He blushed and stepped over.

"Now I didn't say *interrogate*, Shelley." Margaret turned toward Dan. "Actually, I have a business proposition."

He raised his eyebrows.

"I need some painting done."

He grinned.

"At the gallery. The ceilings."

"When?"

Margaret shrugged. "ASAP."

"Tonight?"

"Sure. The sooner it's done, the better."

He glanced at Shelley. "Would you care if I started right away?"

"It's up to you." She sounded sincere.

"I can ride down with you to the gallery," Margaret said. "Show you the paint. Explain the plan. I've already got everything you'll need. I just need to take Adelaide home first. Allan's in his shop." She checked her jacket pocket for her keys. They were there.

"The kids and I can walk her over," Shelley said.

Adelaide was holding Emma now, and Aiden was pulling on the leg of her sweatpants. Margaret hoped he didn't tug them off.

"Thanks," Margaret said. "Tell Allan I'll be home shortly."

Dan quickly changed into paint-flecked coveralls, then he and Margaret got into his truck. He didn't say much on the way to the gallery, but that changed when he stopped his truck out front. "I've been praying for some extra work. I appreciate it."

"Well, I've been praying for someone to finish my gallery repairs, so I appreciate you too." She unlocked the front door to the gallery and swung it wide open. The evening light was wafting in through the high windows and illuminating the dust particles all the way down to the floor. "I have some spotlights you can use if you paint tonight. Or you might just want to get set up."

He shook his head. "I work best in the evening. And I'd just as soon get as much done as I can before Monday."

Margaret agreed. She just wished she'd asked Dan sooner. "Do you have overtime work lined up this coming week?"

Dan blushed. "I never know that far ahead."

Margaret cocked her head.

Dan's face reddened more. "Did Shelley tell you what's been going on?"

Margaret cocked her head. "No."

"I've been doing some extra work for a friend. Then Detective Little got all suspicious of him and asked Shell some questions. Yesterday he came down to the dock and questioned my friend."

"And?"

"Well, he hasn't questioned me yet, at least not specifically. He did come down on the dock before yesterday and asked me—and John—some general questions. But not to single me out or anything. So I think I'm good."

Margaret's eyes narrowed. "Are you?"

"Absolutely." He pulled his cap off and put it back on backward. His eyes looked clear and sincere.

Margaret liked to think she could spot a liar, and she was pretty sure Dan wasn't lying. "Who's the friend?"

"Brett Leburt."

"Leburt? Is his dad Bob?"

Dan nodded.

Margaret pursed her lips. She'd done the guy's taxes when she'd worked as a bookkeeper, but she wasn't going to tell Dan that. "I used to be acquainted with Bob. He's a pretty fast talker, if I remember right. Always one to push boundaries." He'd gotten into some trouble for shipping whiskey from Canada illegally.

Dan flinched a little. "Sounds like Brett."

Margaret laughed. "Like father, like son?"

"Maybe not the boundaries part." Dan's face had faded to gray. "But the fast talking sounds familiar."

Margaret showed him the paint, the pan, the roller, and the brushes. She had drop cloths and tape too. She started a pot of coffee for him, gave him the extra key, and said for him to call if he had any questions. "Until ten," she instructed. "After that, you're on your own because I turn into a pumpkin."

He thanked her again, and she slipped out the front door and locked it behind her. As she started down Main Street, a bolt of lightning flashed across the sky. She counted, reaching ten before the sound of thunder came. She quickened her pace. The storm was two miles away. She probably had enough time to get home before the worst of it arrived.

Rain fell, a few light drops at first. But within a minute, it was coming down in sheets. Another flash of lightning struck, but this time she counted to only five before the thunder came. One mile away now. She increased her speed, darting down Newport Avenue toward her house.

Another bolt of lightning flashed, and before she could even count to one the thunder crashed, shaking the ground. A dog howled, probably Rocky next door, as Margaret flew up the steps to her front door.

She crashed through it, trying to shake the water from her short hair, and she was greeted by Aiden, Shelley, Emma, and Adelaide, who all stood at the window watching the storm.

"You okay?" Adelaide asked.

"Ay-yup," Margaret said. "Boy, what a storm." And it had come on so fast.

Allan came out of the kitchen holding the phone. "It's Dan, calling to see if you made it home all right."

"Tell him yes and thanks, and then hang up. Don't you know you're not supposed to be on the phone during a lightning storm?"

Allan retreated into the kitchen, not hanging up fast enough for her. It was sweet of Dan to call. A man who did that could not be doing something illegal. It wasn't in his character. And once a person's character was formed, it was usually set for life.

She thought of her cousin Buddy again and shivered. He'd been a bully growing up. And then, when she and Allan had gotten married, he'd drunk too much and ended up throwing up in the bushes. But not before he'd managed to thoroughly embarrass her with a horrible toast about her upcoming wedding night.

After that, back when she still saw him, he used to rib her and Allan about starting a family. Allan told him a couple of different times that it was a hard topic for Margaret, but Buddy wouldn't let it go. The last time she saw him, Adelaide was a baby. Buddy had glanced at her, whispered something to one of their cousins, and smirked. That was it. Margaret had avoided him ever since.

Margaret went into her room to change out of her wet clothes. The storm pounded the house for fifteen minutes, with lightning and thunder coming every few seconds. Emma cried and clung to Shelley. Once, the lights even flickered off and on, which sent Aiden to his mother too. But then the storm began to move off farther inland.

"We'd better get going," Shelley said.

"Maybe you should wait a few more minutes to make sure there's not any more lightning," Margaret said.

"The rain's stopped." Shelley peered out the window. "The storm definitely has passed by."

Margaret stepped closer. "Got to love Maine storms."

After Shelley and the kids left, Margaret didn't close the door. She stood on the threshold welcoming the freshness of the evening. Oreo rubbed up against her leg, hoping to escape out the screen. Margaret scooped him up and held the cat close.

Adelaide plopped back down on the couch.

"Oh no, you don't," Margaret said. "Let's make some granola for tomorrow." She wouldn't let Adelaide veg out on the couch and watch other people's lives instead of living her own.

★ ★ ★

When Diane saw Shelley crossing the street from Margaret's house with Aiden and Emma, she hurried to her porch. "Hey, you three. I just took a pan of brownies out of the oven. Want to join me for some with vanilla ice cream?"

Aiden's eyes lit up.

"Oh, that sounds so good," Shelley said. "But I need to get the kids in the tub, and then I have some more baking to finish up."

"Some other time," Diane said, forcing her voice to be cheery. It seemed like everyone was extra busy lately. She knew Shelley was hoping to open a business down the road, but she couldn't imagine why she was doing so much baking just lately. What could she possibly do with all of those goodies?

Diane returned to her house, pulling the front door shut behind her. Was she turning into one of those lonely old ladies who stalked their neighbors? Suddenly she felt more sympathy for Mrs. Peabody.

Making her way to the kitchen, she wondered if her friends were avoiding her on purpose. Perhaps she had been braggy without intending to be when she'd talked about getting an agent and then an offer from a publisher. She pulled a knife out of the drawer and cut into the brownies.

She retrieved the ice cream from the freezer and dished her dessert into her favorite blue bowl, the last one left from the set of dishes that her parents had given to her and Eric at their wedding.

She went into the living room and settled on the couch with her feet up, looking over at Shelley's house. Dan's pickup was still gone. He'd left with Margaret, which Diane thought was a little odd. And then Shelley and the kids had walked past with Adelaide, and then they'd just come back without her. Maybe something had happened, but Diane was pretty sure if there had been some kind of emergency, Shelley would have told her.

She took a bite of the cold ice cream and warm brownie. Although it tasted good, there was nothing satisfying about it. She took another bite, but it wasn't any better than the first. She put the bowl down on the coffee table.

What was wrong with her? She stared out the window again. She needed to get a grip. She needed to stop moping around.

She stood and took the bowl back into the kitchen, scraping the contents into the garbage. Dessert was meant to be shared. It was only 7:45 PM. It wasn't too late to take a plate of brownies and the ice cream over to Mrs. Peabody.

*   *   *

An hour later, Diane returned to her house, smiling. She felt loads better. The dessert had tasted so much better sharing it with someone else, and Mrs. Peabody had been genuinely pleased to have Diane drop by, although she'd offered Diane her own brownie recipe, stopping short of outright saying it was better. That had made Diane smile. She'd graciously accepted the recipe.

As she closed the door to her house, she realized her cell phone was ringing. She dashed around trying to find it and finally located it on the bathroom counter. It was Justin.

"Hello!" She was a little out of breath.

"Hi, Mom. I've been meaning to call. How have you been?"

Diane walked down the hall, calculating that it was eight in the morning in Dubai. She settled back on the couch in the living room.

"I've got some leave coming up, and I thought maybe we could meet."

"Great. When would you be coming?"

"I'm actually flying out in three days."

"Seriously?" She sat up straight. "And you're coming here?"

"To Marble Cove?" He laughed. "Sure, for a day or two during my leave. I'm not sure when, though. I'll be staying at Jessica's, mostly."

She slumped against the couch. "Of course." She tried to make her voice sound cheery. She shouldn't have expected him to rush up to Marble Cove from the get-go. It wasn't home to him.

"Hey," he said, "I wanted you to know how proud I am that you have an agent. I know that's a big deal."

Diane smiled. "Thank you."

"So how's it going?"

"Actually..." She explained about the publishing house and that she hoped she would see a contract soon.

"Wow! Mom, that's fantastic!" The volume of his voice nearly made her drop the phone. "That's such a big deal. I'm so proud of you."

Tears sprang into her eyes. Justin got it.

"Dad would be so proud of you too. You must miss him so much right now."

The tears spilled over and started to run down Diane's cheeks. "Yes," was all she could manage to say.

"I'm sorry. I didn't mean to make you cry." Justin's voice was tender now.

"No, it's fine. Crying is a good thing, right? And I know you miss him too. I can't tell you how much that helps."

Justin was silent for a moment. "Yeah. Every day I miss him. Every minute."

"He'd be so proud of you too," Diane said.

Justin had been a little lost after Eric had died. Even though he'd been only a few classes short of graduating from college, he'd dropped out. Diane wasn't sure if the military would be a good fit for him, but it had been, so much so that he'd finished his college classes and was now considering officer training school.

Justin grunted a sort of acknowledgement and then changed the subject. "Have you started your next book?"

"Not yet."

"Shouldn't you? Before you start revisions on the first? It seems like now would be the perfect time to at least have a firm idea ready for the next one."

Diane bounced a little on the couch. He was right. She would need a proposal and the first three chapters, but not the entire novel this time. Of course, she should get started now. She probably had a good chunk of time before the revision process on the first novel began.

"I've been thinking that too," she said, hoping she didn't sound like she was talking down to him. "Let me know when you arrive. If you can't get up this way right away, I'll come see you."

After they said good-bye, Diane slipped her phone into the pocket of her jacket and padded down the hall to her office. She felt a hundred times better after Justin's call. And she did have an idea for another story. There was a Korean War vet in it. A young woman. And a mystery in a small town on the coast of Maine.

*   *   *

Shelley stirred when Dan came to bed just after two. "How did it go at the gallery?" she mumbled.

"Good. I think I can finish tomorrow. I had to put primer on first." He pulled the covers up to his chin. "How was your evening?"

"I got more baking done. The freezer is getting pretty full." There was still a shelf left. Maybe she'd see if Adelaide could come over and help again so she could finish filling it.

Dan turned toward her, face to face. "I've been thinking more about Brett. I've been pretty trusting with him. I probably didn't ask all the questions I should have. I think I'll do that. Maybe tomorrow."

Shelley yawned. "Good idea."

He touched her nose with his. "Good night." Rolling onto his back, he reached for her hand. In no time, he was asleep.

But as the minutes ticked by, she became more and more awake.

Finally, slipping her hand out of Dan's, she rose, plucking her robe off the end of the bed and padding barefoot down the hallway and pouring herself a drink of water from the filtered pitcher in the fridge. She walked to the living room window and turned to the east slightly, taking in the waves crashing against the shore in the light of the full moon. The tide was in, and the rocks were completely covered.

Then she turned her head in the other direction, up the street. Diane's office light was on. Shelley stepped closer to the window, wondering if her friend was working. She hadn't said anything about her novel in the last couple of days. In fact, she seemed generally subdued about it. Shelley figured that if she'd had good news of that size—if she'd won a national bake-off, for instance—she wouldn't be able to contain her excitement.

Diane was truly both a modest and a gracious person. And she probably had no idea what an absolute blessing she was. Since Shelley lived so far from family, she was doubly blessed to have Diane as a neighbor and to have her interested in her kids. She was turning into a sort of grandmother to them.

But Shelley had to be careful not to expect too much from Diane in helping with the kids. She didn't want to take advantage of her. She couldn't trust Adelaide as wholly as she could trust Diane, of course, but she was thankful that the young woman was available. That way, she could ask Diane sometimes and have Adelaide help the other times. It was a nice balance.

Diane's light flicked off, and Shelley startled a little. She needed to get back to bed too. Emma wouldn't care at all in the morning that her mama had been wide awake at three.

Shelley put her glass in the sink and tiptoed back down the hall toward bed, but she took a detour into Aiden's room. He slept on his back, just like his dad did, with one arm slung back over his head, and he'd completely kicked off his blankets. Prize was in her kennel, in keeping with the agreement they'd made in order for her to sleep in Aiden's room. Shelley covered her son and kissed his forehead. He didn't stir a bit. Neither did the dog.

Next, Shelley stopped at Emma's room, pushing the door open enough so she could peek in. Emma had rolled over to her stomach but was still covered, with her head pointed toward the hall. Shelley said a prayer for both her children as she watched the rise and fall of her little girl's back under the blanket.

After a moment, she crawled into bed next to Dan, slipping her hand back into his as if she'd never been gone.

Chapter Twenty

The next morning during church, Margaret watched Adelaide snuggle next to Allan as the preacher began his sermon. Adelaide had a very special relationship with her father. Oh, Margaret knew her daughter loved her too, probably more than she could comprehend, but Adelaide absolutely adored her dad.

Granted, Allan was an easy person to adore. He was generous and easygoing, and he offered Adelaide endless security. He was amazingly patient with her, encouraging her to try new things. Because of his patience, Adelaide trusted him completely.

Though they'd been coming to church since Margaret's near drowning, she still didn't feel entirely comfortable here. Some of her old agnostic arguments still cropped up from time to time, though her growing faith was putting them to rest one by one. Allan's faith was maturing too as he remembered his upbringing. But Adelaide took to Christianity as if she'd known it all along. Her faith put Margaret's to shame.

The pastor opened in prayer and then asked everyone to turn in their Bibles to Proverbs 3:5–6. "Notice the four statements," the pastor said. "First, 'Trust in the Lord with all your heart.' Second, 'Lean not on your own understanding.' Third, 'In all your ways acknowledge Him.' And fourth, 'He will make your paths straight.'"

Margaret let the truths soak in. Before her rescue, she wasn't sure what she believed about God. But over the last few years, bit by bit, she knew He existed, knew He cared about her, knew He had orchestrated her survival. Now she was trying to truly put her trust in God, starting with her business and the huge risk she'd taken.

"You can't pick and choose what you're going to trust God with," the pastor said. "If you have faith in God, you're going to have to trust Him with every detail of your life."

Margaret's shoulders stiffened. Some things were easier to trust God with than others. Margaret thought about Adelaide. Her daughter trusted Allan with every aspect of her own life. Could Margaret do that with God? Could she completely trust Him with Allan as he aged? With Adelaide and her future?

God knew how much Margaret liked to be in control of things. She sighed, feeling a little defeated. It was hard to imagine coming to a place where she trusted God with everything. She stole a glance to her left again. Adelaide had her head against Allan's shoulder, her eyes closed, her whole being as trusting as a three-year-old's.

The thing was that, besides trusting her dad, Adelaide trusted God more than anyone Margaret knew too. This was a sermon she *could* sleep through—she understood intrinsically what it was to have faith.

Margaret directed her attention back to the sermon.

"We think we know better than God. We think we know our finances better and our relationships—and our own needs, even. We don't. And we think we know about God's love for us, but we can't begin to comprehend that either..."

Sighing again, Margaret wondered if she would ever be able to grasp God's love. To think He loved her more than she and Allan loved Adelaide. She shivered a little, and glanced at her daughter again. The comparison shouldn't be that God loved her more than she and Allan loved Adelaide. No, the comparison should be that He loved her more than Adelaide loved them.

Adelaide was the one who loved unconditionally. She was the one who loved constantly. She was the one who saw the good and instantly forgave the bad when forgiveness was needed. She expected the best. She celebrated the simple things and saw value in all things.

"We think we know how to run our lives better than God does," the pastor continued. "And the lives of others. But we can't. If we try, our path won't be straight. If we're willing to live by faith and trust God, though, we'll be able to let go of control and travel the path God has laid out for us."

The pastor flipped to the New Testament and started talking about fear being the biggest detriment to trust. It made sense to Margaret. Adelaide was the bravest person she knew. She never lived in fear. Oh, she'd get upset if Oreo got lost, but when it came to the big issues in life, she had absolute trust.

Margaret closed her own eyes as the pastor continued with the sermon. Here she was, sixty-seven years old, with still so much to learn. She felt like a child grasping at concepts just a little too advanced for her, and yet her daughter, who was developmentally about nine years old, understood all of it without trying.

"Besides learning to trust God with the future," the pastor said, "you also must learn to trust Him with the past. With everything that can't be changed. With people who have harmed you..."

Margaret stiffened and then glanced at her watch. It wouldn't hurt to leave a little early. She'd need to work around Dan painting, but she definitely wanted to open the gallery for the day. She slipped from the pew. If Dan had finished the ceiling in the first gallery she would re-hang the paintings and hope for some business as he worked in the second. Then by Monday, everything would be back to normal—and the painting done in plenty of time.

She shivered, thinking about the family reunion. It was one thing to aim at trusting God with the present and the future. But the past? Who was the pastor trying to kid? What had happened had happened. Now it was all about protecting herself.

And she could only trust herself to do that.

★   ★   ★

As Diane turned left, away from Margaret's church, the sun came out from behind a cloud, dazzling the day with glorious light, so glorious that she began fumbling in her purse for her sunglasses. She found them and pushed the plastic frames onto her face.

She was glad she'd decided to visit her friend's church. It was something she liked to do from time to time to meet new people in town. She'd gotten there late and hadn't seen Margaret until her friend had gotten up and left. Otherwise she would've sat with her.

The sermon had encouraged her. She hadn't been trusting God with her relationships with her friends. She hadn't even been trusting Him with her writing—not really. He'd provided her with an agent and a contract offer, and here she'd been down in the dumps, worried about what other people thought and feeling sorry for herself because she didn't have Eric to share all of this with. Yet God had reached out to her through Justin's timely and encouraging phone call.

Instead of turning to go down the street toward her house, she decided to head downtown. Margaret was probably at her gallery, opening it up for the day. She admired that her friend squeezed in church before work. It made a long Sunday for her. Maybe there was something Diane could help with.

As she neared the shop, Diane noticed Dan's truck out front. She quickened her step. When she pushed through the gallery door and smelled paint, she finally put two and two together. Margaret had hired Dan to do the painting, just as Diane had suggested.

She looked up at the ceiling. Margaret had chosen the haint blue paint. That encouraged Diane further. Her friends really did value and pay attention to her. She stopped, mesmerized by the color. It was like the sunlit ocean, turned upside down. And like the summer sky. It was the most hopeful color she'd ever seen.

"Back here," came Margaret's voice from the second gallery.

Diane stepped across the first room and through the door to the second.

Dan perched on a high ladder, painting the ceiling with a roller brush. He wore a mask over his face and once-white coveralls over his body.

"Thanks for the suggestion to hire Dan," Margaret said, a painting in her hands. "It's working out brilliantly."

Dan gave her a nod, and his eyes lit up behind his goggles.

"He painted halfway through the night and then started again right after church."

Diane thought she'd heard his truck late last night. Even with his muffler repairs, she could still hear it coming and going. "Need some help hanging pictures?" Diane asked Margaret.

"That would be great! Thanks so much."

Diane placed her purse behind the counter and slipped out of her light jacket.

"I'm going to put a 'work in progress' sign on the door, but I hope people will still come in. I don't want to lose a whole day of business."

"When's that reunion you plan to go to?"

"This week. Wednesday night."

"Funny time for a reunion."

"I know—but my cousin's hoping we get a better turnout in the middle of the week. People are gone too much during the summer on weekends. And most of the family lives close by."

"But you'll have to take a day off work..." Diane followed Margaret into the back room.

"Just the afternoon. Actually, I've been meaning to ask you to mind the shop for me then."

"I'd love to," Diane said, barely giving it a thought. "I like helping out at your gallery. Makes me feel artsy myself."

The two women hung painting after painting until the doorbell chimed. They were in the back room.

Margaret smiled. "First customer of the day. Gotta love 'em." She hurried out of the room, and Diane rested for just a moment, until she overhead Margaret say, "And I thought I had a customer."

"Adelaide wanted to see her mama." It was Allan's voice.

"*Oooh*, I like the color," Adelaide said.

Diane ventured out and said hello to the two.

"This will be nice for the party!"

No one said a thing for a moment.

"Yes," Margaret said, "it will be so good to go off to our reunion knowing this is done, won't it?"

Allan nodded, and Adelaide looked a little confused.

Diane looked around, wondering what party Adelaide was talking about. Maybe she had been referring to the reunion, but that had sounded more like a cover on Margaret's part. Maybe Margaret was planning a gallery reopening or something. But why wouldn't Diane be invited? She took a deep breath, trying to quell her reaction to being left out. It couldn't be intentional.

Allan helped hang the rest of the pictures. Diane asked him about his carpentry work.

"Things have been a little slow," he said.

Diane knew that keeping up with Adelaide had to take quite a bit of his time, especially with Margaret so busy during the summer months. She anticipated that Allan would ask about her writing or her book, but he didn't. Maybe Margaret hadn't told him about the agent or publisher. She tried to push that thought aside, remembering the sermon and a little embarrassed at her sensitivity. Honestly, she needed to get over herself.

★   ★   ★

When Dan came home for lunch, Shelley had tuna sandwiches and apple slices ready, plus a couple of scones from the baking she'd done. It was the beginning of their austere budget.

"Hey," Dan said as he came in through the front door. The children scampered to him, and he scooped them up in his arms as Shelley stood watching at the archway to the kitchen.

He plopped Aiden into his booster seat at the table and slipped Emma into her chair. Shelley placed the children's plates in front of them and went back for the others. Dan headed down the hall to wash up.

"I wanted chicken nuggets," Aiden said with a whine.

Emma nodded her head.

"This is better for you," Shelley said, settling into her chair. And cheaper—but she knew that didn't mean much to a child. For once, neither of the children touched their food before grace was said.

When Dan came back, he said the blessing. When he was done, the children each picked up an apple slice and ate that.

"Tuna sandwiches!" Dan picked up half of his. "These were my favorite when I was a kid. I'd choose them any day over PB&Js. Even over chicken nuggets." He took a bite, and his eyes grew wide in delight as he chewed.

Aiden picked up his sandwich and took a little bite. He swallowed.

"Delicious, huh?" Dan took a second bite.

Aiden nodded, although he didn't look entirely convinced. Shelley offered Emma a little tuna on a small piece of bread. Emma stuck her finger in the middle and licked it. She made a face and returned to eating her apple slice.

Shelley began eating her sandwich, and after another minute Emma picked up a chunk of tuna with her finger and thumb and tried it again. This time she didn't make a face. She took another bite.

"Good, huh?" Aiden had nearly finished his half a sandwich.

Emma just took another bite.

When the kids had finished, Dan herded them down the hall to wash up. He returned to kiss Shelley good-bye and get back to work at the gallery. "I'll stay until I'm done," he said. "Probably around eight or so."

"What about dinner?"

"I'll eat when I get home." He turned to go, but then stopped. "Brett called to see if I would work tonight."

"And?" She realized she'd crossed her arms, so she quickly let them drop to her sides.

"I told him I couldn't." He took a deep breath. "But it was weird. He said he had some stuff he was moving from his cabin up north."

Shelley cocked her head. "That's a familiar story."

"Exactly what I told him. And when I helped with that load, he'd said he'd moved everything he owned out of the place. That his dad was renting it out to someone else."

"What did he say when you brought it up?"

"Not much. Just laughed and said I must not have heard him right before." Dan shook his head. "It's like he can't even keep track of his own stories."

Shelley wrinkled her nose.

"Anyway, I'll see you later." Dan turned back toward the front door.

"Thanks, Dan," Shelley said.

"What for?"

"For working so hard for us."

He waved a little, as if telling her it was no biggie, but she could tell he was pleased with her praise.

She stood at the door and waved as he backed his truck out of their driveway. As he drove off, she noticed Diane in her yard.

"Want me to watch the kids for a while?"

"That's okay," Shelley called out. "I've got it covered. It's almost nap time, and then I'm going to try a new recipe." She waved. "Thanks anyway!"

Diane looked a little dejected as Shelley closed the door. She couldn't imagine that Diane was actually disappointed not to watch the kids. She shook her head a little. Her friend had her writing and gardening and reading and her relationships with all the other neighbors. She was busy, busy, busy. She was just being kind to offer to watch the kids.

CHAPTER TWENTY-ONE

Beverly came to a stop in front of Mr. Maker's house. "We're here," she said.

Her father stirred in the passenger seat beside her, and Mrs. Peabody yawned dramatically in the back seat. Both of them had slept most of the way from Marble Cove.

Celia, on the other hand, already had her door open. Beverly wondered if she was going to go inside without them, but the woman scurried around to the other side to help her sister out of the car.

Beverly did the same with her father, reminding him to watch the curb. As the four made their way up the walkway, she searched Mr. Maker's yard and the front of his house. She didn't see him, and the blinds weren't moving at the windows. They were a half hour late—traffic had been a little heavier than she'd anticipated.

Once they reached the first step of the porch, her father stopped. "It's too hot."

Beverly helped him take his sweater off and held it for him. Celia led the way to the front door and knocked firmly.

And then they waited. And waited. But no one came to the door.

"I'll go around to the back and check," Beverly said.

She headed around the side yard and unlatched the gate. "Mr. Maker," she called. "Are you back here?" No one answered. She made her way around the grape arbor.

There he was, in his chair. "Mr. Maker?" Panic rose in her throat. Was he all right? "Mr. Maker!" Beverly ran to him and placed her hand on his shoulder.

He startled. "What's wrong?"

Relief flooded through her. "Nothing, nothing. You scared me, that's all."

"I scared *you?*" He was standing now, glaring at her.

"I'm sorry. I thought—" Clearly, he was fine. "Never mind."

He glanced at his watch. "You're late. I thought you weren't coming."

She shook her head. "Traffic was bad. The others are on your porch."

His hand flew to his full head of salt-and-pepper hair and raked through it quickly. Beverly smiled and wanted to tell him how handsome he looked, but she was afraid that would embarrass him.

"Is everyone here?" he asked.

"Yes." Beverly smiled. "Celia's here too."

"And she wants to see me?"

Beverly wanted to laugh. "Of course she wants to see you. She wouldn't have come all this way if she didn't." She put her hand on his shoulder. "In fact, I think she's very eager to see you."

"Should I go around front? Or through the house?" His face suddenly looked young and vulnerable.

"Through the house." She followed him up the back steps and into the kitchen, past his empty table, and into the living room. He paused a moment, and Beverly positioned herself where she could glance from his face to Celia's.

He opened the door.

Celia's face turned upward like a lily to the sun. Mr. Maker stood frozen, his expression blank. And then his faded blue eyes began to water. Regaining his composure, he reached for Celia's hand and squeezed quickly. "Come in, come in," he said, as he let go of her hand. "All of you." He gestured to the living room. "Sit down, please. I have some lemonade and shortbread cookies."

"Let me help," Beverly offered as the other three sat on the couch.

Mr. Maker seemed grateful for the offer, and in no time they had five glasses filled and on a tray. He already had the cookies arranged on a blue glass plate. Together they carried everything into the living room.

He served Mrs. Peabody first, then Celia, Beverly's father, and then Beverly, who had settled in one of the two dining room chairs he'd brought into the room. He sat in the other straight-back chair. Quickly, before Celia could ask about him, he asked what she'd been doing all these years.

She explained that she did become a teacher and had taught in a community an hour north of Marble Cove her entire career. Next he turned to Mrs. Peabody and said he hadn't had the pleasure to meet her all those years ago, but that it was good to meet her now. He added that their brother had talked a lot about the two of them.

"You served with him, isn't that right?" Mrs. Peabody asked.

"Yes," Mr. Maker said. "In Korea. But not for long, I'm afraid."

All three were silent for a long moment.

"Oh dear," Celia said. "It's still so sad, isn't it?"

Mr. Maker nodded. "It didn't take me long, once we became acquainted, to realize you were his sister. Like I told you all those years ago when I came home. He had nicknames for the two of you. They were quite cute." He tilted his head a little.

"Cece and Coco," Mrs. Peabody said. "For Celia and Coral."

"That's right. You'd think I'd remember that."

"Oh heavens. Why would you?" Celia laughed a little.

Mr. Maker didn't seem to hear her. "I wasn't with him the day he was killed, but I always felt so horrible. I always wondered if there was something I could have done."

Celia shook her head. "I'm sure there wasn't."

"You came from such a good family." His eyes were watery again, and Beverly was surprised at his transparency. "I couldn't imagine what the heartache did to all of you."

Mrs. Peabody took her sister's hand. "We got through it. Didn't we?"

Both of their heads bobbed a little, in unison.

"Did you make a career out of the army?" Beverly asked.

"I did. After Korea, I ended up in Colorado at Fort Carson. I met my Dolly out there."

Beverly stole a look at Celia. The woman was listening intently but didn't react to his mention of a wife.

He continued. "Then we were at Fort Bragg when I was sent to Vietnam in the midsixties. After that, I was transferred to Anchorage. When I retired, we were stationed at Fort Lewis in Washington State. But after Dolly passed, fifteen years ago now, I decided to return to Maine." He paused. "I missed the winters."

His eyes sparkled a little, but then he grew serious again. "My daughter had settled out here and raised her son. She was one of those people always searching for her roots." He paused. "Otherwise I wouldn't have come back to Augusta."

It was by far the most Beverly had heard the man say in one sitting. She was sure there was a sad story about his daughter, but she wouldn't be so rude as to ask. She was appreciating this private man more and more.

"That tells about what you've been up to since you joined the army." Mrs. Peabody leaned forward, toward their host. "But what about the photo taken by the lighthouse? How long did you live in Marble Cove?"

He gave Beverly a desperate look.

Coming up with a rescue plan was made even more difficult by not knowing what the dilemma was. Besides, she wanted to know too. But she quickly eased his discomfort. "Celia is an avid gardener, Mr. Maker. And Father and

Mrs. Peabody both enjoy it too. Would you give us a tour of your yard?"

"Of course." He stood quickly.

They placed their nearly empty lemonade glasses on the tray on the coffee table.

"Let's go out the front door," Mr. Maker said.

By the time they reached the backyard, Celia was walking beside him as he pointed out different plants and what he'd added just this summer.

"These," he said, pointing to a large clump of greenery, "when they're blooming, are my favorites. They bloom in the early summer. I've forgotten the name. A little flower." His eyes twinkled.

"Blue?" Celia seemed to be in on his joke, but Beverly had no idea what he was talking about.

"Yes. Pale blue."

"The color of your eyes." It was a statement on Celia's part, not a question.

He nodded.

"Would they be forget-me-nots?"

"Yes," he answered, his voice was low and full of emotion yet with a hint of teasing.

After that, Beverly did her best to engage her father and Mrs. Peabody in conversation, trying to let the old friends have some space. They walked ahead to the vegetable garden, while Beverly pointed to the dahlias along the fence line. Her father said that his mother used to grow sweet peas there. They'd wound their way up and down the fence, blooming in the early summer. He and his friends used to pick the pink blossoms and bring them into the house to her.

Beverly thought of her grandmother. Even as an old woman, she'd loved to have people over. She'd never been a flashy entertainer, but she'd welcomed people into her home, even into her much smaller place across the river, the only home of her grandparents that Beverly ever knew. She was always quick to invite a visitor to stay for a meal, even if all she had planned was soup and bread. She valued people, and Beverly was sure that was what Edward Maker remembered about her grandmother. That was what had led him back to this house, to this yard. He wanted to remember the good of his childhood, not the bad.

Mrs. Peabody was ready to leave much sooner than Celia was. The older sister and Mr. Maker were on the far end of the garden talking about natural pesticides when Mrs. Peabody plopped down in the lawn chair and declared they should be on their way.

Beverly ignored her and stepped over to where her father was standing in the shade of an apple tree.

"I wonder if this is the same one I climbed when I was little." He touched the gnarly trunk with the palm of his hand. He looked out over the yard, and his gaze landed on Celia and Mr. Maker. "Do you think he loved his wife?"

"Sure," Beverly said.

"He certainly seems taken with Celia."

Beverly smiled, sure her father had been, too, before he saw what had survived between the two friends through the years. "Father, if you become romantically involved with someone, I promise not to doubt your love for Mother."

He snorted, a little too loudly.

"Just saying," she said.

"There's no worry of that." He sighed. "No one could replace your mom."

"Cece," Mrs. Peabody called. "Mr. Wheeland's getting tired!"

"Oh." Celia looked startled. "I'm sorry."

As they walked around the side of the yard, Beverly overheard Celia ask Mr. Maker if she could get his phone number. He pulled a card from his wallet and gave it to her. "I have this for my produce delivery. So the old folks can give me a call when they run low."

"You sell produce?" Celia sounded confused.

"Oh no. I give it away."

"To the old folks?" She was clearly amused. "I guess I do too. I mean, my produce. And to the younger families around too."

"It's not like the Depression," Mr. Maker said. "That's for sure. Times aren't that bad. But there's no denying that they're tough. I like to do what I can."

They all said good-bye and climbed back in the car. As they pulled away, Mr. Maker waved. Beverly glanced in the rearview mirror a couple of minutes later. Celia held onto the card in her hand and stared out the window. Mrs. Peabody was absolutely quiet.

Beverly wasn't sure if she'd ever get the answers she wanted from Mr. Maker, especially if she kept rescuing him. But she was pretty sure Celia had gotten hers: he remembered her... fondly.

★   ★   ★

The next morning, as Beverly started her workday in the alcove at her father's house, her cell phone rang. She fished it from her briefcase, thinking maybe it was Mr. Maker calling, because she'd just been thinking about him.

It wasn't. It was her new boss, Phil Miller. "Hey, you know that budget report you gave earlier in the month? They want you to give it again."

"They?"

"The finance committee. The full committee this time. Plus some others."

"Oh." Beverly's stomach flopped. "When?"

"This afternoon—one o'clock in the second floor boardroom."

Beverly's stomach flopped again. "Today? Seriously?"

"Believe me, I wouldn't kid you. I'll be there too."

"Well...I guess I'll see you then."

She held the phone in the palm of her hand for a moment. The presentation had all sorts of information about benefits, vacation time, and furlough days. They were probably trying to figure out if they could squeeze even more out of the budget.

She took a deep breath and sat up tall and straight. She could do this. She needed to skim the PowerPoint presentation and anticipate their questions, but she was good at this. She sighed again and looked around the kitchen. She might as well head into the office and prepare.

★   ★   ★

The five members of the finance committee, along with her boss and half a dozen other folks she had seen only once or twice, were all on time. Phil introduced her—as Bev— and then quickly added the rest of her name, even though everyone already knew her.

Beverly felt a wave of panic, something she hadn't experienced for years. She was feeling less and less comfortable with her job as time went on. And she had to be honest: she didn't have the same drive as she'd had five years ago or even two years ago. Work was no longer the escape for her that it had been.

Still, she put on her business persona and started to speak. It wasn't that she couldn't do it; it was just that she didn't enjoy it the way she used to. The presentation clicked along, one slide after another. She ad-libbed a little and got a couple of laughs, just as she had last time, and she made eye contact with each person around the table, including her boss.

At the end, after a few clarifying questions about the new copays and deductibles and how the furlough days would be monitored, Phil thanked Beverly.

As the others left and she packed up her laptop, Phil waited for her. "That really was great," he said. "You definitely have a knack for presenting."

She zipped her briefcase. "Thank you."

He placed his hands on the table and leaned forward. "So why didn't you apply for the director job when it was open? For my job."

It had occurred to her to apply for it, but there was no way she could telecommute if she was the director. "A few years ago, I would have been interested."

"Will you be, in the future?"

She shrugged. "I don't know." She really didn't. Sometimes, like when she was giving the presentation, she enjoyed what she was doing. But most of the time her work definitely didn't have the pull it used to.

Once she was back in her office, she decided to go ahead and leave, even though it was only a quarter till two. She thought about stopping by her house, but there wasn't really any reason to.

On the way out of town, as she crossed the bridge, she thought of Mr. Maker. He still hadn't given her any information about the photo or about Marble Cove. As she came to his street, she decided at the last minute to turn down it. Seeing Celia seemed to have softened him. Perhaps he would talk about his childhood now. Perhaps Beverly would have more of a story to tell Diane after all.

She pulled to a stop in front of his house and got out quickly, before she talked herself out of it. She knocked rapidly on his front door. No one answered. Even though the afternoon had grown hot, he was probably working out in the garden. Between harvesting and preserving his produce, he had his hands full.

She walked around the side yard, taking deliberate steps in her heels, careful not to trip. She scanned the garden but didn't see him. "Mr. Maker?" His Chevy truck was parked next to his garage. Perhaps he was delivering vegetables to nearby neighbors.

She turned, ready to leave, when she heard a sound. And then another. Maybe it was the creak of a branch of the maple against the garage. But then she heard it again. It sounded like someone was saying her name. She stepped closer to the garden.

"Back here. By the ditch." It was definitely Mr. Maker's voice. "I've fallen."

Beverly hurried back behind the garden, her heels sinking into the soft soil. She was almost to the irrigation ditch and still hadn't seen Mr. Maker.

"Down here."

There he was, on the bank of the ditch, his legs and feet in the muddy water.

"Oh dear." Beverly tottered at the top of the bank, but then her heels sank into the muddy soil. "Do you need a hand?"

"Please. I've hurt my leg. Much as I've tried, I can't get up the bank."

Beverly yanked the cell phone out of her purse. "I'll call 911."

"No, please don't. Go across the street and get my neighbor. In the yellow house. He's strong. And then get me my walking stick by the back door."

Beverly hurried to the neighbors' house. A young woman about Shelley's age answered. She said her husband was sleeping after having worked the night shift, but she'd wake him up.

"Oh no. Don't do that," Beverly said.

"Are you kidding? To help Mr. Maker? I'd be in big trouble if I didn't. You go on back. I'll send George right over."

Beverly thanked the woman, hurried back across the street, and grabbed the walking stick, using it herself as she made her way back behind the garden again. "He's on his way." Beverly handed Mr. Maker his walking stick and then squatted down as ladylike as she could in her dress.

"You're a godsend," he said.

Beverly smiled. It'd been a long time since she'd felt sent to do good. She liked the feeling.

"I haven't felt this helpless in years. One of the worst feelings in the world is to not be able to take care of yourself, although not being able to take care of others is even worse."

Beverly cocked her head. "Are you talking about Korea?" Or maybe Vietnam. He would have had heartbreaking experiences there too.

"I was thinking further back than that. To Marble Cove."

"What happened back then?" Her voice was soft, barely audible, even to her, over the chirp of the birds and the breeze dancing with the leaves of the hemlock tree.

He shook his head and looked toward the garden.

"Did you live at the lighthouse?" Beverly asked.

Mr. Maker took a deep breath. "For a couple of years. When I was little. " He looked directly at her, as best he could.

"Is there anything you can tell me about it?" She paused. "Anything special?"

He had a faraway look in his eyes. "I remember…" He took a deep breath and then met Beverly's gaze and then shook his head. "I don't have anything to say about the lighthouse, not now."

She nodded. She'd pressed enough. He had a right to what information he was willing to share. Perhaps he'd be willing to talk more about it some other day.

"Mr. Maker?" A man, at least six foot five, came running into the backyard.

"Over here." Beverly stood and waved.

The man looked like a weightlifter with his bulging muscles tight against the sleeves of his white T-shirt. He assessed the situation. "I'm going to pull you out. Then we'll call an ambulance."

"I don't need an ambulance," Mr. Maker said. "Just some help."

The man positioned his hands under Mr. Maker's armpits and pulled slowly, dragging him up the bank. Once he had him up and on one foot, he helped Mr. Maker hobble to the lawn chair.

George knelt down and pulled Mr. Maker's pant leg up over his knee. "You may have torn some ligaments. You definitely should have your doctor check it out."

"I can take you," Beverly said.

"No, that's too much. I'll call my grandson."

"He lives in town?" Beverly hadn't gathered that from any of their earlier conversations.

"Yep," Mr. Maker examined his knee. It was swollen and discolored. Then he looked at Beverly. "Could I borrow your phone?"

Beverly reached for hers, but George already had his out.

Mr. Maker took it and dialed. "I might as well stay out here until he comes."

After a quick phone conversation with his grandson it was obvious the man was on his way.

"I'll wait with him," George said to Beverly.

"Shouldn't you be sleeping?"

He shook his head. "I don't work tonight. I was going to get up soon anyway."

Beverly hesitated.

"Please," Mr. Maker said. "I'll rest easier if you're on your way."

Finally she agreed. "I'll call you tomorrow," she said. "Just to check in."

"I'd like that. Thank you, young lady."

She was tempted to kiss the old man on the forehead the way she did her father, but decided against it. He'd admitted to living in Marble Cove; that was probably a huge step for him. She didn't want to push things any further—at least not right now.

She said good-bye to George and started to leave but turned around abruptly. She took the photo from the front pocket of her purse and showed it to Mr. Maker. "I think you should have this. You can show it to your grandson." She placed the photo in his hand.

Mr. Maker met her eyes. "Thank you." His faded blue eyes shone. "For everything."

Chapter Twenty-Two

Tuesday evening after bath time, Shelley brushed out Emma's hair while Dan helped Aiden with his Spider-Man pajama top. Dan's phone beeped. Shelley stiffened as she watched Dan read the text.

"It's Brett." His voice fell as he spoke. "Listen to this. He says he needs help moving more stuff out of his cabin." Dan groaned.

Shelley didn't say anything.

He searched her eyes. "Do you have Detective Little's card?"

She nodded. "Or you could go knock on his door."

"I'd rather call," Dan said, standing.

"The card's on the desk," Shelley said. "In the middle cubby."

Dan went down the hall as he made the call. She couldn't hear his words, only his muffled voice. A minute later he came back into the living room. "He's going to come over. He said it's easier to talk in person."

Shelley stood, Emma in her arms. "I'll get the kids to bed."

For once, Aiden didn't protest, and Emma actually rubbed her eyes when Shelley lowered her into her crib, looking as if she might go to sleep soon.

By the time Shelley returned to the living room, Dan was in the middle of his story. Detective Little took notes and asked several clarifying questions. Finally, Dan asked if he'd been complicit somehow. "I mean, am I in trouble too?"

Detective Little's face was serious. "We'll have to see how the investigation pans out." He stood to leave. "If I have any more questions I'll call you or stop by."

Shelley didn't sleep well that night, though both her children did. She was pretty sure Dan was awake off and on too. They didn't talk, though. She felt as if they were both holding their breath, afraid to say a word.

In the morning, Dan got ready for work as normal, but as he was eating his bowl of cold cereal, his phone rang. From Dan's side of the conversation, Shelley could tell it was his supervisor calling to say there wasn't any work for the day.

"What about tomorrow?" Dan pushed his bowl toward the middle of the table. There was a pause. "Okay, thanks. I'll wait for your call. Bye." He flipped the phone shut.

Shelley's heart sank. Fewer hours meant less money, which meant more unpaid bills. Thankfully, Margaret had paid Dan yesterday. The money would help even more than they'd anticipated.

Dan rubbed his face with his hands. "Do you think this has to do with the investigation?"

"No," Shelley said. "It's coincidental, that's all." But she wasn't convinced herself.

Aiden turned *Blue's Clues* up louder in the living room. She'd let them choose a video to watch after they'd finished their breakfast. Dan stood and headed toward the front door. It took her a second to realize that someone was knocking. Her heart raced. It was too early for a visitor.

Dan swung the door open. There stood Detective Little. Shelley felt as if the wind had been knocked out of her. Had Dan been lying all along? Was the officer here to arrest him?

"Got a minute?" The detective looked unshaven and as if he hadn't slept all night.

"Sure," Dan said, stepping outside.

Detective Little nodded to Shelley. "You too, please."

She glanced at the kids. The show had another ten minutes. "Aiden, we're going to be on the porch. Come get me if you need me."

He nodded solemnly and Emma imitated him perfectly.

They stepped out into the chilly morning.

"Thanks for the tip," Detective Little said to Dan. "It was just what I needed. We ended up with enough evidence to make the arrests."

Dan's hand went to his forehead. He raked his fingers through his sandy hair. "Did you make all the arrests already or do you have more to make?"

Shelley's heart raced faster.

"Why do you ask?" The detective crossed his arms, and his light jacket made a crinkly sound.

Dan opened his mouth, but no sound came out.

Detective Little smiled. "Are you asking if I'm going to arrest you for being number than a hake?"

Shelley crossed her arms. *Number than a hake* was one of those Mainer sayings that only made sense to people from Maine—it meant foolish.

"Nope," Detective Little said. "Brett Leburt confirmed your story. He said you knew nothing and saw nothing. And I didn't tell him I got the tip from you. They came in on the beach in a rowboat. I met them there. They thought I was just snooping around and happened to get lucky. So as long you keep mum, no one is ever going to know."

Dan sighed deeply. "Thank you."

"Just be more discerning about extra work you take on, okay? Make sure it's aboveboard. If you have any suspicions, I'd be happy to advise you."

Dan nodded.

"Thank you," Shelley whispered.

"How much time do you think Brett will get?" There was an edge to Dan's voice.

"It's too early to have any idea. He's just a pawn in all of this too. There's a big electronic smuggling ring out of Bangor that's moving stuff down to Boston and New York. Brett's talking, though, so chances are the whole thing will be coming down in no time." With that, Detective Little said he was headed down to the station to fill out his report. "Thanks again, Dan. You did the right thing."

As Detective Little headed to his pickup, Diane appeared, coming up from the beach with Rocky. She called out a hello to the detective and then to both of them. She stopped at the end of their walkway. By the expression on her face, Shelley knew her friend was concerned. She gave her a thumbs-up, and Diane's face relaxed a little. Shelley waved to her friend and said she'd see her soon.

As soon as Shelley followed Dan into the entryway, he had his arms around her. "I'm so sorry," he said, holding her tight.

"It's okay. You didn't know."

"I should have figured it out."

"Next time you will."

"There won't be a next time."

The credits were rolling for *Blue's Clues*, and the kids both started toward them. Emma had her thumb in her mouth and was dragging her ratty blanket.

Aiden had his blanket tied around his neck like a cape over his Spider-Man pajamas. "What's wrong?" Aiden wrapped his legs around Dan's knees.

Dan lifted him up, and Shelley bent down for Emma, lifting her next to Aiden, between her and Dan. "I'm just thankful, that's all," Dan said. "For God protecting us."

Aiden tilted his head a little. "This is like a familyship."

"A what?" Shelley said.

"You know, instead of a spaceship, it's a familyship." He grinned.

Emma took her thumb out of her mouth and smiled too.

"Oh, I like that," Shelley said, as Dan wrapped one arm around her and Emma and drew Aiden closer with his other. Spaceships and familyships. "We're the Bauer Familyship," she said. "Who knows where we're going—but hopefully we'll arrive together."

"Since you're home today," Shelley added, "I'll be able to finish my baking."

"Perfect," Dan said. "If you need us, check the front yard. You might even catch us between flights. Maybe you can join us."

"We better go get dressed!" Aiden said.

He and Emma wiggled down to the floor and ran down the hall as Dan leaned in and stole a kiss from Shelley.

⋆　　⋆　　⋆

"Any questions?" Margaret asked Diane, glancing around the gallery. Even Margaret thought the paintings looked gorgeous against the newly painted walls and haint blue ceiling.

"No. I've got it. I'll call if anything big comes up."

"Thanks so much," Margaret said. "I really appreciate it." She gave Diane a quick hug.

Just then, Adelaide came into the gallery. "We're here!" she announced. "Out front. Dad told me to come get you." Adelaide had on a lime green short-sleeve top, pink capris, and low-heel but strappy sandals.

Diane *oohed* and *ahhed* over her outfit. "You look picture-perfect!"

Adelaide beamed.

After they said their good-byes, Adelaide called out to Diane, "See you Friday!"

"Okay," Diane answered but she had a confused look on her face. Margaret tried not to cringe as she hustled Adelaide out the door.

It was an almost two-hour trip to Acadia Park. The reunion officially started at five, which gave Margaret, Allan, and Adelaide an extra half hour buffer time.

As Margaret crawled into the front seat of her van, Allan asked if she had the name tags.

"Uh-huh," she answered. "Did you grab the cooler?"

"Affirmative."

She'd made potato salad, a veggie tray, and chocolate pie. Beth was picking up chicken for the entire group, and everyone else was bringing side dishes and desserts too. There had been an e-mail message to the whole crew last night from Buddy, saying how much he looked forward to seeing everyone. Margaret still didn't believe he'd actually show up, but if he did, she didn't know what she would do. Just the thought of seeing him made her queasy.

As Allan drove out of town and up the coastal highway, she gazed out over the vast Atlantic and at the scruffy trees leaning inland, blown practically sideways by the relentless winter winds and occasional hurricane. But they were still standing, holding on to their rocky foundations by their tenacious, gnarly roots.

That was how Margaret felt. She thought about Sunday's sermon. *God wants us to trust Him with every area of our lives,* the pastor had told the congregation. *The future. The present. And the past. And with people who have harmed you...*

She thought about her miraculous rescue by that stranger on the beach. Surely that alone should be enough to make her more willing to trust Him with her present. God had seen her flailing in the water, and He had sent someone, maybe her personal angel, to save her.

She was doing her best to trust Him with the future, Adelaide's future, in particular. But trusting Him with the past seemed the hardest. She was afraid it was going to pop back up and bite her again.

She remembered Buddy's punches when they were little. He would hit her in the arm, saying he was just playing. But when none of the adults were watching, he'd smack her in the back too. He'd also trip her, and one time he shoved her out of his tree house.

She remembered now, almost sixty years later, grabbing for the rope ladder as she fell, but to no avail. She'd landed on her back, the wind whooshing out of her. With no breath in her, she couldn't even cry. She could only gasp and gasp as Buddy laughed. Her mother found her that way, and then Buddy had acted all concerned and had hustled down the ladder, saying Margaret had just fallen.

"Boy, she sure is clumsy," he'd said to her mother, a look of concern on his face. Buddy was so charming that everyone believed him. But it wasn't like she tried very hard to tell her mother what was going on. Back then, kids weren't taught about bullying. She'd thought it was somehow her fault and that she needed to deal with it on her own.

Even now, Margaret wasn't sure what had made him so mean. But she couldn't imagine what someone like him could do to someone as vulnerable as Adelaide, given the chance, even though he was well into his sixties now. She closed her eyes. It felt as if she couldn't trust God with the past and protect herself and others at the same time. She had to stay vigilant, that was for sure, for both her sake and her daughter's.

At some point she must've fallen asleep, because the next thing she knew, Allan had turned into Acadia State Park. "Wow, that was fast."

Allan reached over and patted her hand. "You were tired."

"I guess so." She glanced in the backseat. Adelaide was wide awake, looking out the window.

They wound around in the park to the group picnic site.

"Pull up by the tables," she told Allan. "We can unload, and you can go park the van."

As they rounded the corner, she spotted a big diesel pickup truck idling in front of the pathway to the shelter. A man was unloading folding chairs. She squinted, positive it wasn't Buddy. The man didn't have a beer belly, and he had a bounce in his step. As Allan came to a stop, the man pulled an ice chest from the truck.

Margaret stepped from the car, staring.

The man smiled at her. "Margaret? Is that you, cuz?"

Cuz. A wave of nausea swept over her. She hurried toward the shelter.

Her cousin Beth started to wave. She wore peach-colored shorts that hit just above her knees and a short-sleeved sweater set. Her bottle-blonde hair was cut in a bob. "Great to see you, Margaret!" she called out. "Where are the name tags?"

Margaret held up the paper bag in her hand. "Right here." When she reached the table, she gave Beth a quick hug. She opened the name tags and spread them out on the table, along with two permanent markers.

Beth glanced toward Buddy. "Isn't it great? He's clean and sober. The rumor is he went through some wild experience that shocked him into it."

Margaret's eyes widened. Could it be true? She looked back toward the truck. Buddy was talking with Allan, and Adelaide was listening to the two of them. Margaret took a deep breath. "I'd better go help unload."

By the time she reached the car, Buddy seemed ready to try again with her. He stepped forward. "I was happy to see you were coming," he said. "Honestly, that's one of the reasons I decided to come. I wanted to have a chance to talk with you."

Margaret must have looked as confused as she felt.

He lowered his voice. "I don't want to make this more uncomfortable than it probably already is. It's just that I wanted to say that...I know I was horribly unkind to you growing up."

She nodded.

"And after we were grown too."

She nodded again, this time more adamantly.

"And I wanted to apologize."

She stopped nodding and held his gaze.

"I'm sorry," he said, his eyes moist. "I hope in time you can forgive me."

Allan and Adelaide were standing just a few feet away. She cleared her throat. Never in a million years had she expected this. It was as if she'd had the wind knocked out of her again. "Forgive you?" she stammered.

"In time," he said.

Could she forgive him? He was admitting that what he'd done was wrong. That should change something in her. And it wasn't that she wanted any harm to come to him. Still, she didn't know if she could forgive him, just like that.

She turned away.

"So be it," Buddy said, matter-of-factly. Even though her back was to him, he said, "Adelaide has grown into a lovely young woman."

Margaret wanted to believe he was being genuine, but he'd tricked her so many times before. She felt even more on edge now than before.

Buddy helped unload their van. As he carried their cooler, he walked beside Adelaide to the tables.

Allan, carrying the picnic basket, caught up with Margaret. "You okay?"

She shot Allan a look. "My head is spinning."

Adelaide laughed at something Buddy said.

Margaret hadn't felt so flustered in a long time.

Over the next hour, Buddy orchestrated the games for the young people. Margaret kept an eye on him as she helped set out the food. He'd recruited Adelaide as his helper, and she was enjoying herself immensely. Allan stayed close by their daughter and stepped in to help when he was needed.

When all seventy-two of them gathered for dinner—it turned out a midweek reunion was a great idea—Beth asked Allan to say the blessing, and he did. Afterward Margaret held back, letting the older relatives go first and then the younger. Allan went through the line with Adelaide. By the time Margaret was ready, Buddy and Beth were just in front of her. It looked as if they'd waited too.

"So," Beth said to Buddy, "rumor has it you've been clean and sober now for…?"

"Five years," Buddy said.

"And just how did that come about?" Beth asked, taking a plate off the stack. The line ahead had backed up, and they were standing still. Margaret stayed close enough to her cousins to hear.

"It's really a two-part story," Buddy said. "First, one thing happened and then another. The first thing landed me in the second, which was Alcoholics Anonymous. By the grace of God, I'm living one day—one moment—at a time."

"I see." Beth picked up a napkin and cutlery. She looked at Buddy quickly. "And what was the first thing?"

"Well, it's a little unbelievable." He grabbed a plate and took a deep breath. "I don't tell this story very often." Margaret was sure he wasn't aware of her behind him. "Several years ago, I was headed down to Portland for a business meeting the next day. My plan was to hit the bars that night—I was drinking pretty heavily back then. I'd try to quit, but nothing would work, and I'd be back at it again, feeling as defeated as ever. When I reached Marble Cove

I decided to stop for old times' sake. I parked above the boardwalk and headed down to the beach, by the rocks, toward the lighthouse."

Beth nodded.

"I took off my shoes and jacket and put them on a log, and I rolled up my slacks." Buddy was following Beth now as the line moved slowly. "Walking toward the lighthouse a ways, I saw something thrashing out in the water. At first I thought it was a hurt seal, but then I realized it was a person."

Beth looked back toward him, her eyes wide.

"Without thinking, I ran into the water, but the waves were churning and high. A big wind was blowing in. The person kept going under, over and over. I was certain I couldn't save her."

"It was a woman?"

"Yeah," Buddy said. "She was wearing a cap and an old lady swimsuit."

Margaret gasped, but Buddy didn't notice.

"Anyway, I don't know why, but for the first time in a long time I cared more about another person than I did myself. I begged God to help me. I said if He did, I'd go to AA and stick it out. That I'd do whatever it took. Weird, I was out there in the water, but I couldn't find her. She'd gone under. But right when I prayed, a wave pushed her up, without me moving an inch. She was right in front of me. I grabbed and caught the back of her suit." He chuckled. "If that wasn't strange enough, I swear, to this day, a beacon flashed from the lighthouse right then." He shook his head.

There was a look of disbelief on Beth's face. It matched the surprise in Margaret's heart.

Buddy continued. "The woman had swallowed a bunch of water, but she was sputtering by the time I got her on the sand. A man and a woman came running toward us, and I figured she'd be okay then."

He continued. "I was so overcome with emotion, I didn't feel like I could cope. I ran to my truck and thought about stopping for a drink. Then I remembered what I'd prayed—and that God had answered. The storm blew in full force then, and boy, was it an apple shaker. It started to thunder and lightning, I kid you not, like God Himself was there." He laughed. "I found an AA meeting in Marble Cove that was going on right then, and I went, soaking wet. I've been going ever since."

Beth stopped at the salads and turned toward him again. "Buddy, you're pulling my leg, aren't you? Just like when we were little?"

"No. I wouldn't lie about this sort of thing. Scout's honor."

"I though you dropped out of the Scouts."

He cocked his head. "You're right. But I wouldn't lie about this, honest."

Beth shook her head in a playful way. The line was moving now, and she stepped to the chicken.

Margaret narrowed the gap to Buddy. "I overhead your story." Her voice shook.

He turned toward her, meeting her eyes. "It's the truth. I promise."

"I believe you." Margaret felt clammy all over. "Every word."

Buddy shook his head, a confused expression on his face. "Why would you, if Beth doesn't?"

"Because I was that woman."

His eyes grew wide. "W-what?"

"I'm the woman who you rescued." The words tumbled out of her mouth. "I had no idea, not in a million years, that it was you." She put a hand against the table to steady herself.

He reached out, his napkin in his hand, and touched her shoulder. She grabbed his hand and squeezed it, tears welling in her eyes. Buddy didn't answer, but the tears streaming down his face said it all. In that moment, Margaret was sure Buddy had changed into a person she could trust. Even more, she knew she could trust God—with her present, future, *and* past.

"I forgive you," she stammered. "And...thank you."

CHAPTER TWENTY-THREE

Beverly sat in her alcove on Friday afternoon glancing at her watch every few minutes. They needed to leave for their special appointment by two thirty, but that was still half an hour away. Mrs. Peabody was going to go with them, but she'd gone home to change her dress. Her father was in the library, probably dozing. He'd given up on doing yard work again after their second trip to visit Mr. Maker. That was for the better: his balance wasn't good enough to garden by himself anymore.

Mr. Maker, on the other hand, was regaining his. He'd bruised his knee pretty badly, and although he'd have to be off his feet for a couple of weeks, he would recover. At least that's what he'd told her two days ago. She'd told him she'd call again and check in. She glanced at her watch. She might as well do it now.

He answered on the second ring. When she broached the subject of working in his yard next week, he said he had plenty of help.

"Your neighbors?" she asked, a little disappointed that he didn't need her. "Or friends?"

"Yes and yes," he said. "In fact, Celia's here today. She's been harvesting. She's getting ready to make some of my regular deliveries."

"Oh." Beverly forced herself to smile, hoping it would make her voice cheerier. "That's great." But then she smiled for real. "Maybe you could come out here sometime with Celia. Visit Marble Cove. See the lighthouse again."

She was always amazed at how one could sense tension over the phone. He didn't answer.

"Maybe in a month or two," she added.

"No, I don't think so," he said. There was another awkward pause.

On a whim, Beverly went for it. "Isn't there something you can tell me about the lighthouse? Could you share just one memory you have of it?"

After a long moment, he asked, "Have you explored all around the lighthouse?"

She pushed back from her desk. "We were able to go inside once."

"I don't mean on the inside," he said. "On the outside. The east side of the building."

"What's there?" Beverly asked.

There was a long pause and then the sound of Mr. Maker exhaling. "Sometimes I'm not sure what is there. Maybe it was all a dream."

"I'll take a look," Beverly said, wishing the man would come to Marble Cove with her. Her phone beeped. She had another call coming in, probably work. "I need to go," she said. "Take care. Please tell Celia hello. Oh, and I'll stop by and see you sometime soon."

The incoming call was Margaret, and her voice was a little desperate. "I don't know what's got into Diane. She's in some kind of funk. Have you ever known her not to agree to something? As planned, I asked her to come by and help me hang a couple of paintings, and she said no."

"Oh dear." Beverly stood.

"This could ruin everything. Beverly, could you ask her to go for a walk or something? And then, you know, swing by here."

"I could try." Beverly didn't like the idea of trying to manipulate Diane. She was just too nice and sweet to try to trick.

"You have to do it. Shelley can't. I can't. I'd have to close the gallery. And besides, our special guests are due to arrive any minute. It won't work if you can't get her here."

"I'll see what I can do. I'll call you if she refuses." If that was the case, they'd probably have to tell her what was going on to get her to cooperate.

She hurried over to Mrs. Peabody's house. The woman came to the door carrying her purse. Obviously she was ready to go. "Can you get Father over there by yourself?" Beverly asked. "I've been put in charge of Diane."

The older woman stood up straighter. "Do you think the mister can walk that far?"

"There's a cane in the hall closet. Have him use that. Later, I'll run home and come back with my car."

"In that case, we'll manage."

Beverly thanked her and hurried on down to Diane's. Her father would take the plan better coming from Mrs. Peabody than from her. In no time, she was knocking on her friend's door. But no one answered. She knocked again and listened closely. She couldn't hear a thing. Not even Rocky barking.

"Diane!" she called out as she tried the doorknob. It was locked. She pulled out her cell phone and called Diane's numbers, first her house phone, which she could hear ring inside, and then her cell. No one answered.

Beverly headed back to the sidewalk and looked up and down the street, but she didn't see Diane anywhere. Maybe she'd gone for a walk on the beach after Margaret had called. Or maybe she was headed to the gallery after all. Shelley's car was already gone, but Dan's truck was in the driveway. She decided to check with him to see if he'd seen Diane.

A minute later she was inside their house. Dan hadn't seen her, but Aiden had. "With Rocky. They were headed out for a walk."

"Which way?" Beverly asked.

He pointed toward the ocean.

"Great! Thanks so much." She hurried toward the door.

"See you in a few minutes," Dan said.

"Hopefully," she answered, rushing outside.

She squinted in the bright light, wishing she'd grabbed her dark glasses. The afternoon sun shining off the sand was nearly blinding. She could see the lighthouse in the distance.

The lighthouse. Mr. Maker *had* lived there. And there was something on the outside, on the east side, perhaps, that he remembered. She longed to go look. But she couldn't right now. Maybe later in the evening.

She turned toward town. There were several families on the beach, but she didn't see a woman and a dog. She looked back toward the lighthouse, squinting this time. The tide was out.

There, by the rocks in the tide pools, someone was bent down. Beverly started down the pathway. The figure stood up, and then a dog bounded away and back toward the person. It had to be Diane and Rocky. Beverly started jogging, trying to look as nonchalant as possible, watching as her friend bent back down.

* * *

Diane poked her finger at the sea anemone, delighting in the feel of the creature grabbing on to her. She sighed. She was a lonely person indeed to be thrilled by the touch of a sea creature.

She hadn't written another thing on her new story idea since last Friday night. She was avoiding her friends, hurt they hadn't invited her to their secret gathering. Would publishing a novel mean losing all her friends?

Justin had called the day before and said his flight had been delayed, and he wasn't sure when he'd be flying home. He hadn't mentioned the novel, and he shouldn't have. It wasn't like she could expect her family and friends to want to talk about it all the time.

She hadn't heard from Jessica, not even a text, for over a week. She stood straight again and rubbed her lower back. Maybe Jessica just didn't care.

Rocky tiptoed over the rocks, a stick in his mouth. Diane took it and flung it out into the sand, straining her elbow as she did. "Oh good grief," she muttered. "I'm a mess."

Rocky ran in an arc, heading back toward town.

"Come on, boy!" she called. Off to the north a figure was jogging toward them. Diane shook her head. It was Beverly, of course, waving. But then Beverly stopped and held her cell phone to her ear. That was odd. She didn't think Beverly usually took her phone with her when she ran. And she didn't seem to be in jogging clothes. As Beverly neared, Diane heard her say, "Okay. See you in a few. Bye." And then, "Diane! How are you?"

Diane flopped her hand around in a so-so gesture.

"That was Margaret on the phone. She needs some help in her gallery. I was going to head her way. Want to come along?"

Diane shook her head. "I'm headed to the lighthouse."

Beverly's gaze fell beyond Diane, to the point. "Looking for some inspiration?"

Diane didn't answer. *More like comfort.*

"How about if I walk with you a little ways?"

"Isn't Margaret waiting?"

"I'll run back. She'll be okay." Beverly fell in step with Diane but didn't say anything more.

"Is Margaret rearranging things?" Diane asked.

"Hmm?"

"You said she needs help in the gallery. But on Wednesday the paintings all looked fine. She's rearranging, then?"

"Oh, I don't know. Maybe she sold a couple and needs to balance things out."

That made sense. Wednesday seemed like a long time ago. It was lonely being in the gallery without Margaret. Diane didn't get lonely writing, but she didn't like doing most other endeavors by herself. Speaking of writing, she hadn't asked Beverly about her visit with Mr. Maker. She perked up a little as she asked for the details.

Beverly told her about Sunday's visit, Monday's accident, and the phone call in which she'd learned that Celia was over at his house.

"Wow," Diane said. "That's amazing. I was so taken with Celia when I met her. What a nice friend for Mr. Maker. Or do you think they'll turn out to be more than friends?"

"I have no idea," Beverly said. "But I think either way, they're both going to be happier."

Diane used to tell her kids that in order to have a friend one had to be a friend. She'd also told both of them at the beginning of their freshman years that all it took was one good friend to make all the difference during their high school years. She supposed the same thing held true in the golden years too. She sighed.

They were halfway between the rocks and the lighthouse, but Diane stopped in her tracks. Here she had three good friends, and she wasn't acting like a friend at all.

"We should go help Margaret," she said. "I've been moping around long enough." She squared her shoulders and pivoted around. Rocky nuzzled her hand, a stick in his mouth. She took it and lobbed it forward. "Let's go."

"I was hoping you'd say that."

*   *   *

Beverly pushed through the door of the gallery and held it for Diane while Rocky settled down on the sidewalk. The front gallery looked like it always did, and Beverly stepped ahead, leading the way to the back gallery.

Beverly had just a moment to take in the scene in the second room. Her father and Mrs. Peabody were sitting in chairs. Dan stood with Emma in his arms, and Aiden stood beside the table that was covered with his mother's confectionary creations. Shelley had a wide smile on her face while Margaret had a look of absolute relief. Allan and Adelaide were next to Dan, and Detective Fred Little and his wife Cindy stood by the punch bowl.

"Margaret," Diane called. "Are you back here?" She came into the second gallery and came to an abrupt stop. "Oh my!"

"Surprise!" they all shouted.

That was when Beverly noticed the two young people in the corner. The young man's blond hair was in a buzz cut, and he was tanned, tall, and muscular. The young woman had shoulder-length brown hair and a willowy build, much like Diane's. They stood side by side under the sign that Margaret had made that read: *Congratulations, Diane. We're All So Proud of You!* followed by a drawing of a book.

"Oh! What is going on?" Diane cried, her hand flying to her chest. She looked around the room, a smile spreading across her face. But she froze when her eyes reached the corner. "Jessica? Justin?" She flew toward them, and they met her in the middle of the room.

Diane's shoulders were shaking, and Beverly wasn't sure if she was crying or laughing. She finally decided she was doing both. Tears stung Beverly's own eyes. Seeing Diane with her grown children was bittersweet. Beverly rejoiced for her friend but grieved for her own losses, both what was and what would never be, acutely.

Diane stepped back as she held on to her children's hands. "I didn't think you'd even left Dubai yet," she said to her son.

His brown eyes twinkled. "I caught a flight. Jessie picked me up at the airport."

"And we drove straight here," Jessica said.

"And you've been keeping this from me all this time?"

They both nodded. "That's why *I* called last," Justin said. "We both know I'm a better liar than Jess." He laughed, and Diane squeezed his hand harder. She turned toward Margaret and Shelley and Beverly, shaking her head. "Thank you."

"We've been planning the party for a couple of weeks," Shelley said, gushing. "Since your agent contacted you."

"Shelley's been baking up a storm." Margaret gestured toward the table.

"I know." Diane laughed, wiping away tears. "I just had no idea it was for me."

"Isn't it great?" Beverly said. "A published author right here in Marble Cove!"

They all cheered.

"Oh, but wait." Diane patted the air with her hands, trying to get them to calm down. "Nothing's official yet. I've decided I want to accept the deal, but my agent is still hashing out the contract with the publisher. She said it could take months before I sign anything that—"

"Oh, pish-posh," Margaret said. "We all know it's going to work out. Don't we?"

They cheered again.

Diane didn't think it was worth it to press the point anymore. Better just to enjoy what they'd done for her. She turned toward Beverly. "Thank you."

Beverly swiped at her own eyes. "You didn't make it easy."

"I know." Diane was wiping her own eyes now. "I was feeling so sorry for myself, thinking you all didn't want to hear about my book anymore. And all the time you were doing this!" She looked at her hands, which were shaking. "I think I learned a valuable lesson."

Beverly gave her a hug.

Diane turned back toward the group, pulling her children along and introducing them to each of her friends. Beverly watched for a few minutes and then headed over to the table, filling plates of Shelley's goodies for her father and Mrs. Peabody.

The party lasted for over an hour. People visited merrily, moving from one group to another. Diane's children fit right in, asking questions about Marble Cove and telling stories from when they'd visited as children. When Beverly's father said he was tired, Allan said he'd give him and Mrs. Peabody a ride home so Beverly could stay and help clean up. A few at a time, the other guests, including Dan and the kids, left too.

Beverly urged Diane to go on home with her children, but Justin cleared his throat. "Actually, Jess challenged me to a game of miniature golf—eighteen holes."

"Go with them, Diane," Beverly said.

Diane and her kids burst out laughing.

"Mom's not allowed," Jessica said. "She has a reputation for flying clubs."

"And wild balls," Justin said.

"And falling in the little pool by the windmill," Jessica said.

"I did not."

Jessica raised her eyebrows. "You almost did. More than once."

"I did get my shoes wet a couple of times." Diane sighed. "It's true. I was the comic relief for a few years until the kids hit middle school. Then I was the colossal embarrassment."

"We're not embarrassed anymore," Jessica said sweetly.

"Just concerned." Justin's eyes lit up. "For everyone's safety."

After the two left, assuring Diane they'd meet her at the cottage in an hour, Beverly told the other women about what Mr. Maker had said about the east side of the lighthouse.

"Let's go!" Diane said. "Before the kids are done."

Shelley said she'd gather up the leftovers when they returned. She sent Dan a quick text saying she'd be home after a while. Mrs. Peabody had already said she'd fix dinner, so Beverly didn't need to rush back.

"I'll just leave Allan a message," Margaret said, picking up the phone.

★   ★   ★

Once they hit the beach, Rocky ran ahead, tearing through the sand and darting in and out of the incoming waves. The women walked at a brisk pace. Diane thanked them over and over until Margaret burst out with, "Enough already! It was our pleasure."

"We are so excited for you," Shelley said. "And it was so fun to plan the party."

"You certainly did a good job!" Diane sounded like her old self. Positive, enthusiastic, and encouraging.

Beverly realized she felt "in the moment." She was enjoying the women and walking down the beach. For the first time in a long while she wasn't thinking about the past. She smiled. There she went again—thinking about the past.

But Margaret's story about her family reunion pulled Beverly back. As she finished the story, Margaret stopped just past the rocks and the others gathered around her.

"It was right about here where Buddy saved my life." She looked at the other three women, one by one. "Can you believe it? God used the person who had hurt me the most to save me, and bring me around to believing in Him. And then He also used that action to change Buddy's life." She shook her head. "And I didn't think I could trust God with the past." She started walking again and then burst out laughing. "Here I am, sixty-seven, and He's still changing me. Maybe because I gave Him such a late start."

Beverly fell behind the others a little. Could *she* trust God with the past? She wasn't sure she'd ever be able to change the way Margaret had.

Diane turned to wait for her. "You're usually leading the pack."

"Oh, I was just thinking about things."

"Like Margaret?"

Beverly nodded. "And Mr. Maker."

"Maybe his friendship with Celia will be what he needs to help him get through." Rocky dropped a stick at Diane's feet, and she picked it up and threw it with ease.

"Maybe." Beverly couldn't imagine carrying a heavy hurt for over seventy years. Five years had been long enough. But she still wasn't ready to share her own story.

Diane kept throwing the stick for Rocky as they walked, hurtling it closer and closer to the lighthouse. When they reached it, the dog tore around it, completing the circle a couple of times.

"Whatever Mr. Maker was talking about, if it exists, he said it was on the east side," Beverly said, leading the way.

There were several thick bushes up against the foundation. They looked ancient; the bark and thick trunks appeared practically petrified.

Beverly slipped between the foliage and the lighthouse, making her way down the foundation. A gnarly branch from a bush poked her, making her gasp as she wiggled away from it. She went to her hands and knees. Maybe there was a trap door in the dirt that led to a tunnel. Or maybe, as a boy, Mr. Maker had stashed his favorite toy somewhere between the lighthouse and the ocean.

"Found anything yet?" Margaret asked from the other side of the bushes.

Beverly started to answer but stopped herself. There were flakes of white paint ahead in the dirt as if someone had been chipping at the outside of the lighthouse. She crawled forward.

"What is it?" Diane peered over the bushes.

"I don't—" Beverly stopped. There was a panel of wood with a knob and a hook on it about three feet high in the side of the lighthouse. Two hinges on one side had been painted over. She yanked on the knob. "I found something. A hidden door, maybe."

Diane stepped between two of the bushes and knelt beside Beverly. "Someone could come in and out through here and then go up and flash the light. They wouldn't have to go through the front door at all."

"You're right," Beverly said. "If they can get this open." She yanked on the hook as hard as she could. "Because I can't." They were one step closer to solving the mystery. Someone was entering through the secret door and flashing some sort of light. It wasn't a supernatural mystery after all, as Beverly had known all along. If only she could get the door open.

As the other women gathered around, Beverly pulled again, but still nothing happened. Margaret took a turn next. She couldn't get it to budge, either. Diane had a little knife on her Swiss Army key chain, and she tried prying through the paint around the latch and hinges, but that didn't work.

Diane stood. "Well, we definitely know there's a way in and out of the lighthouse besides the front door."

"We can come back with tools," Shelley said. "I bet we can pry it open." The other women agreed.

Beverly stepped back from the shrubs and stared at the door. Mr. Maker had been correct about there being something on the east side of the lighthouse. But why had he been so unsure of exactly what it was?

Just as the lighthouse attracted her and her friends, it seemed to repulse him. While the mysterious beacon of the present called to the four women, the beacon of the past flashed memories so painful that Mr. Maker refused to return to Marble Cove. She couldn't imagine.

Or maybe she could. She certainly knew that shadowy areas of a person's life, even if avoided, were still a powerful force.

As the other women stepped away and Margaret led the way toward home, Beverly felt compelled to say a quick prayer, asking for healing for Mr. Maker. And then for herself. Shelley came alongside her and they walked together. Beverly breathed another prayer of thanks for the friendships she'd found in Marble Cove.

"I have to tell you a funny thing Aiden said," Shelley announced to the group. "He called Dan, Emma, himself, and me a 'familyship.'"

"Ooh, I like it," Diane said. "Like a spaceship, right?"

Shelley nodded. "But it got me thinking about another word. *Friendship*. And how it also 'transports' us—just like spaceships and families."

Beverly let that soak in for a minute. "Wow."

All the women stopped walking and moved closer to each other. It was Diane who put an arm around Shelley and then one around Beverly. "That's exactly what I realized here on the beach, with Beverly, before I got my sorry self over to the gallery. Although my revelation wasn't as eloquent as Shelley's."

They all laughed, and Margaret stepped closer and completed the circle, drawing all of them together.

"I'm so thankful for this friendship," Beverly said.

The women hugged as Rocky ran around them barking.

"Speaking of ships, um, familyships," Diane said, "I'd better get back to my cottage. For once, I get to cook dinner for someone besides myself."

Tonight they all, even Beverly, had families to return to. Her family of two—three, with Mrs. Peabody—counted.

Beverly turned to look at the lighthouse one last time. The evening light bounced off the glass and glimmered against the sea. For a second she thought she saw a flash, and it made her smile. With that flash, she made a decision.

She turned back and increased her stride, quickly catching up with her friends. She might not be able to imagine carrying a lifetime of hurt, but there was one thing she could imagine.

Calling Marble Cove home—for good.

ABOUT THE AUTHOR

Leslie Gould is a best-selling and award-winning author of numerous novels, including five in Guideposts' Home to Heather Creek series and two in Stories from Hope Haven. She received her Master of Fine Arts in creative writing from Portland State University, and besides writing for the last two decades, she's also held the positions of museum curator and magazine editor. She lives in Portland, Oregon, with her four children. Her husband is currently deployed to Afghanistan. Please visit Leslie at www.lesliegould.com.

A Conversation with Leslie Gould

Q. How did you research a setting in Maine, clear across the country from your home in Oregon?

A. I drew on a trip to Maine years ago. Thankfully I keep a detailed journal of nearly every trip I go on, which has paid off more than once. I also gathered information from people who have spent more time in Maine than I have, collected information from the state's tourism department, and watched videos and read accounts online.

Q. Do you involve your family in researching your books?

A. I do. For *Beacon's Call*, we visited a lighthouse on Vashon Island west of Seattle, just days before my husband left for Afghanistan. I took a gazillion photos, which I looked at over and over as I wrote. Later that same month, my daughters and I also spent spring break on the Oregon Coast with their aunts and uncles and cousins, walking along the beach and visiting a lighthouse, as I was working on the novel. Obviously Oregon's coast isn't Maine's, but the two states are at similar latitudes, and both lighthouses I researched inspired me.

Q. *Who were your favorite characters to write about in Beacon's Call?*

A. I adore the four friends, of course. I have a couple of different groups of women in my life, and when I wrote about the friendships in the novel I thought of my own friends.

However, I especially enjoyed writing the scenes with the children in the story. I incorporated the borrowed idea of a "familyship" that my friend Kate's son Lucas came up with a few years ago. I passed it on to Shelley's son Aiden in the story. That inclusion brought me a lot of joy.

Q. *What advice would you offer to aspiring writers?*

A. First of all, write, write, and then write some more. Even if you can only write one page a day, do that. But do it every day. (In a year, you'll have a novel written!) Also, read books about writing. You can find them at your library, local bookstore, or online. Then find a critique group so you'll have deadlines and feedback. Once you know you can complete a project, start attending writers' conferences to learn more about the craft and to meet other writers, editors, and agents. Expect to work hard, and to find both frustration and fulfillment in the process!

Q. What do you hope readers take away from reading your books?

A. I hope when a reader finishes one of my novels she knows she is not alone. I want her to know there are other women that share her struggles, her joys, and her heartbreaks. Including me.

Baking with Shelley

Dan's Favorite Lemon Cake

¾ cup and 1 tablespoon lemon juice, divided (Use fresh-squeezed lemon for the best flavor!)

3 cups all-purpose flour, plus flour for dusting pan

¾ cup and 2 tablespoons milk

2 sticks melted butter

2 cups sugar

4 large eggs

½ teaspoon baking powder

½ teaspoon baking soda

Heaping ¼ teaspoon salt

½ cup chopped walnuts (optional)

Add 1 teaspoon lemon extract to wet ingredients for more intense lemon flavor (optional)

Preheat oven to 350 degrees.

Combine milk and ¼ cup plus 1 tablespoon lemon juice in a small bowl. Set aside.

Prepare Bundt pan by greasing it and dusting lightly with flour, and then turn it upside down and tap lightly to remove excess flour. In a large mixing bowl, cream butter and sugar. Add eggs, blending until smooth. Add the milk mixture plus

½ cup lemon juice and lemon extract into the mixing bowl and blend.

Using a separate bowl, mix together dry ingredients (flour, baking powder, baking soda, and salt). Add them into the wet ingredients, blending together just until smooth. Stir in walnuts, if using.

Pour batter into Bundt pan. Bake for fifty to sixty minutes or until a toothpick comes out clean. Cool in Bundt pan for ten minutes and then flip the cake carefully onto a cooling rack.

The glaze:
½ cup powdered sugar
3 teaspoons lemon juice
2 tablespoons butter

Combine powdered sugar, lemon, juice, and butter. Add more lemon juice if a thinner glaze is preferred. Drizzle glaze evenly over cooled cake with a spoon. Slice, serve, and enjoy!

FROM THE
GUIDEPOSTS ARCHIVES

This story by Lloyd B. Wilhide of Keymar, Maryland,
originally appeared in
the May 1982 issue of *Guideposts.*

"Ask and it shall be given you," Jesus said. I've always believed this, but never so totally as the day of the accident in 1978.

I was seventy-five years old. The grass on our 121-acre dairy farm needed cutting, so I hitched a set of mower blades to my tractor and went to work. The tractor was huge, and for added traction on our up-and-down Maryland terrain, its rear wheels were filled with five hundred pounds of fluid, and a two hundred-pound weight hung from each hub.

When I finished the job, I was on a slight uphill grade near our chicken house. I switched off the ignition and climbed down from the high seat. I was unfastening the mower blades when the tractor started moving backward.

I tried to twist around and jump up on the seat, but I didn't make it. The tractor's draw-bar hit me in the knees, knocking me flat, and the seven hundred-pound left wheel rolled over my chest and stopped on top of it. I struggled for breath. The pain was agonizing. I knew I was facing death, and I made my request.

"Please, God," I begged, "release me."

At that moment the tractor began to move.

It went forward enough to free my chest, and—to my astonishment—it moved uphill!

My dog, and then a farmhand, found me; and after six broken ribs, two fractures, and twelve days in the hospital I was back home, talking with the Maryland state trooper called to investigate the accident. "I won't try to explain it officially," he told me. "Why, a dozen men couldn't have moved that tractor off you."

Twelve men or 1,200, it didn't matter. Asking God's help did.

Read on for a sneak peek of the next exciting book in
Miracles of Marble Cove!

Autumn Light
by Dan Walsh

S tanding on the beach, just a few yards from where the
promenade deck came closest to the sand, Diane Spencer
closed her eyes and took a deep breath. This was why she'd
moved to Marble Cove. This had to be the freshest-smelling
air on God's good earth. The rush of crashing waves filled
her ears, and she couldn't help but smile. She opened her
eyes again and noticed that the sky shone with autumn light
that spoke of summer's end and fall's beginning.

It was the day after Labor Day. It should prove to be a
very big day, Diane thought.

She knew Shelley, Margaret, and Beverly would be just
as excited. She looked up at the Orlean Point lighthouse.
She was supposed to meet them fifteen minutes ago but was
running late. They're probably already there, she thought. In
just a few moments, they would all be inside the lighthouse.
But this time they wouldn't be coming through the front
door. Today, they'd get in through the *secret* door, the one
they had discovered in the lighthouse foundation a few
nights ago, after her surprise party.

As Diane climbed a narrow pathway through the rocks,
she heard voices on the other side of the lighthouse.

"Ladies, we've got to do this now. I can't wait here all day."
It was Detective Little. He was the reason the friends had had
to wait until after the Labor Day weekend to come back.

"Can't we wait a few more minutes, Detective?" That
sounded like Shelley Bauer. "Diane just called. She'll be
here any moment. We can't go in without her." Shelley was
the reason Detective Little had gotten involved in the first
place. The rest of the women had all been set to return on
Saturday with tools to pry open the secret door themselves.
Shelley had had serious misgivings that if Detective Little
found out they had gone in themselves, he might get angry.
Might even consider it trespassing.

"I'm here!" Diane dusted the sand off and walked
around the base of the lighthouse to the east side. As she
cleared the structure, she looked down a slight incline that
led to the foundation, and she saw Shelley, Margaret, Beverly,
and Detective Little. She also saw that new young policeman,
Officer Crawley, standing behind Detective Little.

"We told him you'd be here any minute," Margaret said.

"And here I am. Sorry I'm late."

"It's good to see you, Diane," Beverly said.

"Isn't this exciting?" Shelley asked.

Officer Crawley smiled and nodded at Diane.

"Hey, Diane." Detective Little was the last to greet her.
He held a crowbar in his right hand. "We're getting ready to
bust this door open." He turned to face it. "I can't believe I
let you all talk me into this."

"What's the harm, Fred?" Margaret said.

Officer Crawley held pruning shears. A pile of branches
lay off to the side. "Those were some gnarly old branches,"

he said. "It took some effort cutting through that biggest one."

"Yes," Margaret said, "they've been growing here quite a while."

"No wonder no one ever saw this door before," Shelley said.

"Well, someone knew about it," Diane said. "Do you see all those paint chips on the ground, Fred?"

"I see 'em," he said, bending down. "They're definitely the same as the trim on this door. But all that proves is someone tried to get inside. It doesn't prove they succeeded."

"They had to have succeeded," Beverly said. "How else would we have seen the lights turning on inside?"

Detective Little looked up at her but didn't answer. Facing the door again, he stood up. He wedged the edge of the crowbar between the door and the jamb, just above the knob. Then he paused. "I don't know about this."

"You don't think you can get it open?" Diane asked.

"No, I'm sure I can pry it open. It's made of wood, not stone. It's just that, once I do, I'm going to have to hire a locksmith to come back here and replace the lock. Which means I'm going to have get the city to pay for it, which means I'm going to have to do a bunch of paperwork. And worse, now that this *secret* door is exposed, I can't just leave it here unlocked when we're through. Anyone can come back here and get inside. You know how curious people are, especially kids. Look," he said, pointing.

Diane and the others looked toward the road where he pointed. A group of four boys had gathered by the edge to watch, standing beside their bikes.

"I should have figured that would happen," he said. "We need to call this off. We can come back when I can have a locksmith standing right here. You know those kids will be over here the minute we leave."

"You can't call this off, Fred," Margaret said. "Look how many days we had to wait to get you here."

"Well, Margaret, I'm afraid curiosity's going to have to take a backseat to public safety. Besides, I might be able to get the locksmith here later this afternoon. The guy I use usually gets right back with me."

"But I can't come back this afternoon," Shelley said.

"Me either," Beverly said. "Can't you get us in there now? Then after, you could post Officer Crawley by the door until the locksmith comes. He can make sure no one gets in."

"I can't have Officer Crawley standing around here all day on guard duty, he's got—"

"Detective Little?" It was Officer Crawley. "Sorry to interrupt you, sir, but can I have a word? I think I might have a solution to all this."

Detective Little looked at him, then walked away from the door. Officer Crawley followed. They stopped just out of earshot and began talking quietly.

"What do you think they're saying?" Shelley said.

"I have no idea," Diane said. "But if it gets us inside that door now, I'm all for it." She noticed Fred Little finally nod. The men walked back.

"Officer Crawley acquired a certain skill before we brought him on the force," Detective Little said, moving to the right side of the door. Diane thought she saw Officer Crawley's cheeks flush.

Crawley bent down in front of the knob. He pulled something out of his pocket and held it with both hands in front of the knob.

"What, is he going to pick the lock?" Margaret asked.

"That's right," Detective Little said.

"Isn't that against the law?" Diane said, smiling.

"Very funny," he replied. Officer Crawley stopped and looked up at his boss. "You keep going," Detective Little said. "I said it's okay. Better this than hiring the locksmith. If it works, we'll just lock it back up when we go."

Everyone stood in silence for several minutes as Officer Crawley picked away. At last, Diane heard a strong clicking sound.

"There, that should do it." Officer Crawley stood up.

"Well," Detective Little said, "see if it opens."

"It'll open." Crawley turned the doorknob and pulled a little, and the door gave way, creaking on its hinges. "There you go." He stood back.

It was pitch black inside.

"Good job." Detective Little tossed his crowbar in the grass and lifted his flashlight. "You ladies wait here. Let Officer Crawley and I check it out."

"Don't be silly," Margaret said. "We're coming right behind you. It's not like you're going to run into any monsters."

Diane laughed. It was so exciting. Detective Little walked inside, followed by Officer Crawley, then the ladies in single file.

Diane's first impression was that it looked more like a tunnel than a room. It was maybe thirty feet long, angling upward.

"Where's this thing go?" Margaret said. "Can you see?"

"It looks like it goes nowhere," Detective Little said. "It just dead ends up ahead."

"Do you think maybe it's just an old storage room, sir?" Officer Crawley said. "Look at all these shelves along the top half of this one wall. They run the whole length."

"Maybe."

Diane also noticed what looked like a workbench under the shelves, with more shelves below that. "This can't be just a storage room," she said. "There has to be a way into the lighthouse itself from here. How else could someone get inside?"

Detective Little stopped, which caused them all to stop. "Well, Diane, look for yourself." He shined the flashlight forward. "It's just a wall, a paneled wood wall."

"Say, Fred, shine that light back up near the top again." It was Margaret. He did. "See that, just along the top below the ceiling? Looks like a seam to me."

It did to Diane too.

"You may be right, Margaret." Detective Little reached up and felt along the edge. "There's definitely a cut running along here." He traced it until it stopped. "It's hard to see because of the way the boards meet, but I think there's a seam running down the side too. Hold this." He handed Crawley the flashlight then traced his finger down the other side too. "It's got a seam on both sides. This may be the way in. I can't pull it toward me, though. There's nothing to grab. Here, everybody stand back."

As the four friends backed up, he began to push against it, but it didn't budge. He put some weight into it a few times. Finally, it gave way, and he almost fell forward. "Well how about that?" he said. Light from the other side flooded into the tunnel.

"There had to be a door," Diane said. "I just knew it."

"This is how that man has been getting inside," Beverly said, "to turn on those lights we've been seeing."

Detective Little walked into the open room, everyone right behind him. As soon as they came out of the tunnel, Diane recognized the room. They were in a part of the lighthouse that they had explored the last time they were here. "Well, look at that," she said as Detective Little closed the makeshift door over. A number of shelves had been built onto it from top to bottom. When closed, it almost disappeared and became a part of the wall.

"You know what I think?" Detective Little asked as he opened the door again. "This is some kind of hidden room. That's why we didn't see it before. We weren't meant to."

"Look, sir, under that workbench." Officer Crawley walked back into the tunnel and bent down. "Old wooden crates. There's a whole bunch of them. They're all lined up on the floor under these shelves." He slid a few out and set them on the workbench.

"Bring those in here," the detective said. "Let me look at them."

As Crawley set them on a counter, Diane noticed faded writing on the crates, and also that they were caked with dust.

"Is that the word *peaches*?" Detective Little said. "I can't make out the first one. It's some kind of company name."

"It is," Margaret said. "And that other word is definitely *peaches*. These are just old peach crates."

"I don't know," Beverly said. "You don't see many peach orchards in Maine."

"No, you don't," Detective Little agreed.

"Which means these crates probably contained something else," Diane said. "They must have stored other things in this room."

"It looks that way," Detective Little said.

Diane thought a moment. "I wonder what."

"And who? Whatever they were doing," Beverly said, "they needed a secret way in and out of this place to do it."

"Well," Shelley said, "it proves someone has definitely been coming in here these past few months, right through this tunnel."

The women looked at Detective Little, waiting for his response. "Okay," he said, "I can buy into what you're saying. To a point. But you still can't prove it is happening, just that it could be. What point would a grown man have to sneak into the lighthouse off and on just to turn on some lights? He's obviously not living here. There's nothing in here worth stealing. Why would someone do that?"

The women stood there, exchanging puzzled looks.

"We don't know," Diane said. "I guess we still have to figure out that part of the mystery."

"Mystery," Detective Little repeated. "I really don't think there's any mystery going on here. I wish you ladies would just drop this thing."

"Drop it?" Margaret said. "After this?"

"After what?" he said. "There's nothing here."

"We can't drop it, Fred," she said. "But we really do appreciate you taking time out of your busy day to help us here. Really, we do. You and Officer Crawley."

All four of them added their thanks.

"Officer Crawley and I need to get going. Which means you ladies do too."

After Detective Little and Officer Crawley left, the four friends went to lunch in town. They discussed the peach crates and the secret door and what it could all mean. None of them could figure out why someone would sneak in there just to turn lights on and off.

"I'll be the first to admit it," Margaret said over the last of her meal. "I'm a little disappointed. On the one hand, it was so exciting to make this new discovery about the secret tunnel room. But then...I guess I'd hoped we'd find something more. At least something significant enough to win over a skeptic like Detective Little."

They all agreed.

"Still," Shelley said, "it was a good day overall, don't you think?"

"Absolutely," Beverly said. "I'd have to say that we made real progress in solving this mystery."

★   ★   ★

Later that afternoon, Diane came back to the beach with Rocky near Orlean Point. Right away he ran off immediately, chasing seagulls near the water's edge. He never caught them but never gave up trying. The sand felt cooler between her toes than it had only a week before.

As she walked, Diane thought about what Eric might think of this new development at the lighthouse. She'd love to hear his take on all this. She still missed him terribly, but at least the emotional ambushes that used to overwhelm her had subsided. Now she could recall fond memories of their times together. She could savor the sweetness without lapsing into depression.

"Thank You, Lord, for that." She knew it was God's healing touch that been helping her, not the mere passing of time. Still, if she dwelt on it too long...

Rocky came bounding back and dropped a small piece of driftwood at her feet.

"You are so good for me," she said and tossed the stick as far as she could.

As he ran off, she recalled that another thing that had been so good for her had been her great visit yesterday, Labor Day, with her two children, Justin and Jessica. After the surprise party her friends had thrown for her at The Shearwater Gallery last week, Justin and Jessica had stayed through the holiday weekend.

With every step, her toes got more and more frigid. She had to get her feet off the cold sand. She walked back toward the promenade deck. "Rocky, come! It's time to go." It was amazing how quickly summer had disappeared. But that was one of the things she loved about Marble Cove: its four distinct seasons. Each seemed to arrive at just the right time, and none ever stayed too long.

Rocky walked beside her. His stomach and paws were covered in wet sand.

"You're going to need a bath when we get home." Diane climbed up to the walkway, relieved to be walking on wood.

She glanced back at the lighthouse, half-hoping to see a light appear. She knew what they had confirmed today meant that at least one part of the lighthouse mystery was manmade. But she was convinced something more was going on. Something supernatural, something...miraculous. What else could explain all the people who'd been rescued from the water around the lighthouse just after the mysterious light had appeared?

She heard the familiar sound of her cell phone ring. But by the time she'd pulled it out of her pocket, she'd missed the call. On the screen were two voice mails, both from Frieda Watley, her literary agent. There was also one text message from her. All three had come in the last thirty minutes. The sound of the surf was just too much for her phone's ringtone to compete with. She read the text first:

Diane, please call me ASAP. Urgent!

A Note from the Editors

We hope you enjoyed Miracles of Marble Cove, published by the Books and Inspirational Media Division of Guideposts, a nonprofit organization that touches millions of lives every day through products and services that inspire, encourage, help you grow in your faith, and celebrate God's love.

Thank you for making a difference with your purchase of this book, which helps fund our many outreach programs to military personnel, prisons, hospitals, nursing homes, and educational institutions.

We also create many useful and uplifting online resources. Visit Guideposts.org to read true stories of hope and inspiration, access OurPrayer network, sign up for free newsletters, download free e-books, join our Facebook community, and follow our stimulating blogs.

To learn about other Guideposts publications, including the best-selling devotional *Daily Guideposts*, go to Guideposts .org/Shop, call (800) 932-2145, or write to Guideposts, PO Box 5815, Harlan, Iowa 51593.